THE DECEPTION INCIDENT

THE INCIDENT SERIES, BOOK TWO

MARLA HOLT

eBook ISBN: 978-1-7338518-4-8
Paperback ISBN: 978-1-7338518-5-5
Cover Design by: Suite Six Studios
Edited by: Jacqueline Hritz

for all the chosen families

CONTENTS

Author's Note & Content Warning   7

Prologue   9
Chapter 1   15
Chapter 2   31
Chapter 3   45
Chapter 4   57
Chapter 5   71
Chapter 6   84
Chapter 7   94
Chapter 8   107
Chapter 9   115
Chapter 10   122
Chapter 11   128
Chapter 12   142
Chapter 13   144
Chapter 14   146
Chapter 15   151
Chapter 16   161
Chapter 17   170
Chapter 18   179
Chapter 19   202
Chapter 20   209
Chapter 21   220
Chapter 22   228
Chapter 23   235
Chapter 24   241
Chapter 25   250
Chapter 26   259
Chapter 27   266
Chapter 28   273

Chapter 29   281
Epilogue   288

Afterword   295
Acknowledgments   297
Also by Marla Holt   299

AUTHOR'S NOTE & CONTENT WARNING

Dear Reader,

Thank you so much for picking up a copy of *The Deception Incident*. Before you begin, I want to warn you that in this book, like *The Van Birch Incident* deals with themes of sexual assault and the court of public opinion. In addition, the narrative explores themes of addiction and mental health. If these are difficult or triggering issues for you, you have my permission to walk away. Though I hope most of you stay and read Bryant and Minnie's story.

While *The Deception Incident* does not shy away from difficult issues, I guarantee it ends with a happily ever after.

XO

Marla

PROLOGUE

MAY 2020

*I*f Minnie thought a couple of years of pretending to be a New York socialite had prepared her for the marvel that was Van Birch's wedding, she had been mistaken. When she'd gone out in New York, it had always been a group endeavor. She'd been surrounded by people who, even if she didn't know them very well, all claimed her as one of their own. The only people Minnie really knew at this event were all in the wedding party. While some of the local population was sprinkled throughout the crowd, a good portion of the guests were some of the most well-known names in music, film, television, and politics. As she watched them, Minnie struggled with the strange dissonance of being surrounded by people she recognized but didn't actually know.

Naturally, Minnie was handling it in the most mature way she could imagine, cowering in the shadow of a marble pillar and peeking through the leaves of a split-leaf philodendron while she tried to get herself together. The movie stars weren't the real problem, of course. It might have been years since Minnie had been adopted by Renee and her whole set, but Minnie had been around famous people every now and then. She'd been to her fair share of swanky parties since she'd fled New York, thanks to her obligations to her father. But at least then she'd had Rocco along for moral support and could delight in her father's frustration each time they'd convinced him they were a couple. They weren't; they never had been. Rocco had been her best friend since she was five years old, and she had exactly zero interest in him outside of a sort of brotherly friendship, but pretending they were more to get under her father's skin had been worth it every time.

Minnie had invited Rocco along to the wedding, but he'd refused to come. Instead he'd told Minnie to go, to have fun with Phoenix, and to try not to worry about Malcolm, like he didn't realize Minnie was a nervous wreck for reasons that had nothing to do with her son's well-being.

It had been months since Van Birch announced to the world that she was getting married to her stepbrother, Clay Noble, instead of Bryant Wilder, the man the whole world had thought she'd been dating for the last five years. Minnie was one of a select group of people who knew that Bryant and Van had never been in a relationship at all. And even though Minnie had known that for months now, when she thought of it, she still felt like her world was tilting.

August to April had not been enough time to process how much of Minnie's life had been based on a lie. She'd lived in guilt for the entire duration of her pregnancy and for months after, knowing that she held the key to breaking the heart of America's favorite celebrity. When she'd first met Bryant, Minnie had been so busy falling in love, and too wrapped up in her own world, to even notice.

Finding Bryant Wilder had been like breathing air for the first time. It had been like she had lived underwater her whole life, viewing the world through the shifting sheen of light on the surface. And everything had felt like it had been overhead and out of her reach. But the studious, industrious man who had built her bookshelves and taken her dancing had introduced her to what it was like to live a little. Through his lens, everything had become clear. When she was with him, she had felt confident and in control. Minnie had no longer been buffeted by the swells of life and winds of her father's fancy. She had been strong.

She hadn't skulked behind a plant like a coward; she'd decided she'd wanted Bryant, a bold, brave move after what she'd left New York to escape. Minnie had gone after what she'd wanted then, but would she have if she had known that this was where she'd end up?

Minnie stepped out from behind the plant. See, she wasn't a complete coward these days. But she'd been avoiding Bryant for so long, protecting herself and her son from him and the paparazzi that followed him had almost become second nature. The number of sanctioned photographers here was already enough to make her want to flinch, but Minnie knew if she looked toward the front of the room, she would see him, and the guilt and the turmoil and the hurt might drag her back under the waves she'd been swimming against all these months.

The music changed as Minnie braved the celebrity chef and television detectives—one of whom had spent the entire dinner staring at her breasts—and a couple of guys from Clay's crew she'd been seated next to. A nondescript jazz had been playing during dinner, but now booming bass thumped from the speakers. Minnie could feel it reverberate in through her chair as she sipped her glass of water.

Since dinner, Van and Clay, both dressed in black, had been circulating among their guests, but now the wedding party and most of the assembled crowd headed toward the stage that had been erected at the front of the room. Van pulled Clay onto the stage, a grin on her face as she took the mic.

"He didn't know I was going to make him sing today." The crowd laughed and cheered.

Clay stood in his tux with his arms crossed, but he wore a fond smile as he took a second microphone from one of Van's bandmates.

"You make me sing every day, why should today be any different?" he said into his mic, and Minnie couldn't help her own smile from taking over her lips. She could feel their love, even from all the way back here.

"I married you so you could never tell me no," she said and bumped him with her fluffy tulle skirt.

"I'm not sure that's how this works," he said.

Minnie had never noticed that Clay had sort of a drawl to his words when he'd merely been one of her contractors and a customer at Revival, but when she watched him on *Pop Star* or anytime he spoke with Van, the local accent was slightly more pronounced. He had to be doing it on purpose to impress Van, but Minnie thought it was cute.

Bryant stood on the far side of the stage, laughing and clapping as Clay donned an acoustic guitar and he and Van sang together for the first time as husband and wife.

Bryant hadn't seen her yet today, though she'd seen him scanning the lawn when he'd taken his position next to Clay at the front of the big rose garden in the city park. The sun had been too bright to see much in that direction, and Minnie might have chosen a seat that slightly hid her behind a bush of yellow roses.

Phoenix came for her then and pulled Minnie onto the floor with her. They danced together for ages. Sometimes they were silly; sometimes they chatted over the music. They'd even embraced each other to take on a slow number when Van's dad, Robin Birch, interrupted them. First, Phoenix stiffened, then she sneered, "No, you may not cut in. Minnie and I are having a magnificent time."

Robin quirked a half-smile in Phoenix's direction, which Minnie knew was meant to be charming, so the way Phoenix froze and stepped away from him into Minnie was dramatic and unnecessary.

"Do you mind if I steal Minneapolis away for a moment?" he asked.

Phoenix looked between the two of them, and Minnie could tell she was gauging whether she was being set up. Minnie shrugged, she had no clue why Robin Birch would want to dance with her. She sold him a cup of black coffee most mornings, sometimes a sandwich. They said hi, he asked after Malcolm, that was about the extent of their relationship.

Phoenix threw a warning glare back at Robin, and with a "Fine," she stalked away with an exaggerated sway to her slim, yet subtly rounded, hips.

Robin took Minnie in his arms as if they were dancing a waltz, and Minnie looked between him and Phoenix. Robin was still wearing his half smile, and Phoenix pulled the next unoccupied man she passed onto the dance floor.

"She's still angry with you?" Minnie asked, even though she knew Phoenix would probably die angry at Robin.

MARLA HOLT

Robin's expression turned somewhat pained. "I'm starting to think she'll never forgive me."

"What happened to make her so angry?" Minnie asked. This was a genuine question. As often as Phoenix had complained about Robin and what a cold-hearted bastard he was, she had never confided exactly what it was he'd done to earn her ire. Though Minnie had a few guesses.

"I'd rather not talk about it today, if you don't mind." His jaw clenched, and Minnie recognized that whatever it was, it was still a sore subject for Robin as well.

"All right," Minnie said. "What was the impetus for this dance then?"

Robin shrugged, even as he guided her around the floor in an actual waltz. Minnie was barely keeping up as he swept her in wide arcs through the other dancers, some of whom had stopped to gawk at the 19th-century-like spectacle.

"I am waiting for the right dance partner for you to get up the guts to ask to intercede. He said he would, if for no other reason than to clear the air."

"Oh," Minnie said and searched the crowd for Bryant. She didn't see him. But a moment later, as they slowed their step, she felt a tap on her shoulder.

"May I cut in?" Bryant asked.

CHAPTER 1

*B*ryant had only returned last week from two weeks of filming *Pop Star* in L.A., and the stark difference between downtown L.A. and downtown Wellville had never been clearer. It was eight o'clock in the evening, and there was absolutely nobody out on the street in Wellville, whereas L.A. would have just been getting going.

It didn't help that it was about three degrees in Kansas. Even though he'd been working, putting these bookshelves in for the last two hours, the tips of Bryant's fingers were still chilled, and his toes had taken an hour to thaw after he and Clay had hauled them inside. Of course it had taken almost half an hour just to get Clay to leave. He'd flashed the proprietor his signature panty-dropping half-smile and told her all about the craftsmanship that had gone into making her custom bookshelves. Bryant had only pushed his business partner out the door by reminding him there was a custom set of cabinets for a kitchen remodel that a client was waiting for.

Clay had left with a smile and a little bit of an extra drawl in his farewell. It had taken all of Bryant's willpower not to roll his eyes. Clay's strategy rarely failed. His crooked smile and all-American charm usually landed him whatever woman he wanted. Only, Bryant prayed it didn't work on this particular woman.

It had been a long time since Bryant had been drawn to a woman. Most of his lovers over the past few years had been men. A quick fuck he'd picked up in a club, gave a good time, and wouldn't have to think about again. Things had been easier that way, but this woman. Minnie. Bryant hadn't been able to stop thinking about her since they'd done their first consult before Thanksgiving. She was a petite blonde with boudoir curves and bright eyes that guaranteed nothing but complications.

Bryant normally avoided complications. The entire world thought he was in love with their favorite pop star, so he had to keep his liaisons quick and quiet. Bryant had a feeling there was nothing quick or quiet about Minnie, and his cock had been aching to find out since she'd made eye contact with him for the first time.

Eye contact.

That's all it had taken for him to go hard every time he'd seen her since. Bryant had even convinced Clay that he should be the one to install the bookshelves, even though that was something Clay would normally do. Bryant had pushed the kitchen remodel off on Clay, promising to help out in the afternoons.

Now, he was alone in the old doctor's office downtown, bolting row upon row of heavy oak bookshelves to the floor and trying not to think about his client's tits.

Except he couldn't stop. Thinking about her breasts had

almost become a pastime, he'd spent so much time contemplating the weight of them in his hand, the way they'd overflow his grip, the color her nipples would be, the feel of those nipples against his tongue.

Bryant was beginning to feel like a perv. She was young too, twenty-two at the oldest. She looked nineteen. But Bryant was only twenty-six. It wasn't like he was that much older than her, whatever age she was. Plus, there was no way she didn't know who Bryant was supposed to be dating. She was prime Van Birch demographic. Clay had bet Bryant twenty bucks going in that the only reason she'd called them for the job had been to fangirl.

At their first meeting, Minnie had been nothing but professional. Clay had insisted that Bryant couldn't prove anything until they'd dropped off the bookshelves that night. Clay had slapped a twenty into Bryant's palm and said, "She either doesn't know or doesn't care." Then he'd smiled at her like he wanted to take her bed.

Bryant couldn't blame him. He wanted the same thing. Desperately.

He adjusted his jeans and knelt again in front of the last shelf in the row he'd been working on. "Think about the job," he said aloud to himself, "not the girl."

It shouldn't be that difficult. Bryant loved books, and he loved the idea of what this place could become. The space was massive, and Minnie had big plans for creating a coffee shop with a bakery and a new and used independent bookstore. He didn't know if Wellville was big enough to support something that like that long term, but he sure hoped so. They had a Barnes & Noble in town, but they always had to special order the books he wanted to read anyway. He'd rather ask Minnie to order them for him.

He'd been on an ecology kick lately, which had led him into some interesting territory. He'd read about everything from evolution to libertarian self-sufficiency; he's even read *Prodigal Summer* by Barbara Kingsolver. He'd been looking for a particular book about the ecological footprint of new construction, since that was his business, to support some of the research he'd been doing into green building. He'd only been able to find it on Amazon so far. Bryant thought it sort of defeated the purpose if the book came next-day free shipping.

Just when his mind was back on sustainably sourced lumber, he heard Minnie's soft footsteps approaching him from behind. The hair on the back of his neck stood up as he waited for her to appear.

Bryant's heartbeat ticked up. He hadn't had much opportunity to be alone with Minnie, but he'd been yearning for it. The fantasy of what it would be like to touch her, kiss her, shove her up against one of the bookshelves and test the bracing, had kept him up most of last night.

Minnie was the most beautiful woman he'd ever met. She had the perfect combination of features—dainty wrists, grip-able hips, silky looking skin. Her tits alone could start wars. She was so tiny, the size of her breasts had to give her back pain. He wasn't sure how a woman so small supported them, but he wasn't about to ask her. It took all his concentration to avoid staring like a creep and also form proper sentences.

He wondered if she would believe the excuse that he and Van had an open relationship. It was what he told most of his one-night stands when they tried to act like they had dirt on one of the most famous women in the world. Bryant would only give them a sly grin and tell them not to get cocky. That he and Van had a special relationship.

And they did. Just not the relationship everyone thought they had.

Van Birch had never been anything more to Bryant than a friend. His best friend. He would even go so far as to use the word "sister." It made your personal life ridiculously awkward when everyone thought the woman you had sibling-like affinity for was actually your long-distance lover.

There had been times over the years he'd wished their staged make-out sessions for the camera did something for him, but it was like being back in the high school theatre troupe every time. It was acting. It was fake. Van was gorgeous, kind, generous, but no matter how much Bryant wanted to want a sexual relationship with her, he just didn't.

It would have made his life a hell of a lot less complicated if he did.

He became aware of Minnie watching him, but she stood there without saying anything. After a solid minute, Bryant pretended he had just noticed her presence. When he turned to face her, the pensive expression on her pale, lovely face didn't clarify whether she was admiring him or just exceedingly shy.

Or she might be afraid to be alone in this building with him. Bryant was aware that his stature sometimes frightened people. He was six foot four and still had most of the muscles he'd built while he'd been in the Army. He was a large man. She wouldn't be the first to be intimidated by his size, and she was so small. Bryant would give up both his motorcycle and his truck if it ensured she wasn't afraid of him. He wanted her so much, he would probably have traded his house for a simple smile.

"Is something wrong?" he asked when she hadn't moved.

She shook her head, as if waking herself from the trap of her own thoughts, which was something that Bryant understood. The thing about having an active brain was that it often took over.

"I--" she paused to clear her throat and took a tentative step closer to him. "I just took a batch of apricot scones out of the oven. It's a new recipe. Would you like to try one? Taste test for me?"

Bryant stood and offered what he hoped was a friendly smile. He'd been smelling the scones for the last fifteen minutes, and he'd been trying not to think about how empty his stomach was. He'd read right through dinner again, only taking two bites of his drive-thru burger before it became a cold, inedible stone.

"They smell amazing," he said. "And I could use a break." All his nerves fired in anticipation, just at the sheer excitement of being asked into her presence. His hand almost reached for the small of her back as he followed her to the kitchen. He jerked it back to his side. It was a rule of his never to touch anyone uninvited, but he was having a hard time telling his body that at the moment.

A shy smile twitched across Minnie's lips, and Bryant's heart stuttered. He wouldn't have to give up his house after all. Though he probably would give it to her if she asked for it. He felt as though he'd stepped into a fairy-tale and this woman had bewitched him. He would give her anything. All she had to do was tell him what she wanted.

"I'll make you a cup of coffee too. What do you drink?"

"You don't have to do that," he said, not wanting to be an

inconvenience, but she'd already turned in the direction of the coffee counter.

"I'm still playing with the espresso machine, so really, you'd be doing me a favor if you let me make you a latte. I need to make sure the grind on the espresso is perfect."

"A latte sounds amazing."

Bryant followed Minnie, trying and failing not to notice the generous roundness of her derriere as she led him behind the counter. She lifted a plate with half a dozen warm scones on it and handed it to Bryant.

"What kind of milk do you prefer?" she asked. "I have them all: skim, whole, soy, almond, oat."

"Regular old milk is fine for me," he said, barely containing a chuckle.

As she made his latte, Bryant hopped up on the counter behind her. He set the plate beside him and scooped off one of the still cooling scones. The pastry tasted as good as it smelled. He'd seen just enough of that British baking show to know that it was supposed to be biscuity and not too sweet. Minnie had nailed it. He devoured the first one in about three bites and was on to the second when she brought his coffee.

She said nothing about his appetite as she handed over a mug with a heart rosette swirled into the foam and joined him on the counter.

"How do you know how to do all this?" he asked.

Minnie shrugged as she picked the corner off one of the triangular scones. "I started working in a little coffee shop and bakery when I was fourteen. Only stopped when I left for college."

"You've worked since you were fourteen?"

"I lied on my application and said I was eighteen."

"You barely look eighteen now," Bryant said. When a furrow appeared between Minnie's brows, he said, "No offense. You're lovely, actually." Her frown deepened, and Bryant hankered to slip a drop of whiskey into his coffee as he knew he was making a fool of himself. "But I'm not sure I could guess your age."

God, why was he such a fumbling ass in private? Put him on a red carpet and he'd have reporters eating out of his hand, but here, now, when something actually mattered, he was a complete idiot.

"I'm twenty-three," she said. "And I looked about eight when I started at the cafe. The manager took pity on me and paid me under the table until I turned sixteen because she knew I needed the money. It was just me and my mom growing up. We didn't have much."

Bryant tucked away that Minnie was only a year younger than Van as he said, "It was just me and my mom growing up too. She pretty much single-handedly ran the *Wellville Daily News* my entire childhood. Now she's here about three weeks out of the year because she's a freelance travel writer. She's pretty fantastic actually, but she had to work hard to get where she is."

Minnie nodded, crumbling her piece of scone between her fingers. "My mother died during my senior year of high school."

"I'm sorry," Bryant said. "That must be hard."

Minnie took a deep breath, then exhaled through her nose. "It is. But I think she'd be proud of what I'm doing. She loved to read, especially while she was sick. It was what got her through her days."

"I get it. Reading is one of the only things that makes me feel calm," Bryant said.

Minnie's eyebrows rose. "You read?"

He had to breathe out through his nose so he didn't choke on his latte. "I know you don't expect your contractor to be an intellectual or anything, but books are the only things that help me focus. The rest of the world is just boring, you know?"

Minnie cocked her head to the side, and her mouth twitched into a grin. "It can be. It can also be infinitely entertaining."

"What do you mean?" Bryant asked.

"I mean, the endless interpersonal drama of just living."

Bryant shook his head as if he didn't understand, even though the role he'd taken on for Van had introduced drama into almost every part of his life. His mother had been asking lately if he and Van were ever going to get married. And Clay, who had been in love with Van for a decade, had erected a wall between them recently.

Bryant didn't blame him. Clay needed to protect himself, and Van and Bryant had promised each other not to reveal the true nature of their relationship unless it became necessary to end their arrangement. Which included not telling Clay that Bryant wasn't really in a long-term relationship with the only woman Clay had ever loved. It was a shit arrangement in so many ways. It didn't benefit Bryant in *any* way, but he'd never been able to say no to Van.

And he hadn't been able to follow her to L.A. and help protect her from the people that might prey on her, so he acted as her beard. He was a part of the fairy-tale she wove for the world because he loved her. And as frustrating as he found navigating his sex life amid the lies surrounding his public persona, for years Bryant had forgone the luxury of developing his own connection with someone so he could be there for Van.

They had both always agreed that if either found someone they wanted to be with--really be with--they would call off the charade, because both of them deserved to be happy. But Bryant wasn't looking for permanence. He didn't know how he would handle having someone around all the time. It was possible Bryant's tenuous hold on his obligations might fall apart completely.

Bryant usually grew bored of company quickly. He grew bored of everything quickly. It had been a curse his entire life, one that had caused him trouble in school. Bryant had trouble with structure. If it wasn't something he cared about, he couldn't make himself care. So he'd goofed off in history class by working ahead in his math and science classes, and then he'd grown bored in math because he'd taught himself everything already, so he'd get in trouble for reading mystery novels instead of paying attention to the lecture.

Clay had tried to convince Bryant to go to college. He'd told Bryant he was too smart, that joining the Army was a waste of his brain. But Clay didn't know how abysmal Bryant's grades were. Bryant had always been good at hiding his struggles. He knew he had the brains for college and would probably find some of the advanced classes in biology and ecology fascinating. But the thought of sitting still through all those general education lectures made his skin crawl, and the writing classes? Bryant had proved in high school that he didn't have the temperament for writing. He'd only passed because he'd used his mom's old tape recorder to dictate his papers. Even then, it had taken him weeks to complete an essay the same caliber as the ones his classmates cobbled together at the last minute.

Besides, Clay was one of the few people who Bryant wanted to be around. And when he found those people, the fear of losing them was something he had to force himself not to obsess over. Once Clay had posed the idea of joining the Army, Bryant had no questions about signing up with him, because friends did things like that to support each other.

It was a point of pride for Bryant that he was nothing if not fiercely loyal.

"Apparently, you have so much drama, you don't even know where to start telling me about it." The laugh in Minnie's voice woke him from his thoughts. He hadn't even realized he wasn't paying attention to her anymore.

He offered an apologetic smile. "No drama. I'm just a simple guy who builds things."

"And reads a lot," she said, a smile curling her lips.

"And reads a lot," he said in confirmation.

"Much to the chagrin of your very jealous significant other, who's probably annoyed you're working late."

Bryant nearly choked on his third scone and had to splutter through a few sips of his latte before he wheezed, "No significant other at home. It's just me, and I don't care how late I work."

Minnie leaned over the half-empty plate of scones between them so her elbow brushed against his. Her sweater gaped at the neckline, and Bryant could see straight down her shirt. She wore a blue lace bra, and he bet that if he took her sweater off, he'd be able to make out the shape of her nipples beneath the lace. "Good, because I have a recipe for oatmeal creme pies I need to test out tomorrow night, if you're interested."

Was it possible that she didn't know who he was? He supposed she just might not care, but somehow, he didn't think that was the case. She was too pure for that. Too sweet.

"I'm interested," he said and raised a hand to hover over her cheek. "May I?"

She dipped her head once in a bashful nod. "Yes."

The skin on her jaw was impossibly soft, he was almost afraid his calloused hand would damage her. But Minnie's eyes closed as she leaned into his touch like she'd been craving him as much as he'd been wanting her.

"Minnie?"

"Hm?" She didn't even open her eyes, like she couldn't stop concentrating on the feel of him.

"I'm going to kiss you now."

She nodded, the same single dip of her head from before, and Bryant stopped holding back. His skin caught fire as their lips met. She was soft and supple beneath his hands, smooth but not yielding against his lips. Her tongue licked at his lips first. When Bryant darted the tip of his out to meet hers, he turned to liquid. He slid off the counter so he could face her and mold every part of himself against Minnie's body.

He had to duck his knees to capture her lips, even with her sitting on the counter, but her breasts pressed against his pecs in the most delicious way. Minnie wrapped her arms around his neck. He felt the scrape of nails in his hair, like she already knew it was one of his favorite sensations.

Bryant pulled her hips to the edge of the counter. Minnie wrapped her legs around him and they each moved the other as if their bodies already knew each other. As if they hadn't barely met.

This was so wrong. Minnie was a client. He couldn't dry hump a client. Clay would have a fit. But even as he thought it, his pelvis bucked, pressing the ridge of his erection against the central seam in Minnie's jeans.

Goddamn, her wanted her.

"Can I touch you?" he asked.

"Please," she breathed against his lips. She hopped off the counter long enough to shed her Toms and slide her jeans to the floor, then hopped back up.

Her skin was the most gorgeous pale color, even and soft like undyed wool. Bryant swept his hands up her thighs, afraid that he was going to pass out from the barrage of sensation. He was certain his brain wouldn't be able to process it all, but when Minnie pulled him back into a kiss, his fingers followed the heat to her center.

His brain latched onto that heat, the slickness, the soft swollen sweetness of her. He teased her nub with his thumb, then slipped one finger inside her. She squeaked as if in surprise, then opened her legs wider. Bryant stepped between them, matching his strokes to the rhythm of her hips. Minnie cursed, and his cock pulsed against his zipper.

God, he'd never wanted anything so badly as he wanted to fuck this woman. If he'd had a condom in his pocket, he would have. Asking her about her health and her birth control was on the tip of his tongue, but Minnie moaned and pulled him closer. She was going to come soon, and Bryant wanted to see that more than anything. He added a second finger and pressed just that much more deeply into her.

"God, yes!" she gasped and clung to him as her breath caught in her throat.

Bryant felt her clamp down on his fingers, and her legs squeezed him in close as she pulsed around him.

A moment later, her head fell against his shoulder and she was panting in his ear.

Bryant slowly withdrew his fingers. He had the urge to touch them to his lips, but Minnie's arms were draped over his.

"Jesus, that was good," she said. "I didn't expect it to be that good."

Bryant laughed despite himself. "What did you expect?"

"Something awkward and fumbling that would prove that this crazy strong attraction was just in my head."

Bryant shook his. "I feel it too," he said.

She smiled up at him, looking relieved, and Bryant had the impression that Minnie was stepping way out of her comfort zone. He ghosted a kiss over her lips.

"I'd like to return the favor," she said.

Bryant resisted the urge to adjust himself in his jeans. He was uncomfortably hard and worked up enough that he knew he'd go off like a rocket. He was desperate for her to touch him, but he said, "You don't have to."

"I want to," she said. Her eyes were so green. Like sea glass. Or clovers. The color of new grass in the spring.

Bryant reached for his belt, but she knocked his hands aside and worked the leather free herself.

"When was the last time you were tested?" she asked.

"Last month." He was barely able to choke out the words as her slender, nimble hands worked his fly.

"And?"

"Clean," he said. "I always use condoms. Haven't been with anyone since. You?"

"I haven't been with anyone in months," she said as she pushed his jeans and his boxer briefs down his thighs. "But I had all the tests after. I'm healthy."

Bryant wanted to ask about birth control again, because she still wasn't wearing any pants and he wanted to feel those legs wrapped around his hips, but she wrapped her fingers around his dick before he could. The sweet pleasure-pain of being touched when he was this aroused rendered him silent. And when she sank to her knees? How could he argue? He couldn't remember the last time someone had gone down on *him*.

She took him into her mouth, and the heat almost undid him. Her hand wrapped around the base of him, while she took him in as far as she could. Bryant tangled his fingers in her hair, guiding himself toward her throat. It took about three thrusts before his balls tightened and his back tingled. It was not the best first impression of his stamina, but he didn't have a choice. He came so hard he forgot how to breathe, and she swallowed everything she could. Some of his release dribbled down her chin, but Bryant licked her clean as he pulled her to her feet, and the two of them kissed each other like they might never taste another person again.

Their embrace was a tangle of tongues and teeth and fingernails that slowed into languorous licks and soft caresses.

"That was amazing," Bryant whispered against her lips.

Minnie grinned. "It was." She bent down and pulled his clothes back up his legs, then punched her own legs into her jeans. When they were both dressed again, she faced him and said, "So, oatmeal creme pies tomorrow?"

Bryant's grin was so wide, his cheeks were starting to hurt. He had been waiting for this for so long. Whatever had just happened. He wanted more. "If you keep baking for me, you might not be able to get rid of me."

"I don't know about that," Minnie said, tendrils of her sly smile curling up to sparkle in her eyes, and Bryant's heart raced. "Let's see how the cookies turn out tomorrow."

CHAPTER 2

*C*lay's text woke Bryant way too early the next morning. After leaving Minnie's shop the night before, Bryant had gone home and read his book while sipping a glass of whiskey. Only he hadn't made much progress in the book. He'd been too busy replaying the encounter with Minnie in his mind over and over again. This morning he was groggy, and his eyelids felt like sandpaper over his eyes. The last thing he wanted to do was go to the gym.

The last thing he wanted to do most mornings was go to the gym, which was why Clay texted him until he showed up three days a week. Clay liked working out; he had fitness goals that he tracked and meal plans he wrote for himself. Bryant mostly just went because it was time he could spend with Clay outside of work. And gossip columnists would probably start publishing all sorts of dire stories if Bryant's physique changed.

Bryant pulled himself from bed and guzzled roughly a gallon of water. He had three more texts from Clay reminding Bryant that he needed to take care of his body by the time he heaved himself into his truck. He sipped his coffee and fantasized about the sausage sandwich he was going to buy himself when this was all finished, even though he was certain Clay had a protein drink ready for him to have for breakfast instead. Bryant still hadn't been able to bring himself to tell his friend that his protein drinks were disgusting. Bryant usually dumped them down his garbage disposal before bringing the bottle back to Clay, pretending he'd downed the whole thing.

The urge to tell Clay about Minnie had been on the tip of Bryant's tongue the whole time they'd spotted each other on the weights. And when they'd hopped on treadmills next to each other, Bryant had had to turn his music up to unhealthily loud levels to drown out his thoughts. Otherwise, Bryant would have said something. He would have told Clay that he'd fooled around with the most beautiful woman he'd ever met, and sure she was a client, but that didn't even matter because Bryant was so besotted. It was a non-issue.

Only telling Clay would mean betraying Van's secret and explaining to Clay that Bryant *wasn't* actually in love with the pop star. It was possible Van would never forgive him, and then Clay would probably be pissed that Bryant had lied to him for years. Then Bryant would be without both his best friends, and he didn't think he'd be able to function without them. Clay and Van were his tethers. Without Van to drag him out in public, it was possible Bryant's inner introvert would take over and he'd perpetually hide behind a teetering pile of paperbacks.

Clay was basically Bryant's anchor. Bryant had followed Clay's lead for so long, he wasn't sure he would be able to function without him. He'd joined the Army because Clay had wanted to, had passed the contractors exam because Clay had pushed him, had started this business because Clay had wanted to. Bryant loved what he did. Construction was measurable work with attainable goals, and Bryant could get lost in the work without feeling bad about it. But Bryant never would have gone that route if it hadn't been for Clay. He probably would have worked in the same grocery store he'd worked at in high school. Or begged Van to let him be her drummer.

No matter how much Bryant wanted to tell Clay about how there might be something good starting in his life, he couldn't do it. So he turned his music up and kept running.

Minnie would just have to be his own special secret for now.

Minnie had never been so daring with a man before. All through high school, if she'd liked a boy, she'd languished in her solitary crush, hoping he noticed her. Sometimes he did, sometimes he didn't. In college, she'd learned how to cock her head to one side and stick her boobs out while giving just the right sort of smile to signal she was interested, but Minnie had always let the guy make the first move. From the moment Bryant Wilder had first visited her shop to bid on the bookshelf project, Minnie had wanted to climb him like a tree.

Bryant was the tallest man she'd ever met. He had to be a foot or more taller than she was. And his frame was just muscular enough to show through his clothes without being ostentatious. He was quiet and let Clay Noble, his partner, do most of the talking, but Minnie glimpsed the light of mischief in his eyes on the rare occasion that he met her gaze. She had a feeling he didn't show that hint of a bad boy to everyone.

But boy howdy, had Minnie needed to know where that little kernel of trouble might lead the moment she'd seen it. It wasn't a coincidence that she'd arranged to be baking when he was scheduled to put up the shelves. She told herself that it was only practical. It was easier to call book reps and coordinate food deliveries during the day when all those people were open, and she wouldn't have to worry about accidentally burning her scones. She was also self-aware enough to know that her excuses were bullshit. She wanted to have Bryant all to herself so she could woo him with baked goods.

He'd seemed interested. She'd caught him staring at her boobs a few times, and she could see him scolding himself in his head. Not only were his self-recriminations endearing, but they let Minnie know she would be safe with him. She'd known instinctively that Bryant wouldn't touch her unless she invited him too. Last night, he'd asked her every step of the way if he could touch her, and it had only made her want him more.

She'd never come just from a man's fingers before. Any other time someone had touched her like that it had been a quick, fumbling prelude to intercourse, but Bryant Wilder's fingers on her had felt like worship and absolution all at the same time. And when she'd gone down on him? Minnie had never felt so powerful. Here was this behemoth of a man, tall and well-muscled and well-hung, fisting his hands in her hair and begging her for pleasure and release.

Minnie blushed when she thought of her own daring, but that didn't stop her from wanting him again.

So the second night, Minnie made him oatmeal creme pies and passed so close behind him as he stood where the register would be that the tips of her breasts brushed against his back. He'd leant her back against the prep table and pressed her top up enough to suck on her nipples through her bra and dry humped her until she came. The night after that she made tiny savory tarts and chucked him in the shoulder in a playful way, like they were best buds. He'd propped her up on the counter and feasted on her like she was the one made of brie and caramelized onions, not the tarts. Yesterday she'd made brownies, and he'd run his fingers over her forearm, and he'd finally let her stroke him until he'd come all over her shirt. He'd apologized, but Minnie hadn't cared. Shirts would wash, and he hadn't let her touch him for days.

Minnie's skin had broken out in goosebumps and heat had pooled between her legs. Now that it was Friday night and they'd been stoking this fire through whatever strange dance they were doing, Minnie was ready to serve him his cinnamon rolls and throw him down on the floor and ride him before he didn't have an excuse to come back.

The bookshelves were starting to form stacks now. After five nights worth of work, Bryant had almost finished installing her shelves. They were gorgeous. Tall and sturdy with a dark walnut finish. She could already picture them full of the books she'd been stockpiling in her apartment and was anxious to start shelving them. That was the only reason why she was going to give Bryant an hour and a half to work tonight before she seduced him.

She hadn't planned on him coming to her after only an

hour. Minnie had just taken the cinnamon rolls out of the oven when his deep voice spoke over her playlist.

"Any chance I can get another one of those lattes?"

Minnie bumped the oven door closed with her hip and tried to hide how much his arrival had startled her. Over her racing heart, Minnie turned down the volume and smiled up at him. She'd worn her "going out" blouse tonight. It was a silky, flowy white shirt with a deep V in the neckline that made her breasts look even bigger than they already were and showed a generous amount of her cleavage. To her delight, Bryant's eyes went straight down her shirt. Score one.

"Got you addicted, did I?"

A sheepish grin curved over Bryant's lips as he forced his eyes up, over her collarbone, chin, and nose until they finally met hers. "My body thinks I need coffee at 8 p.m. now."

"I can help you out with that--too bad I won't be open that late once this place is up and running."

Bryant leaned over the front counter, and rather than feeling like he loomed over her, Minnie felt herself leaning in closer to him. "Maybe I can finagle myself an after-hours invitation. I happen to know the owner."

"I don't know," Minnie said as she braced herself on the edge of the counter, pressing her chest forward, plumping her breasts against the fabric of the shirt, and feeling triumphant as she watched Bryant swallow against the desire she was fanning. "I hear she can be hard to get to know. Most people think she's pretty shy."

Bryant shook his head, and Minnie was so focused on how much closer his face was coming to hers that she hadn't noticed he'd raised one of his hands until a rough finger traced down the hem of her gaping neckline and tickled across the top of her breast.

She shivered as he said, "Shy? No. I think she has her own reasons for being quiet though."

"I'm not always quiet," Minnie said and proved her point by moaning as Bryant dipped his finger beneath her shirt and caressed first one breast, then the other, and traced that single finger back up the other side of her shirt's neckline.

"Can I take you out for a drink?" he asked.

"Only if you come upstairs with me afterward," she said and tried not to bite her lip. Minnie had never been so forward about what she wanted as she'd been with Bryant these last few days. If she didn't take him inside her soon, Minnie thought she was going to combust.

Bryant leaned over the counter and caressed the stray hairs that had broken free of her braid away from her ear and brushed a soft kiss over the shell. "What are we waiting for?" he asked.

Minnie shut down her kitchen in a flurry of nerves and desire while Bryant went to pack up his tools. When he returned, he wore his black leather jacket that, paired with his ripped, dusty jeans and faded Henley, made him look exactly like the bashful bad boy she wanted him to be. Minnie had the feeling that he'd look just as appealing in a tweed jacket and elbow patches, and just as uneasy, like neither role suited him exactly. Minnie wondered if the leather jacket was part of a costume. Then dismissed the notion as silly. Why would Bryant need a costume?

He helped her into her expensive navy wool coat and wrapped the matching plaid scarf--a present from her father after parading around as his dutiful daughter for a week--around her neck. Bryant's fingers were warm and sure as they skimmed over her collar and whispered against her neck. The scant touches chased any thoughts of her father from her mind.

"There's a place down the street, Tessa's. Do you know it?" he asked.

"I've never been, but I heard it's one of Van Birch's favorite places when she's in town."

Bryant flinched ever so slightly at the celebrity's name but smoothed Minnie's scarf and said softly, "With any luck, she's not in town, and the place will be relatively civilized."

"Is it chaotic when she's here? I don't think she's been back since I moved in."

"How long have you been in Wellville?"

"Three months."

"Then no, she hasn't been back since then, and won't be until March."

"You know her schedule?"

Bryant's eyes darkened, for just a moment, and then he said, "Clay is Van's stepbrother, so I know a little bit."

"Oh," Minnie said, trying to recall if one of them had ever said something about the contractor's relation to the super star. "I didn't realize. Wow."

Bryant shrugged. "I figured you didn't watch the show. Most people who do would have asked us about her by now."

"No, I don't watch the show. I know some of her songs, but I didn't move to Wellville because she's from here or anything."

Bryant moved closer, his fingertips played with the tips of her braid where it landed just below her shoulder. His voice was soft as he asked, "Why did you move to Wellville?"

"My cousin, Rocco, lives here—well, he's not really my

cousin. He lived in the apartment next door to us growing up, and our moms were as close as sisters, so he's like my cousin." Minnie realized she was rambling and pulled in a deep breath. "Anyway, he's the closest thing to family I really have left since my dad is an asshole I like to pretend doesn't exist, and after I left school, it seemed like it only made sense to move to where he was."

"And what does Rocco do?"

"He works third shift at the flour mill. He's an engineer."

Minnie wanted to brag on how he'd worked so hard for his scholarship and then to maintain his GPA. She wanted to explain to Bryant how big of a deal it was that Rocco had graduated summa cum laude with his degree in Manufacturing Engineering because she and Rocco had come from nothing. They'd lived in the same slummy apartments outside Denver, had both been born to single mothers who'd barely scraped by. Only, unlike Minnie, Rocco hadn't had a rich father step out of the woodwork when he'd turned eighteen the way Minnie's had. Rocco had done everything on his own.

Rocco was the success story of the two of them. He'd worked for everything he had. Minnie had basically blackmailed her dad into supporting her. She hadn't earned the start-up money for her store, Revival, unless you counted her childhood spent in poverty while her father had hoarded his millions. Minnie would probably never forgive him for that. That he'd never stepped up to take care of Minnie's mother was something Minnie would punish him for the rest of her life.

Bryant smiled and traced a hand down the length of her arm until he twined his fingers with hers. "Shall we?"

Minnie allowed him to lead her out of the bookstore and

down the street for a block and a half until they reached a club, which, despite the fact that it was about five degrees out, had a line around the building. Instead of getting in line, Bryant pulled Minnie to the door and nodded at the bouncer.

"Hey, Speck. Just headed in for a drink."

Speck cocked his shaved head to the side, then looked Minnie up and down. "I don't know your friend."

"She's new in town. I'm showing her the sights."

Speck frowned but opened the door for them. "Tell Van I said hi," he called after them, and Minnie giggled. She hadn't thought much about the pop star since she'd moved to Wellville but figured being business partners with Van Birch's stepbrother had its advantages. That he'd known they could get into the club immediately and ignored the shade from the bouncer told Minnie he was used to the perks.

Bryant pulled her up to a gap at the busy bar. There were no stools free so he stood behind Minnie, his front pressed against her side, his arms boxing her in as he defended their space. Minnie shimmied against him for just a second and wanted to do more, but almost immediately, two shots of amber liquid were set in front of them. Bryant handed her one of the shot glasses and raised his own as if in a toast

"What is it?" Minnie asked over the noise.

"Jameson," he said. Then, "Irish whiskey," when she looked confused.

Minnie was not a big drinker. She'd never had alcohol straight. She was more of a Malibu and pineapple or a Bahama Mama kind of girl.

"Hey, Jojo, can I get a lemonade back?" Bryant shouted over the din, and the bartender, whose torn black shirt hung off her shoulder, flashed a thumbs up before plunking another shot glass of lemonade in front of Minnie.

"You drink the lemonade after the shot to cut the burn," Bryant said. Minnie knew she still must look confused, and a little like a young, naive idiot, because he added. "I bartended here for a couple of years when we were still getting the construction business off the ground. Jameson shots were kind of our thing. You don't have to take the shot, if you don't want. I'm still planning to buy you a real drink. Maybe dance for a while."

The way his eyes scrunched with fear that he'd already screwed up set Minnie at ease. "So I'm being initiated into the local service industry," she said, picking up the whiskey.

"Yes," he said. "You should get in with this crowd. They'll be fiends for your caffeine when they have to be back here at ten in the morning for staff meetings."

"Noted," Minnie said and clinked her shot glass against his. It was all she could do not to choke on the intensity of the whiskey, and she was thankful when Bryant shoved the lemonade into her hand. The sweet, cold tartness of it cooled and opened her throat. She smacked her lips as the lemonade settled the fire from the whiskey. "That isn't half bad."

"I should have Jojo make you a real whiskey sour. It's a similar flavor combination."

"Sure," Minnie said, embarrassed to order a Malibu and pineapple in front of a man who'd been a bartender. "What are you going to drink?"

"American whiskey, neat."

"Yeah, I don't have that in me," she said. "But I'll take whatever you recommend."

He ordered the drinks. She found the smooth, tart

creaminess pleasant, and as she neared the bottom of her martini glass, a similar smooth, relaxed feeling came over her.

Bryant pulled her to the dance floor, where he surprised her with his fluidity. For some reason, she expected someone of his height to be gawky and awkward, but he wrapped his limbs around her, moving to the frantic beat of the house music until Minnie was sweating and gasping for breath.

"Another drink?" the whisper of his breath across the shell of her ear made her shiver as she nodded her emphatic yes.

She fanned herself as she drank her second sour, aware of Bryant's hand on her hip. There had been a free bar stool this time, and Bryant had snagged it, guarding Minnie in much the same way he had before. Only now they were equal in height, him sitting as she stood between his legs.

"You are the most beautiful woman I've ever laid eyes on," Bryant whispered in her ear. "I haven't been able to stop thinking about you since we met. Your hair, your shape, your mouth. That delicious glint in your eyes that promises more. I want everything you have to offer, and I am worth absolutely nothing, but I want to be better than I ever have been, for you."

Minnie drained the rest of her drink and settled her arms around Bryant's neck as he drew her between his spread thighs, "You're one of the best men I've met," she said, wishing it to be true more than knowing. But after this week, it was easy to believe. Bryant had been gentle with her when she'd needed it and passionate when she'd wanted him. She could tell he was kind and considerate, and

Minnie indulged herself by nipping at his lower lip. He caught her lips with his in a pressure that burned.

Like every time she kissed him, Minnie felt as if she'd caught fire as she fell into the kiss with an intensity that surprised her. Her blood ignited, and her core went molten as she fought to press as much of her body into Bryant's as she could. At the same time, his tongue traced soft velvet caresses over her lips that rocketed through her like lightning strikes.

It only occurred to her that they were making out in public when someone jostled her from behind as they tried to squeeze onto an abandoned barstool. She broke off their kiss, her senses returning to her just in time to hear their new neighbor say, "So fucking gross."

Minnie giggled and hid her face against Bryant's collarbone. She could feel the deep flush coloring her face as Bryant ran a soothing hand up and down her back.

"You live above the bookstore?" Bryant asked, his voice a caress against her ear. She nodded, her forehead still in the crook of his throat. "Then what are we waiting for?"

Minnie raised her head to meet his gaze. In the low light, his blue eyes shone silver. "I thought we were keeping up the pretenses of having a real date first."

"Well, I don't want you to think I'm only after your body."

"But you do want my body?"

Bryant slid forward on his stool and pulled Minnie hard into his chest. "Your body is like finding an oasis after wandering for years in the desert, and I plan to drink my fill," he said, running kisses down her neck.

White hot heat seared through Minnie at his words. She

knew men appreciated her assets, but she'd never thought she'd inspire this kind of worshipful praise.

Bryant kissed his way back up to her ear and whispered, "But I want everything, Minnie. I want to know all there is to know about you."

Minnie was so full of heat and pleasure that she thought her molten core might burst like the heart of a volcano if she didn't find some relief soon.

"Let's go," she said and practically pulled him down the street and up the outside entrance to her apartment.

CHAPTER 3

*A*ny other time, Minnie would have been mortified about the stacks of dirty dishes in the sink, but as she and Bryant stumbled through the rear entrance to her apartment, she was too centered on him to care. Bryant's chilled lips traced soft kisses over her jaw, ghosted against the corner of her mouth then skipped back down the other side of her chin. The skin over her neck, still tense from the cold night air, prickled with anticipation. Minnie fisted frantic fingers into Bryant's coat pockets, seeking out the leverage of his warmth anywhere she could find it.

Bryant eased back and shushed her when she whined at the loss of his heat. "We don't have to rush," he said. "We have all night."

Minnie didn't agree. If she didn't have him now, her entire flat was going to be covered with molten Minnie, because she would have succumbed to the pressure building deep inside her.

She fumbled blindly for his zipper and plunged her hand beneath his coat to push it over his shoulder and down his arms so it dropped onto the floor. He let out a soft chuckle as she pushed him into the stove and whipped the scarf from around her neck as she attempted to undo her own buttons with her body still crushed against his.

"It's not funny," she said. "If you don't fuck me now, I am literally going to explode. Don't you understand?"

Bryant's fingers wrapped gently around her wrists, stilling her hands. "We can take our time," he said, but she hadn't missed the urgent press of his arousal against her stomach. The hard, thick evidence of his desire only made her want him more.

"We can take our time later. Right now, I need--" Minnie didn't have time to tell him what she needed because his lips crashed down on hers in such a searing, urgent kiss that Minnie could do nothing but buck against him as her coat finally fell away.

She shivered in her flimsy blouse and let Bryant's inherent warmth surround her. If she could crawl inside him and share his skin, she would, but she'd have to settle for the second best thing.

"My bedroom's this way," she said and yanked his wrist so that he followed her across the hall and into the bedroom, which was, thankfully, marginally neater than the kitchen.

She expected there to be a moment of shy hesitation, because that was the way she had always been in intimate situations before Bryant, but all she felt was the magnetic pull of him. She slipped off her shoes at the same time Bryant reversed her hold on his wrist so that he could tug her toward him. He trapped her in his embrace then covered her lips with his as his tongue pummeled through her mouth.

Yes, this. This is what she wanted. She wanted hard and fast and brutal, and she didn't want to wait. Bryant swept his hands up under her shirt, and his fingers felt icy against the need boiling just behind her ribs. The contrast was delicious, and she urged his hands up and over her breasts. Bryant let out a heavy sigh as his palms closed over her flimsy bra and squeezed her breasts hard. Despite his large hands, her giant tits still overflowed his grip. That didn't stop Bryant from trying to squeeze every part of her breasts into his palms at once. The pinch and pull of his hold on her was exquisitely painful.

"Jesus, Minnie. Your breasts," he said and used them as leverage to pull her tighter against him. "I've been dreaming about these." And with that, he whipped her top up over her head, and tore her bra from her so quickly, she suspected he'd ripped the hooks from the cloth.

Bryant took one nipple into his mouth, sucked so hard she felt it reverberate through her core, then switched to the other side and repeated it.

Minnie moaned and felt the urge to rake her fingernails over his shoulders, but she couldn't find purchase through his clothes. That's when she pushed him back onto the bed and stripped herself bare in front of him.

There was nothing delicate or seductive about it. She shimmied her jeans down her hips and threw her socks over her shoulder. Then she tugged Bryant's boots off his feet before starting on his fly. He had propped himself up on his elbows to watch her work, an appreciative smile on his lips. His glasses sat crooked on his nose as he let her unfasten his belt, then the button underneath. Minnie carefully pulled the zipper down over his swollen length, then lost all pretense of carefulness again as she pulled him free.

There was no question what to do next. She descended upon him, taking as much of him into her mouth as she could in one go, wrapping her fingers around the base of him and sucking the salty, earthy taste of this man into her.

He cursed, then groaned and flopped back onto the bed. She could tell he wanted to fight her, to pull her off and make her stop so he didn't come too soon. But Minnie could also see that she had rendered him incapable of resistance. Minnie felt her own rush of arousal as she realized how easy it was to bring the large, robust man under her own power once again. She pushed deeper, opening her throat as Bryant's hand came to rest on the back of her head.

He guided her through a few long, deep thrusts of his hips that almost hit her gag reflex, but backed off just before, as if he inherently knew how much of him she could take. Her own hips moved to the rhythm he set, and she yearned to be filled as she continued to suck his cock deeper and deeper into her mouth until she knew she couldn't do anymore without coming herself.

She sat back on her heels, and Bryant lay on her bed, cock at attention and eyes glazed. One hand in his hair, the other fisting her comforter.

"I need you inside me," she said. "Now."

That was all it took for Bryant to spring into action. "I think I'm going to die if I don't get to fuck you after that," he said as he pushed his jeans to the floor. He tore his shirt off and Minnie was so busy marveling at the way the light from the street played over the defined muscles on his abdomen that she missed when he'd produced a condom. She hadn't even thought about the need for one until he rolled it on.

Minnie was glad one of them was thinking practically,

because all she could manage was to center herself on her bed and open her legs.

Bryant crawled over her, centered his palms over her nipples and squeezed as his lips consumed hers again. She could feel the hard, heavy weight of him against her entrance. She flexed her hips, and taking the invitation, Bryant thrust inside her, filling her so quickly and so completely that she let out a groan of satisfaction.

She had expected him to pause and give her time to adjust to his girth inside her, but he withdrew and slammed back into her with the same intensity again and again and again. It was exactly what her body craved after the week of mutual teasing, and she met him for every thrust, grinding into his hips, guiding him deeper inside her as her muscles clenched around him.

He balanced on his elbows and brought his lips to her breasts, sucking hard in time to the rhythm of their hips.

Minnie's orgasm slammed into her hard and fast and pulsing with heat so intense that she thought she might actually be erupting like the volcano she'd felt like earlier.

Bryant sucked on her left breast hard at the same time he pinched her right nipple and she all but screamed as the highest crest of pleasure shot through her. He cursed as he leveraged himself up on his hands and rode out the way her body gripped at him, cursing so hard she knew he was trying not give in to his own rising release.

Minnie hooked her legs around his hips, drawing him deeper and clamping down with her inner muscles. He cursed one final time and pressed into her hard as his abs contracted, and she knew she'd pushed him over the edge right along with her.

~

Bryant thought he might have died. On some level, he knew he lay in bed next to the voluptuous woman he'd been lusting after for weeks. That was the only way to account for the otherworldly satiety that had him feeling as though he'd left his body behind altogether and reached some other level of consciousness.

His mind was not functioning. Bryant couldn't form thoughts, couldn't speak words. This tiny woman, whom he'd thought so shy when he'd first met her, had rocked his world. It was as if her touch had electrocuted him onto a new plane of existence, because he was certain that he was no longer the same Bryant Wilder he had always been an hour ago.

Was that even possible?

The only thing he was sure of was that as soon as his body rematerialized and his thoughts could coalesce into coherence, he was going to have a new obsession. This woman. She was going to be the undoing of him.

The first conscious thought he had that didn't have to do with the freewheeling pleasure centers in his brain was that he had to tell Van.

Telling Van what was harder to grasp. That he'd just had the most amazing sex of his life? Sure, he'd guess that might be something they'd discuss, but it wasn't what he wanted to talk to her about. He couldn't articulate why. He and Van talked about everything.

Then Minnie stirred in his arms, and Bryant fell back into his body. His limbs were heavy, his muscles relaxed, and he thought maybe he had been asleep for a little while. He didn't remember getting rid of the condom, but he must have at some point. All there was in his memory was his skin on Minnie's in a chilly room. He pulled her closer, not sure if they'd knocked all the covers to the floor or if the bed was still made.

Minnie rolled in his arms so her breath tickled his ear, then she skimmed her finger tips up his arm and over his collarbone. She scratched in the three day's worth of stubble on his chin, then trailed up to tap on the hinge of his glasses.

"You still have your glasses on," she said, a giggle in the back of her throat.

"Of course," Bryant said. His voice came out in a decidedly unsexy croak. "I needed to be able to see every expression you made, every sensuous writhe, every shudder of delight, and I'm blind without my glasses."

Minnie removed them, and Bryant opened his eyes for the first time. No wonder the room was chilly. The walls were exposed brick. The ceiling had to be fifteen feet high. Maybe more. He couldn't see the top of it.

"Well, you wouldn't be able to see anything out of these anyway; they're covered in smudges."

Bryant stretched his legs, pleased when his feet didn't fall over the edge of the bed, then cozied back up against Minnie. She burrowed her nose against his collarbone and shivered.

"You're cold," he said.

"It's January," she said, as if he were stupid.

"Then we should get under the covers."

Minnie wiggled closer, and Bryant trapped her legs between his. "That would require moving, and I like this too much.

"What if I'm cold?" he asked teasingly. He wasn't uncomfortable, but he wouldn't mind a blanket.

Minnie made a *tsk*ing noise and wriggled free of him, then gave him a spectacular view of her full, beautiful ass as she leaned over the foot of the bed and pulled up a quilt they'd kicked to the floor. She flung it over him, then burrowed beneath it so that she was once again entangled with him.

"That's better."

Bryant dozed off and on for what might have been an hour, warmed by the heavy quilt and the woman in his arms, but there came a point when the woman in his arms grew more enticing than fading in and out of sleep. He couldn't stop his hands from roaming over the curves of her body. Her waist was so tiny, and the flair of her hips was so round, the weight of her breasts in his hands so heavy. His fingers traced up and down her torso, taking her measure from the roundness of her ass to the delicate clavicle and slender shoulders. She was so soft and so pleasingly curved that Bryant never wanted to stop touching her.

He ducked his head under the quilt and nuzzled his nose between her breasts. She smelled like cinnamon and sugar and sweat and sex, and his arousal surged and flared into need. He licked his way down her tiny stomach, navigating his way by feel to the small strip of blonde hair between her legs. He traced the seam of her sex with one light finger, and Minnie, who had been feigning sleep, stretched languidly into his touch. He chuckled and searched out the top of her mound, circling, but never quite touching her clitoris as she whimpered.

Bryant smiled and sucked the nub until he'd pulled it between his teeth. He held it there so lightly, applying the barest bit of pressure before he soothed with a long hard lick that had Minnie's hands connecting with his hair.

Satisfaction swelled, and Bryant plunged his tongue inside her. Tasting her musky sweetness was like tasting whiskey for the first time. Sharp, sweet, and intoxicating. He couldn't sip from her fast enough. He wanted to drive her as wild as she had done him when she'd had him in her mouth. Just the memory was enough for his cock to throb painfully. He ran a hand over his own length to relieve some of the pressure and Minnie mewled above him, holding his face against her. She was going to come, and God, he wanted to be in her when she did.

Bryant pulled up, dragging his lips up the length of her torso and over her chest until he at last found her mouth. At the same time he plunged his tongue between her teeth, he guided himself inside her. She was so hot and so wet and ready for him, he slipped right in. He stroked into her twice, deep and slow, and she quivered beneath him.

"Bryant," she said. "Bryant, please."

He lost himself as she said his name. He didn't know up from down or right from left. All he knew was this dark room and the warm pleasure of being inside this woman. His entire existence had narrowed down to this fine ecstasy.

Minnie gasped, her body going taut with the beginnings of her release. Her pussy clamped down on his cock as Bryant pushed as deep as he could go, and he couldn't hold himself back this time. He didn't want to. He rode out his orgasm, his muscles quivering from the strength of it.

He collapsed over Minnie, noticing for the first time that the place where their bellies met was wet with sweat. A dazed smile stole over his lips as he met her eyes. Was it possible that time had been better than the first? He wanted to go a third round to see if it was a trend, but he could tell his body was spent.

Bryant rested his head on Minnie's chest this time, and he could hear her heart beating, feel the rise and fall of her breath, and he also heard the deep rumble of her stomach through her sternum as it growled with hunger.

"I forgot to eat dinner," she said by way of explanation.

"I haven't forgotten about my cinnamon rolls yet. You still owe me."

Minnie spluttered. "Your cinnamon rolls? I don't think I owe you anything."

He raised his head and grinned up at her. Her silvery hair was a tangle, but he could see how languid her body had become in the relaxed droop in her shoulders and the unfocused drowse in her eyes, even through her outrage.

"You made them for me, didn't you?" he asked.

"I needed to refine my recipe."

Bryant leaned down and nipped at the tip of her nipple. "I think you've had your recipes squared away for ages. I saw the state of your kitchen. You've been baking non-stop."

Minnie winced playfully. "Damn, I'd hoped you hadn't noticed."

Bryant only pushed himself off the bed and reached for his jeans. "Can I get down into the store without going outside?"

"What are you doing?" she asked as she propped herself up on an elbow.

"Bringing you cinnamon rolls," he said, sounding like it was obvious. "And I'd rather not freeze to death or get snapped by the paps."

"Snapped by the what?" she asked. He knew he must sound like a street urchin afraid he'd be arrested in London in the 1890s.

"Paparazzi," he said. "They're a hazard for anyone with

the slightest connection to Van. I'm always looking over my shoulder."

"Because of Clay?" she asked.

He paused before he zipped his jeans. He didn't want to lie and say because of Clay. That was so wrong. Sure, they followed Clay around sometimes, but Bryant was the notorious one. He still couldn't believe Minnie hadn't recognized him from the cover of the supermarket tabloids. If he showed up wearing one of his designer suits with his hair styled back instead of falling in his eyes, would a light bulb click in Minnie's head? Would she recognize the man who was famous for being Van Birch's boyfriend instead of just seeing him?

Phoenix would have had a fit if she'd known he'd gone to Tessa's in his work clothes. And she thoroughly disapproved of his leather jacket. She called it ratty, but it was warm and it smelled good and riding a motorcycle without one was just stupid unless you like road rash.

Taking Minnie to Tessa's had been playing with fire, he'd known it from the second he'd suggested it, but the decent part of him had needed to do something for her before he took her to bed. Sure, they'd been fooling around all week, but Bryant hadn't wanted her to think he just wanted sex. He wanted everything.

There was no way she could know the significance of his bringing her to Tessa's. And now that their evening was over, Bryant almost feared the consequences. The bar staff knew him, had never questioned how sometimes he came in and danced with every single woman in the place while Clay flashed his dimple around or how he sometimes sneaked a random guy out the back entrance with him.

But brining Minnie there tonight had basically been

begging to get caught. Part of him loved the idea. He wanted something to finally force the issue of how he and Van needed to end their arrangement. He'd chafed against it for years, but she was insistent she needed him, so Bryant stayed. But with the possibility of Minnie on the horizon. Maybe he was hoping someone would post photographs of them grinding on the dancefloor or kissing at the bar.

But that was completely different from being photographed outside her apartment in the middle of the night afterward. A flirtation was completely different from an affair, and he didn't want to cause Van that much of a headache.

"Yeah," he said, then ducked down to press a quick kiss to her lips. "So, inside entrance?"

"There is a stairway right outside the front door of the apartment. The key to the shop is in my coat pocket."

He kissed her again. "I'll be right back with food."

CHAPTER 4

*M*innie had never had so much sex in her life. Even during her two short-lived relationships in college, they had always had classes or events keeping them from each other. But it was as if Bryant found reasons to see her, spend time with her. He'd continued coming to Revival even after he finished installing the shelves and put himself to work transferring boxes of books while Minnie shelved. Then he'd make her a cocktail, take her upstairs, and give her a few orgasms. Minnie had gone to bed tipsy and satiated every night for a week. He'd even blown off brunch with his mother the next Sunday in favor of making her pancakes and going down on her on her kitchen table.

Minnie hadn't even argued with him. Though later, after her sex-addled brain had time to come to its senses, she had pushed him out the door to take his mother out to dinner instead. It had been a mutually beneficial decision, because Sunday evenings meant obligatory check-ins with her father. The weekly phone call had been one of the many stipulations that had come along with the money to open her bookstore. It wasn't because her father was actually interested in what was going on in his daughter's life but because he didn't want to give her too long a leash.

They'd made a deal when Minnie had dropped out of college. Minnie wouldn't go public with the knowledge that he'd knowingly neglected his daughter for the first eighteen years of her life, and he'd give her the means to be independent, *if* she would keep up appearances of him as the loyal and devoted father that she'd always needed but never had. The Sunday evening phone calls were more business meeting than anything. Jonas Halvarson wanted to know what she was doing with his money, and Minnie pretended he was an investor instead of the most infuriating man on the planet.

She didn't want Bryant to see how humiliating it was. If Minnie could keep who her father was a secret from everyone in Wellville, she would. Thankfully, few people in the small Kansas town knew much about the influential Colorado developer. Few enough people read Forbes in the town, whose main businesses were farming and factory work.

Minnie knew Jonas was attempting to get a foothold in the state next door, especially now that Minnie was living in Kansas. He saw no reason why he couldn't gentrify everything he could get his hands on. He didn't understand the difference in income threshold. He'd wanted Minnie's store to be an emporium and had told her she was thinking small when she mentioned an independent bookstore and bakery. He'd wanted her to rival Barnes & Noble and start a chain of Revival Books & Coffee all over the Midwest.

Buying a building in the town's historic district had been

his start. She knew he'd been petitioning the local historical society for permission to renovate some of the unoccupied buildings into luxury apartments, but so far, his proposals had been rejected.

This week, he wanted Minnie to lobby his case. He didn't believe her that the local population couldn't afford the sort of lofts he wanted to build. "Let me worry about finding the right tenants. You worry about endearing yourself to the locals."

Minnie really, really hated him. Everything about him was smarmy, and he was only ever out for his own gain. She wished she could be rid of him, but Minnie couldn't quite let go of the anger at his neglect of her and her mother. She was going to wring every cent out of him that should have been spent on her mother's healthcare, and she was going to do it gleefully.

Perhaps Minnie was more like him than she would like to admit.

She probably needed to hide that from Bryant as well.

Thus far, Bryant had been satisfied with cinnamon rolls, sex, and learning about her reading life. They'd talked about the classics. She loved Dickens; he preferred Thomas Hardy. They talked about the American writers. He was a fan of the Beats; she wasn't. They'd talked for hours about "A Good Man is Hard to Find," by Flannery O'Connor and learned they had a shared love for most of Haruki Murakami's books and marveled that there were so many new and innovative authors coming out that it was difficult to keep up with everything.

Both had stacks of books on their bedside tables that had the potential to topple and kill them in their sleep. Though, while Bryant had seen the massive collection of books

Minnie had accrued, both professionally and personally, over the years, Minnie's knowledge of Bryant's "to be read" pile was entirely hypothetical. After two weeks of regular sex, they'd only ever been in her space. She wasn't even sure it had occurred to him to invite her to his house. They hadn't even gone out together after that first night at Tessa's.

Minnie tried to tell herself it was no big deal. It had only been a matter of days since they'd started sleeping together, and she had so much work to do around the shop if she was going to have a Valentine's Day grand opening. She had it all planned out, with a sweetheart party and a romance novel display front and center. She'd give out heart-shaped cookies, and there would be hot chocolate and cider, and she was going to give away books wrapped in red paper that asked people to be the book's Valentine. All of that could only happen after she inventoried all her books, hired staff for the bakery, and trained everyone. She was super behind on advertising, but thankfully that was something her father's assistant was handling. On the larger scale anyway. The everyday social media was something she wanted to do herself.

Her small accounts had gained some local traction on Facebook and Instagram, but thinking of new posts all the time had given her some anxiety, so she was posting haphazardly at the moment.

When she stopped and thought about it, Minnie understood that she didn't really have time to begin a new relationship right now, but she couldn't help herself. Bryant was so attractive and had such a commanding presence that she would probably let him walk all over her, the way her father claimed she let everyone do.

Her body felt so good that Minnie didn't have it in her to care.

She enjoyed his company and couldn't deny what an advantage it was having someone tall help her shelve the books. It saved her the trouble of dragging the ladder out to reach the top shelf. Most normal-height women could reach it just fine, but being all of one inch over five feet did Minnie little favors in that department.

That had been one of the first personal questions Bryant had asked her in the guise of a joke. He'd been helping her build the used Western section. He'd been distracted by the books, pausing to read the tattered paperbacks' back covers more often than shelving them. He'd just looked up from one when he'd said, "So, is Minnie a nickname because you're so small, or are you really a Minerva?"

Minnie had grinned. Most people didn't even realize that Minnie was usually short for Minerva. They just assumed she was named after the mouse and moved on. "It's Minneapolis, actually."

He'd had both arms raised over his head, one holding the line of books in place, the other poised to add another book, but both arms fell to his sides, and the row of books on the shelf all leaned to the left.

"Minneapolis? I've never heard that as a given name before."

"My mother was a little eccentric," she said by way of explanation. The truth was, her mother had named her after a character Jeff Goldblum played on an episode of *Sesame Street*, which she'd seen while babysitting Rocco when she'd been pregnant with Minnie. And that was almost too much eccentricity for most people. Better to let them think she'd been named after a city in Minnesota known for its giant mall.

"It's fun," Bryant said. Then sounded out the individual syllables of her name. "Min-knee-app-o-liss." He grinned at her. "I think it suits you. You are a tiny force of nature."

"I'm not sure I'd go that far."

"I don't know many other twenty-three-year-old entrepreneurs who could open a business like this. You must have investors."

"I do," she said. "But that's just because I took the time to write a very thorough business plan." Which was true. That her father was the investor and he would have given her millions if she'd asked for it as long as she promised to help make him look good on occasion was something she didn't want to admit to anyone ever. That was her own personal darkness to bear.

"When I was twenty-three, I was fresh out of the Army and didn't do anything but sleep and party."

"That's not true, you got your contractor's license, and you and Clay started your business. That's not sleeping or partying."

Bryant waggled his eyebrows at her. "We didn't start the business until the next year. And that was only possible because Van helped us out."

Minnie still wasn't used to how casually Bryant dropped a rock star's name into everyday conversation. She supposed to him Van was just a friend of his who happened to be one of the most famous people in the world, but Minnie was only used to hearing her name on the radio.

"That was nice of her to do, to help you out like that."

Bryant shrugged. "We'd be in a lot more debt now without her, that's for sure," he said.

"I bought one of her albums the other day," Minnie said.

Bryant's response was to raise his eyebrows. They'd already gone over how Minnie didn't pay much attention to popular music. She'd grown up listening to her mom's favorites from the eighties and nineties, and those were the tunes that made her happy, but she'd have to be living with her head in the sand to never have heard a Van Birch song.

"You talk about her so much," she said. "I was curious."

"What do you think?" Bryant asked.

"That I'd probably get to know her better if I watched her reality show."

Bryant choked on air, then wheezed, and managed a spluttered, "Don't watch the show, please."

Minnie cocked her head to the side, arms still laden with books for Bryant to shelve. "How come?"

"Because most of it is one choreographed publicity stunt after another. If you want to get to know Van, I can introduce you when she comes to town in March."

That had sent a thrill of sparks up and down Minnie's spine. "In March?"

"Unless you're going somewhere before then?"

He stepped closer so that he loomed over her, a furrow between his brows, his glasses slightly crooked.

"I plan on staying right here," she said.

Bryant placed a hard kiss on her lips, then rested his forehead against hers.

"Good," he said. "I'm not going anywhere either."

The only thing that had made Minnie hesitate about the whole thing was that first night they'd spent together. The second time they'd made love, they'd either been so tired or so lost in each other that neither one of them had thought about protection.

That had been the only time they hadn't used a condom. They'd talked about it directly afterward of course. Bryant had come back with the cinnamon rolls. Minnie had used the bathroom and donned her fluffy robe in his absence, because she'd been cold without him there to keep him warm.

She'd taken the plate he'd stolen from Revival, sat next to him on the bed, taken one bite of her dessert and said, "We didn't use a condom just now."

Bryant nodded. "I'm sorry. I never—I wasn't even thinking. I know I don't have anything, but I'm sorry. I'm usually more responsible."

Minnie nodded. "It wasn't just you. I could have said something, but I didn't think of it until it was too late."

"It won't happen again," Bryant said. He hadn't set aside his cinnamon roll, but he'd been less voracious since she'd started speaking.

"I appreciate that. Really," she said. "The only thing is that I'm a little bit behind on my birth control."

That got him to set down his plate. "Oh?"

"It's irresponsible, I know, and I don't have any excuses, except that I haven't found a doctor around here yet, and I've been on the shot, and I was supposed to get another one just before Christmas, so I'm only a couple of weeks over-due. It shouldn't be a problem. Most people have to wait a year after the damn thing wears off to get pregnant, and it should be too early in my cycle, but I just thought you should know what we're dealing with here."

Bryant reached for the hand that still held her fork, set the fork aside, and twined his fingers with hers. "Well, thank you for telling me," he said.

Biting her lip, Minnie asked, "You're not freaked out?"

"By the idea of being a father?" he asked. "Absolutely. And I think it's far too soon for us to talk about children," his teeth flashed in the dim light from the streetlights outside. "But I'd take care of you if that's what it came down to."

"Oh." Minnie hadn't expected so pragmatic an answer. "I'm not sure I'd need taken care of exactly but maybe a helpful hand."

Bryant resumed eating his cinnamon roll and asked around a mouthful. "Would you like me to pick up some Plan B?"

Minnie, who hadn't been able to think much beyond panic sighed. "No, that's a good option. But I can stop by the drug store in the morning."

Except Minnie had stopped by every drug store in town, and no one had it. Then she'd had appointments with book reps and had called every pharmacy between Wellville and the state lines. She had a Walgreens near the Nebraska border ship it to her.

Minnie hadn't told Bryant that part. Just that she'd purchased some. Which was true, and she'd taken it. The fact that it was almost a week later made her worry just a little bit, but the likelihood of conception actually happening was so minimal, she didn't think it'd make that big of a difference.

She was so busy with the bookstore; it was easy for Minnie to push it to the back of her mind. The chances really were so slim.

It surprised Minnie when Bryant would ask her personal questions in the middle of the night, but after the first week, that was when they had most of their intimate discussions. It was nice in a way. They would go upstairs, blow each other minds, doze, and then as if Bryant couldn't turn his brain off, he would come out with questions like, "What's your favorite book?" or "What's your most memorable birthday?" Hers had been *Persuasion* and the year she and her mother had hiked a popular trail and stayed two nights in a tent together and howled at the full moon like wolves after eating a whole pan of brownies, just the two of them. His had been *Slaughterhouse-Five* and his eighteenth birthday, just before his senior year of high school. He and Clay and Van had stolen a bottle of whiskey and driven out to the middle of nowhere and fallen asleep in some random pasture, drunkenly watching the stars. The bottle of whiskey had belonged to Van's dad, Clay's stepdad, and they'd all three been grounded for the first three months of the school year, but Bryant's fond smile as he related the story told Minnie that the whole thing had been worth it.

Minnie was beginning to get more and more curious about what his life had been like so far. He'd been in the Army, and he'd grown up with just his mother. But aside from the almost worshipful way he talked about Clay and sometimes Van, Minnie couldn't help but feel like he was holding something back. Like maybe there was something Bryant didn't want her to know. Not that she could fault him. There was a lot about her life she wasn't ready to share yet either.

But one night Minnie had been dozing, the steady rhythm of Bryant's arm up and down her spine slowly lulling her into actual sleep when he asked, "How did you lose your mom?"

She'd sleepily asked, "Hmmm?"

Bryant had kissed the top of her head and said, "You said

your mom died during your senior year of high school, and I was curious how you lost her. Was it sudden?"

"How do you mean 'sudden?'"

Bryant shifted around her. He'd somehow wrapped himself around every part of her. "Clay lost his mom a few months ago in a car accident," he said, and Minnie cringed involuntarily.

"Oh, that's so awful."

Bryant kissed her forehead. "Mary Beth was the best," he said. "We all miss her."

"I didn't realize," Minnie said, and Bryant shushed her. "I miss my mom too, every day. She'd love what I'm doing with Revival."

"What happened?"

Minnie shivered and snuggled more deeply into Bryant's warmth, even though, even almost five years later, barely anything touched the bone-deep cold grief that had been watching her mother waste away.

"Well, it wasn't sudden, and it was."

Bryant resumed stroking her back. "How do you mean?"

"It's kind of a long story."

"I'm not going anywhere."

Minnie sucked in a breath and prepared to give Bryant more truth than she'd given anyone in Wellville so far. "So the thing to know before starting this story is that my father is kind of a well-off asshole who met my mother when she worked at a gentlemen's club."

She felt Bryant stiffen around her momentarily before relaxing again. "You've already said he wasn't around while you were growing up."

"No. He sort of kept my mom as a mistress for a while. She was never good enough to marry, but he paid for me to be born, apparently. He's listed on my birth certificate, and then he sort of disappeared. My mom left the stage and started bartending after that, but it's still hard to stay up all night at a club and raise a kid, so she worked the bare minimum of shifts to keep us afloat. I remember spending the night at Rocco's most weekends. His mom was a hairstylist, so at least she kept more regular hours."

"Your dad never helped out?"

"I've never been clear on the details. Mom didn't like to talk about him. But he showed up sometimes. Randomly, it felt like, but our financial situation never changed. My mom started working less when I was fourteen. She had headaches. We didn't know why. By the time I was sixteen, she was applying for disability. When I was seventeen, we found out she had a brain tumor, and by the time I was eighteen, she was gone."

"I'm so sorry," Bryant said. "That's why you started working so young?"

"Yeah."

"And your dad didn't step up to help?"

Minnie pulled in a deep breath, then let it out slowly through her nose. "He said he couldn't do anything because it wasn't his fault my mom didn't have health insurance, but he could have paid for her treatments without it even making a dent in his bank account."

Bryant coughed. "Wow, so when you say 'well-off,' you mean—"

"He's worth millions. And he is the person I hate most in this world."

Bryant was quiet for a moment as his hand stroked soothing circles over her back. "Did you move here to get away from him?"

She huffed a sad, dry laugh. "No, I moved to New York to get away from him. I moved here to get away from all the assholes I met at Columbia."

Bryant made a choking noise, "You graduated from Columbia?"

She kissed the tip of his nose. "I dropped out of Columbia in the middle of my senior year." Minnie didn't tell many people that. She usually let them believe she'd finished. It was easier that way.

Bryant's fingers never stopped caressing her skin as he processed this revelation. Minnie was prepared for the same lecture Rocco had given her, about how she could waste such an opportunity. Didn't she know how many people would literally die for a shot at that kind of education? How could she let her so-called friends bully her out of the diploma that she was only one semester away from claiming as her own?

But Rocco hadn't understood; it was more than just the bullying. It was the public scrutiny. The phone calls, the reporters, the paparazzi, the name calling. One time someone had literally smashed an egg in her face and called her a whore on the street. Minnie wasn't built for that kind of life. Yes, the parties and the gossip had been fun for a while. Opening *Page Six* and seeing herself in a picture surrounded by the glamorous elite had been novel after where she'd come from, but ultimately, that wasn't the sort of life Minnie wanted. She wanted to build something for herself, define who she was for herself, live with the fierce sort of independence her mother had only dreamed of.

"I'm just impressed you were able to get in to Columbia," Bryant said.

Minnie laughed. "My dad's family is originally from New York. He's a legacy. I didn't do anything special."

"But you took a chance, and that chance brought you to me," Bryant said. "I'm sorry the people you met there were assholes though."

Minnie kissed him and snuggled her nose against his neck. She wanted to be done talking for the night. Talking about New York was uncomfortable at best, but she liked the romantic twist Bryant had unknowingly put on her experience. He wasn't wrong, but she wasn't entirely sure he was right either. They still had so much to learn about one another.

CHAPTER 5

*B*ryant knew he should be more careful, otherwise some photographer was going to snap him coming out of Minnie's building with bedhead one of these mornings, but he didn't care. He couldn't bring himself to stop. Better than them photographing her coming out of his house. He couldn't bring her there until he'd had a chance to talk to Van. That wouldn't be until after Valentine's Day, but that was fine. He could wait. Minnie would probably be too busy opening her store to notice that they only ever stayed at her place and never went anywhere.

It was just too risky.

He'd been anxious as hell for the last two weeks that someone had taken a picture of them making out at Tessa's and had been waiting for it to pop up on Twitter. He'd tamped down the fear of waking up to a string of nasty messages from Phoenix because, so far, that hadn't happened. But Bryant knew it was only a matter of time.

Why couldn't he have fallen in love with Cole—the

subcontractor who'd been flirting with him mercilessly for the past year? Cole was cute with dark hair, a scruffy beard, and strong shoulders from hanging drywall all the time. Cole had sensed Bryant's bisexuality the moment they'd met, but Bryant had never been interested. If he had been, he could have hung out with Cole for months before anyone would have guessed that their relationship was sexual.

But with Minnie? A pretty blonde with killer curves? There wouldn't be any claiming "we're just friends." One photo of them standing on the same block together and Bryant would be accused of ruining Van Birch's life from the first blurry image. Maybe that wouldn't be so bad? Bryant hated himself for thinking that way, and he regretted the risk he'd taken in bringing Minnie to Tessa's that night. It's why he hadn't taken her anywhere since. He just needed to man up and tell Van he wanted to be done, because God, Bryant didn't really want to want anybody else. He chafed to be done with his work day so he could go back to Minnie's place and help her shelve books or clean the kitchen or just make her a drink and force her to relax after she'd pushed herself too hard all day.

Last night he'd cooked her the one pasta dish he'd taught himself to make and kept her wine glass topped off. When they'd been reading together on the sofa, finishing off the wine after dinner, Minnie had lain snuggled into his side the whole time. Then, after the wine was gone, she'd unzipped his jeans and wrapped her mouth around his cock, then had gone down on him while she'd touched herself.

He'd let her come that way, but he'd fought his own release until he was inside her. He'd pulled out one of the condoms he'd stashed in the end table next to the sofa and unrolled it over himself while Minnie watched, biting her lip. Then Bryant had pulled her onto his lap and almost expired from ecstasy as she rode him. He'd come with her that time, his orgasm ripping out of him so completely that he would have promised her the moon if only she'd stay with him.

Yes, they had a lot of sex, but Bryant didn't care what they did together; he just wanted to be in her company all the time. It was like nothing he had ever felt before. He was obsessed with her. When he imagined going to L.A. next month for the filming he had to do, he imagined himself stepping off the plane, kissing Van for the cameras, then telling her how Minnie was the one. It had taken Bryant only two hours of being in Minnie's bed to decide that he didn't want anyone else ever. She was it for him. No one else would ever satisfy him or beguile him the way she did.

Now he just had to tread carefully so as not to expose Minnie to any of the wrong things before he had a chance to talk to Van. He thought about calling her every day, about picking up his phone and texting her, *I met someone*, but then Van would have a million questions, and Bryant wouldn't be able to keep ahold of the conversation. In person, he could place a finger over Van's lips and tell her to shut up until he was finished.

Bryant didn't think Van would object to ending their fake relationship. She'd always said that the second one of them felt like they'd found someone, they'd call it off. And it had been four years. Van was so established in the industry now, there was much less of a chance some music exec or smarmy agent would try to take advantage of her. Not now that she had the tenacious Phoenix on her side and Bishop, her manager, who practically worshipped her. Bryant thought there might be something developing between Bishop and Van. Something slow and perhaps meaningful.

When he'd been in L.A. in November to film the Christmas episode, the producers had insisted on pitting Bryant and Bishop against each other as possible rivals for Van's attention. Van was innocent of course. She only liked Bishop as a friend, but they showed a scene—which had been written—where Bishop pulled Van aside and gave her a silver bracelet as a Christmas gift in private. She'd thrown her arms around him, and Bishop had tenderly stroked her back. Bryant's part had been to walk in on them in such a state and have Van show off the jewelry in happy oblivion while Bryant and Bishop glared at each other over her head.

Bryant knew they'd cooked up the story line just to keep viewers interested in the monotony of Van being on tour and doing nothing but performing and traveling and sleeping. That didn't mean Bryant hadn't seen the long, slow caresses of Henry Bishop's hands down Van's back or hadn't recognized the real desire there. They weren't sleeping together yet, Bryant didn't think, but he had a feeling they were acclimatizing themselves to the idea. He'd been her manager for three years after all. It would be a shift for her.

Bryant wasn't always Bishop's biggest fan. He could be a macho asshat, but he worked hard for Van, and Bryant was reasonably sure he'd do the same in a romantic relationship. Bryant would be happy for her, and bonus, he would be free to keep Minnie all to himself without the awkwardness of telling Van he was out.

Bryant was imagining all the things with Minnie. He was already plotting how to rent out his house so that he could move in with her until they actually did away with the condoms for good and started making babies and they would need the extra two bedrooms his house offered over her apartment.

The thought of Minnie carrying his child sent Bryant's mind into a lust-filled daze. He liked the idea of having children with her. They'd be so bright and so soft and probably little hellions the way he'd been before he'd figured out his medication and his routine. But that didn't deter him. Bryant looked forward to it. He was prepared. And maybe his kids would escape the ADHD curse. Minnie was so grounded and organized and focused. Maybe they'd get that from their mother, and he'd keep with him whatever genes had caused him to lose focus on everything except words moving in front of his eyes .

He almost didn't want to wait to find out. It was a daily temptation to ask Minnie if they could have sex without the condoms. He wanted that intimacy more than anything else. He wanted that bond between them, but she'd already been on and on about how much work she had to do to get her business off the ground and how she was only twenty-three and how she was glad that Plan-B existed because it made her worry so much less about any failings her birth control might have had and how finding a doctor was absolutely on her agenda for March, because she wasn't going to have time before then, and she didn't have time or mental ability to even wrap her mind around having a baby right now.

So Bryant didn't bring it up. He didn't mind waiting. He hadn't been in a hurry to have kids—possibly ever—until Minnie had mentioned the remote possibility that her birth control wasn't going to protect them from a mishap. It had taken all of Bryant's control not to pounce on her and make sure she conceived. The idea had stuck in him like something primal, and he was having trouble letting it go.

But she hadn't said anything else, and he figured that meant that all was normal. He didn't think it was polite to ask about her cycle and if she was late yet. Though he'd googled Depo-Provera and found out that most women stopped having their periods while on it, so it was likely that Minnie wouldn't be on a regular cycle.

Bryant distracted himself from wanting to ask by looking for any changes in her body. He hadn't noticed any yet, and he'd been taking a keen, daily inventory. After a month of sleeping together, neither of them had tired of the other's body yet. He woke up exhausted and hung over most mornings and struggled through his work day, but by the time he made his way back to Minnie, he had found his energy again, and it didn't subside until they were both limp with pleasure.

It was more than Bryant could bear some days, how much he wanted her.

"Who is he?" Clay asked, startling Bryant from where he stood at the circular saw, his hand poised on the handle, the lintel to a door frame lined up to cut. It was a good thing Bryant hadn't turned the saw on yet, because he hadn't even realized he'd zoned out.

"What?" Bryant asked.

Clay pulled the pencil from behind his ear and chewed the tip. "The guy that has you about ready to cut your hand off with the circular saw."

"What?" Bryant asked again.

"And more importantly?" Clay asked. "Why the fuck would you mess around on Van? Whoever he is, he definitely isn't worth it."

This is where things with being Van's ruse grew complicated. Clay didn't know that Bryant and Van's relationship was fake. To everyone but Van, himself, Phoenix, and possibly Van's dad, Bryant and Van's relationship was very much real. The kissing, the touching, her sleeping at his place two-thirds of the time she was home in Wellville. That was one-hundred percent to keep everyone deceived. Because if anyone, even Clay, who avoided being on camera as much as possible, mentioned one night at Tessa's that Bryant wasn't really dating Van, all it took was the wrong person to overhear and there would be gossip rag scandal for months.

But Clay wasn't stupid. He knew Bryant had sought out other sexual partners during the times when he and Van were living in separate cities. Hell, Bryant had had a sort-of-boyfriend-slash-fuckbuddy when Van had asked him to make things official with her in public. Bryant hadn't broken it off with Will completely until his service commitment was over and he'd moved back to Kansas. Like a shit-bag, Bryant had never given Clay an explanation, just that Bryant and Van had an understanding when it came to certain things.

Clay was Bryant's best friend, but he had a tenuous understanding at best of what it meant for Bryant to be bi. Bryant had steered Clay into assuming that the understanding with Van meant that if Bryant needed to sleep with a dude every now and then to satisfy himself, Van was cool with it. Clay didn't like it, but since he didn't understand, he didn't push about it too much. It was a shitty move, to promote the misunderstanding of his sexuality, especially as Bryant was beginning to understand more and more what he wanted in a partner. But what else was

Bryant supposed to do when Van had begged him not to tell Clay?

When it came to Van, Clay had all sorts of blind spots. Clay had been in love with his stepsister since the moment they'd laid eyes on each other. He'd been sixteen and Van fourteen when they'd met outside their guitar lessons. Clay had been waiting for Van to be old enough for her dad to allow her date, but in the meantime, her dad had fallen in love with Clay's mom outside those same guitar lessons. The two of them had gotten married just as Van turned fifteen.

Clay had never been easy with having to treat Van like a sister. Bryant hadn't known Van before she'd become Clay's stepsister. He'd only known of her as the girl that Clay mooned over at his guitar lessons. The first time Bryant had met her, Clay had introduced them over sodas in Robin's kitchen. Clay hadn't known what to do with his hands. Van nodded at Bryant like he wasn't worth her notice and had taken her soda and hidden in her room. Clay had buried his head in his hands and said, "Dude, I am so fucked." Bryant had only clapped Clay on the back and told him he'd figured it out. But as Clay continued to be an awkward weirdo, Bryant had decided that maybe if he could show Clay how to treat Van like a sister, his friend would figure it out.

Bryant tried to include Van in their conversations when he was over, and she'd been nice enough. Then, a few weeks into the fall semester, Rick Schroeder, a sleazeball who was in Bryant's class, had tried to grope Van at her locker one day. Bryant had been coming down the hall, dreading his English class, when he'd seen it. Van had told Schroeder to back off, but he'd sneered and called her something foul.

Bryant hadn't even thought. He'd dropped his notebooks

and punched the asshole so hard in the face that he'd rocketed back against the locker. Schroeder was on the football team with Bryant, so he didn't stay down long. He'd thrown himself back at Bryant, and they'd brawled right there in the hallway until two of the bigger teachers had pulled them apart. They'd both been suspended after that and each had to sit out a football game.

But Van had shown up on his doorstep after school on the first day of his suspension. She'd been carrying her guitar case. She hadn't even said hello when he'd opened the door; she'd just said, "You're on drumline, right?" Bryant had nodded. "You have a drum kit?" Bryant had nodded again, not sure what to make of her. But Van had only shrugged and pushed past him into the house. "Cool, I need someone who knows what they're doing to jam with."

They'd been friends in their own right after that, while Clay's main strategy for dealing with his feelings for Van had been to avoid her, though he'd always made time for Bryant. At some point, Clay conceded that Bryant had won Van's affection in high school. That Clay thought Bryant was still in a relationship with the woman he'd been secretly in love with had never been a point of contention between them. Still Clay resented that Van alone wasn't enough for Bryant, and whenever Bryant hooked up with someone, Bryant always let Clay think it was a guy, because otherwise, Clay would be impossible to live with.

And it was another shitbag move. Because if Bryant had more than brotherly feelings toward Van, she absolutely would have been enough for him. Someday, he told himself, he would get to tell Clay the truth, and he would tell him that it was more about the person than the gender, and that if he were ever in a committed relationship, he would never look for sex outside that relationship. That wasn't Bryant's style.

Hopefully that day would come soon, because he didn't think he could put up with playing territory games with Clay when all Bryant wanted to do was worship Minnie.

"I was thinking about Van actually," Bryant said.

It wasn't entirely a lie. He had been thinking about Van a little bit, but it was the easiest way to get Clay to back down.

"And is she why you're never at The Fox after work anymore?"

Bryant only shrugged. He hated outright lying, but there was no way he could bring Minnie to the Fox. Paparazzi aside, the place was a dump. "I'm wondering if there's something going on between Van and Bishop," Bryant said, truthfully.

"She wouldn't cheat on you with that asshole," Clay all but growled. It was no secret that he thought Bishop was a creep. But Clay was surly when it came to anything to do with Van, so no one paid much attention to him. It was clear how he felt about her and how he let it run his life. Just about the only person who didn't see that Clay was head over heels in love with her was Van herself. And until Clay either admitted his feelings to her or moved on, there was no helping how much of an asshole Clay was about the other men in Van's life.

Bryant shrugged again. "We'll see."

"Maybe I should go with you," Clay said.

Bryant stepped away from the saw then and faced Clay. "You want to go to L.A.?"

"Why not?" Clay asked. Clay had gone to help with filming twice before and did whatever logical gymnastics he could to maneuver out of being on *Pop Star*, and here he was, volunteering to go.

"Because you hate L.A."

"But if you're worried about Van, I can help keep an eye on things. Give you a second opinion."

"Like a doctor?" Bryant couldn't help the chuckle in his voice.

Clay rolled his eyes. "More like a brother."

Bryant nodded. There were times he'd wished Clay was his brother instead of Van's. Aside from the fact that Clay and Van had nothing that resembled sibling-like feelings for each other, that's how Bryant had always thought of Clay. From the moment they'd met in the second grade when Bryant and his mother had landed in this tiny town, on the run from his ne'er-do-well father, he and Clay had each other's backs. He'd asked his mother once if she and Clay's mom could get married so they could all become a family, and that's when his mother had sat him down for the first time and told him about how some people did like people of the same sex, but that she didn't.

Bryant had only been nine at the time, and he'd noticed that most couples he saw were made of one man and one woman, but some weren't, and he just assumed that everyone was able to choose what kind of relationship they wanted to be in. It had never occurred to him that not everyone thought they were equally likely to marry a man or a woman when they grew up.

That had been the beginning of him realizing that people thought straight was normal and that being attracted to two genders like he was wasn't normal. Because of that, Bryant hadn't had the guts to date a guy in high school. He hadn't had his first relationship with a man until his deployment. And it had been sort of a revelation, and sort of a coming back to himself. to move past his fears and find that honesty with himself that, yes, he was also attracted to men and that there was no shame in that.

But it still wasn't something he liked to talk about with other people. About the only people who understood were his mother, who had known before he did, and Van, who had the uncanny ability to accept everyone in the world, except Clay, exactly as they were. It was the thing Bryant probably loved the most about her.

"Van and I are lucky to have you," Bryant said to Clay, and Clay patted his shoulder a little too hard. Clay was shorter than Bryant, about five foot eleven compared to Bryant's six foot four, but he was brawnier. Bryant was no slouch, but his muscles were lean. Clay had bulk that often had women drooling after him. He only noticed how women looked at him when he was paying attention, but it happened all the time. And when Clay wanted to put power behind his gestures, he had the muscle to do it. That he did so now was no accident.

Bryant knew Clay was part unable to express his own gratitude and part jealous as hell that it was Van and Bryant and not Van and Clay.

"You know she's going to try to get you to take your shirt off on camera," Bryant said.

"Van will hardly notice I'm there," Clay said.

"No, Phoenix. She'll have your shirtless the whole time."

Clay cursed. He and Phoenix, Van's best friend and right hand, did not get along, but Phoenix knew how to get viewers and keep Van's name in the news. Basically, all she ever said to Clay was "Shut up and take your shirt off," which would have been fantastic if he'd thought Phoenix and Clay could maybe work out some of their mutual sexual frustration. The only problem was that sexual frustration over each other wasn't their problem. Clay would never sleep with Van's best friend, and Phoenix's sex life was an enigma. Van said she'd had boyfriends off and on, but Bryant had never met any of them. Sometimes they hung out together, scoping out possible hook-ups in the L.A. clubs, but if she went home with anyone, Bryant never saw it.

"It's going to be so fucking cold," Clay complained. He hated the cold. Even now, working inside, he still wore his dusty Carhartt jacket, where Bryant had stripped down to his flannel. Even in the unheated house.

"I'll be suffering right along with you," Bryant said.

Clay only harrumphed. "You should come out to The Fox tonight. It'll be better for you than being at home stewing about Van."

Bryant nodded. He didn't want to, but he couldn't forget about all his other relationships. And he owed so much to Clay. He'd basically cock-blocked him for the last four years, and he couldn't even apologize, because Bryant wasn't sorry he'd helped Van when she'd asked. But now that the end was in sight, he was glad. They'd made a huge fucking mess of the whole thing, and in just a few weeks, they could start sorting out all the pieces.

Maybe with Bryant out of his way, Clay could stop pretending he thought of Van as his sister and make a move before Bishop did.

CHAPTER 6

$\mathcal{K}$ansas had outlawed smoking in bars more than ten years ago, but The Fox had been around so long, the smell had permeated the walls and sunk into the woodwork. The place would smell like stale tobacco until it moldered away. It wasn't a pleasant smell but one Bryant had always found comforting. It reminded him of when he'd had a family. Back when he and his mom had still lived in Ohio and he would stay at his grandparents' house after school. Their house had smelled this way—well, it hadn't been as grungy as The Fox, but it was the same idea.

He'd had good memories of staying with his dad's parents. He'd help his grandmother make dinner, and his grandfather had given him his first hammer when Bryant had been in first grade and helped him build a birdhouse. That had all been before.

Before his father had become an addict. Or at least before his addiction had taken over and turned him into a person none of them recognized anymore until he'd held a gun to Bryant's mother's head one night before passing out. Georgie had taken Bryant and run the next day, and Bryant hadn't seen any of his dad's family since.

He'd missed his grandparents at first, but apparently, they'd been salty about Georgie taking Bryant away from them and refused to have anything to do with Bryant and his mom after they'd left. Bryant had long ago decided that he and his mother were better off without the lot of them, but every now and then, that smell made him think about how his childhood might have been entirely different if his dad had stayed sober.

He might have been diagnosed sooner and had an easier time in school. He might have gotten in fewer fights growing up. His mom wouldn't have had to work so hard. And while all that would have been nice, Bryant wouldn't have traded his relationships with Clay and Van for that, no matter how confusing they could be. And he definitely wouldn't trade Minnie.

A smile ghosted over his lips as he reached for the pitcher Clay had just plunked onto the table next to their basket of limp fries.

"That's what I'm talking about," Clay said, pointing a fry at Bryant. "That fucking smile."

"What smile?" Bryant tried to drop his grin, but he couldn't. If he had been in any other situation, this is where he would have gushed about Minnie. Bryant wanted to tell Clay about her. Clay deserved to know that Bryant was falling in love, but the thought of betraying Van's trust weighed so heavily on him that he downed his beer instead.

"That's the same smile you wear whenever you're getting laid."

And the conversation had just gone downhill from there.

~

Bryant had texted Minnie after lunch to say he was going to go out for a couple of beers with Clay but that he'd be by later.

Secretly, Minnie was relieved. They'd been inseparable for the last few weeks, and as much as she wanted him around every minute of the day, she was also having her new employees stay late to help wrap the giveaway books for the grand opening party while she put her finishing touches on her displays.

The shop technically opened three days before Valentine's Day, which was only a week away, and she had so much to do that she was starting to lose sleep. Even with Bryant's help, and now the three employees she'd hired, Minnie wasn't sure they were going to make it.

She should have hired somebody to organize the grand opening party for her. It's what her father's secretary had recommended, but Minnie hadn't wanted to. She'd wanted to do as much of the planning herself, not only to prove that she could, but also to prove that she could execute a successful event and that she could do so while still running the business. She'd need that skill in order to attract customers and stay relevant.

As the night wore on and she'd crossed all the items off her to-do list, Minnie didn't feel the sense of accomplishment she usually did at the end of a busy day. Without Bryant there, she found herself wandering the stacks, pulling a book off the shelf only to put it right back, repositioning the armchair in the Romance section for the millionth time, and rearranging the mismatched chairs around the conference table in the center of the stacks until they were arranged randomly, then back to rainbow alignment, and back to random again.

It was all pointless. She missed him, and she didn't want to be here alone. It was too quiet, and she was too aware of how he was the only friend she'd made in town. She'd moved here to spend time with Rocco. Here it was almost Valentine's Day, and she'd barely seen him since Christmas. Minnie paused to send Rocco a text, inviting him to come by and see her progress and help her eat some of the pastries she wasn't quite sure were perfect yet. She'd just hit send when her phone dinged with a notification.

Her heart pounded when she saw Bryant's name. She hoped everything was okay.

Home. Too many beers to drive. Miss you. Will you come to me?

A second text came listing his address, then, *Park next to me in the carport in the alley. I'll meet you there.*

Minnie didn't hesitate. It wasn't until she passed his house searching for the alley and saw the two-car garage and full driveway that she found his instructions to park in the back peculiar. The alley was dark, and she couldn't figure out which house was his until she passed his work truck parked under a steel awning. There was just enough space for her to pull her Prius in next to it. Bryant opened the gate to the privacy fence as she exited the car.

She could tell immediately that he was drunk. And more than just a-beer-too-many drunk. He leaned his weight against the fence like he couldn't stand up on his own. His arms hung slack at his sides. His smile crooked and sloppy. She took a deep breath, not sure what she'd gotten herself into and realizing for the first time since this affair had started that she didn't really know him that well. It had only been a few weeks. She adored him so far, but there was still so much she had to find out.

When she approached him, he tried to pull her into a kiss, but his lips were loose and wet, and he smelled so strongly of whiskey that she thought he might have bathed in it. Minnie pushed him back with a hand to his chest, and Bryant didn't fight her.

"I thought you went out for beers with Clay."

"I did," he said. "And it was horrible. He interrogated me the whole time." Bryant's words were so slurred, Minnie wasn't even sure he knew what he was saying.

"When did the whiskey come in, then?"

"Oh." Bryant let out a laugh that was almost a giggle, then clumsily fished something out of his back pocket. "Never travel without it," he said, shaking the steel flask so the metal caught the light from the moon, and the scant liquid that was left inside pinged against the sides.

Great. He'd been sneaking shots between beers from a flask. Exactly like her fucking father. That wasn't something she'd seen coming. Bryant had been making her the fancy, craft cocktails he'd learned to make at Tessa's, but she'd just thought he'd been showing off. Not that he traveled with his own personal supply of self-medication at all times.

"I'll take that," Minnie said, plucking the flask out of his hand. When she dumped the last drops onto the gravel below their feet, he whined like a toddler.

"Minnie, that was perfectly good whiskey."

Minnie took him by the arm and pulled him toward the back door. "You've had enough. Come on. You need to be inside a controlled environment."

Bryant followed along without resisting but barely kept from tripping over his own feet. He still wore his steel-toed work boots, and Minnie had to work to keep her toes from being trodden on. She'd been in such a hurry to see him, she slipped on a pair of pink flats, and her toes were icicles.

"Trying to get me in private," he said as she pulled him up the back stoop and had to pause to fiddle with the old doorknob. He placed a sloppy kiss on the shell of her ear. "I see how it is."

"Yeah, I'm about as attracted to you right now as a honey badger would be, so let's go."

"Honey badger, honey badger," Bryant repeated as she pushed him through the door and into the kitchen. Minnie had been so curious about where he lived, but right now she was too busy being pissed to take in any of the details about his house. All that she could tell was that it was old and drafty. It felt like he hadn't turned the heat on inside all day. Which didn't seem right.

"What's a honey badger do again?" Bryant asked.

"It'll maul you with its claws and eat your eyes," she said, annoyed, as she searched for the light switch.

"Well, you can maul me whenever you want," he said, as he tried to run a hand seductively over her shoulders but just succeeded jostling her off balance. When she shot her hand out to steady herself, she found the light switch, so there was that. "But I need my eyes."

Minnie ignored his yammering and drunken attempts at seduction. "Why is it so cold in here?" she asked.

"Is it?" he asked.

"Yes, it's barely warmer in here than it is outside."

Bryant stumbled into the next room where the thermostat hung on the wall and tapped the screen a few times. Distantly, Minnie heard a furnace kick on. "I turn it down when I stay at your apartment," he said, and he almost sounded sober. "No reason to heat the place when there's nobody here."

The idea made Minnie sad, the thought of Bryant coming home to a cold, empty house every morning to shower and head in to work and not bothering to turn the heat up again because he knew he'd be spending the night with her again. She liked that he wanted to be with her but to neglect the rest of his life like this. It wasn't okay.

She maneuvered him into the living room and onto the sofa. She figured out how to turn on the one lamp in the place. Minnie couldn't find a throw to cover him with until the house warmed up, so she seated herself next to him. She leaned into him with her coat still on and left her flats on the floor, tucking her toes beneath her to warm them. Bryant sighed and rested his head on her shoulder.

"I missed you so much tonight," he whispered. "You're so much prettier than Clay."

Minnie snorted. "You should make time for your friends."

"Clay's more like my brother," Bryant said.

"Then you should definitely spend time with him."

"And he loves Van."

"Sure," Minnie said. "She's his sister."

"No, Van's my sister," Bryant said. "And Clay loves her, and he's mad at me because he thinks I have a boyfriend."

Minnie had no idea what to say. Bryant wasn't making sense at all any more. When he raised his head with an imploring look that implied he needed her to respond, she asked the only question she could think of that made any sense out of the gibberish he'd just rattled off.

"Why would Clay think you had a boyfriend?"

"Because when I stop hanging out with him all the time,

it's usually because I have a new boyfriend—well boy hook-up. I don't really do relationships."

Minnie spoke the words before she could stop herself. "Then what are you and I doing?" Because she was having a hard time making sense of anything he said. He usually had sex with other men, and he didn't do relationships, but they'd been together every day for more than a month, and she definitely was not a man. Not to mention that whatever it was they were doing had felt like the beginning of a relationship to her.

"You are my destiny," Bryant said and sighed as he nuzzled her neck. "You are it for me. I don't want anybody else."

While Minnie would have liked nothing better than to hear those words from Bryant's lips when he was sober, right now she didn't know what to make of them. There was too much information floating around in her head, not the least of which that she was pretty sure her boyfriend had just come out to her, which was so, so confusing.

"But why would Clay be mad if he thought you were seeing a guy. He's not—"

"He's just protective," Bryant said, but his voice was fading. "Clay's not a homophobobophone."

"Do you even know what you're saying anymore?" Minnie asked.

"We have to keep this a secret," he said. "For just a little while longer."

That was alarming. "I didn't realize we were keeping our relationship a secret."

"It's the only way to keep it safe."

Bryant sagged against Minnie and she sighed in frustration. He was talking nonsense and falling asleep on her.

Great. Minnie did not want to be trapped under his giant body when he passed out in this freezing cold house.

"Come on," she said. "Let's get you into bed."

"Comfy," Bryant slurred.

"I'm sure you are, but I'm cold."

"I'll keep you warm," he said, but Minnie elbowed him in the ribs.

"Come on, show me your bedroom."

It took them too long to climb the stairs, where it was colder than it had been downstairs, if that was possible.

Bryant led her down a hallway with creaky hardwood floors and into a dark bedroom. The only thing Minnie could make out in the dark was a large bed that, while rumpled, was made. She pulled back the heavy, dark comforter and pushed Bryant back onto the bed. She helped him out of his shoes and then his jeans. Then she tucked him under the covers, not quite able to quell the desire she still had for his body. Even below all the stupid confusion and anger, she still loved him. Or at least, she could love him, she thought, if he could make some sense of out his drunken ramblings come morning.

Minnie placed a kiss to his forehead and folded his glasses onto his side table.

"Stay with me," he said, but she could tell he was already drifting off.

"Not tonight," she said. "But we'll talk tomorrow."

He didn't argue, sleep having already claimed him. She thought about fetching him a glass of water and putting some pain pills at his bedside so he could get a leg up on the hangover that was going to crush him come morning, but she didn't know where anything was in his house, and she didn't feel right about snooping.

Plus, Minnie needed to get out. The coldness, the strange behavior, and the even stranger words had Minnie feeling like she'd walked into a David Lynch storyline. Everything was twisted and surreal. It was her life, but it wasn't, and she wasn't sure she wanted it to be.

Minnie hurried out the back door and made sure to lock the knob before she closed the door behind her. The night air had grown even colder, and where she expected it to be silent, she could hear the light murmur of voices coming from somewhere. Suddenly afraid, Minnie rushed to her car and locked the doors once she was inside. She sped from the alley as quickly as she could. She passed by Bryant's house from the front. It looked dark and quiet from the outside, but five or six people dressed in heavy coats stood on his front lawn. It wasn't until Minnie passed them that she realized they were paparazzi. Not a lot of them, but enough for him to want her to come in the back because he didn't want them to photograph her.

Before tonight she would have assumed it was because he wanted to protect her privacy. But after his ramblings about keeping their relationship a secret, she wondered if he was ashamed of her.

She stayed up half the night, fretting about what he'd said about boyfriends and Clay and keeping secrets, and she had the desperate, sinking realization that what she'd hoped was going to be the last romantic relationship she'd have to cultivate in her entire life was probably just going to be another in a long string of instances of Minnie trusting a man when she shouldn't.

She wasn't sure when she fell asleep, but when she woke to her alarm at dawn, she felt so awful, she almost wished she'd been the one to drink a flask of whiskey.

CHAPTER 7

*B*ryant woke up feeling nothing more keenly than the sharp stab of dread that pounded to the rhythm of his alarm's shrill beat. His head ached, and his mouth tasted like a sewer. He could feel the afterburn of the trail the whiskey had seared down his throat and into his gut. The way his stomach clenched, he knew he was going to throw up. Bryant hurled himself into his bathroom, which was pleasantly warm for a change, and emptied his stomach into the toilet.

Head still spinning, he flipped on the shower, set the water as hot as he could handle it, and washed the stickiness out of his body and the stale sweat from his skin. The muscles in his neck and jaw loosened, and he ached somewhat less by the time he was clean.

He had to admit, it was pleasant not to shiver as he dried and dressed. Most mornings he'd suffered the cold until he pulled on all his clothes, but this morning, he was glad to not rush to pull his socks on and wear his coat while he waited for his coffee. It was possible Bryant's appreciation multiplied because he was too shaky to move at anything more rapid than a tortoise's slow and steady pace.

He lay back down on his bed in his towel, trying to remember the night before. Clay had been surly and unsatisfied with the answers Bryant had been able to give him. Bryant had told Clay to wait, that everything would become clear when they went to L.A. to see Van next week.

Clay had left the bar in a huff, but not before he'd leaned over the table, his face inches away from Bryant's. He had practically growled as he spat, "If you're going to L.A. to break Van's heart in favor of whatever douche you're fucking, brother or not, I will break your goddam face."

Bryant had almost—almost—texted Van to ask if he could tell Clay about their arrangement. But Clay had always been one of the people Van had been most adamant never know that she and Bryant weren't really together. Bryant understood why Van was trying to protect herself from Clay, but he'd never agreed with it. He knew their history. Knew that Clay had policed her sexuality as a teenager, had said things that he didn't mean because he'd been jealous and confused about the woman who was supposed to be his sister.

Van didn't understand how difficult it was for Bryant to keep secrets from Clay. She didn't have to lie to her closest friend on a daily basis. She definitely didn't lose any sleep about how many lies Bryant had to tell just to get through every day.

Bryant didn't do well with celibacy. He had enough different conflicting energies to keep in check as it was. The construction work helped keep him from growing restless, his books kept his mind occupied, booze kept him relaxed, but when he let that sexual energy build up, his temper blew up along with it. And there was only so long that he could let it go. In the past, that had been willing hook-ups, but with Minnie?

God, he was done for when it came to that woman. He had a vague recollection from the night before of telling her how gone he was for her, but he couldn't remember the words he'd said. All he knew was that he had told her too much. He wasn't sure how much of the truth he'd been able to articulate, but it had been enough that she hadn't stayed. If Minnie hadn't stayed with him for the first night in a month, it wasn't a good thing.

First, Bryant texted Clay. He was going to be late. Maybe twenty minutes.

Then he texted Minnie. *Can I see you tonight?*

Neither replied right away, and Bryant peeled himself up off his bed. He shoved his limbs into the least dusty clothes he could find and stumbled down the stairs. He forced himself to drink a glass of soda water with a dash of bitters while his coffee brewed, and by the time he was in line at the drive-thru waiting on his sausage and egg sandwich with hash browns, he was starting to feel half human. Some food and a dose of painkillers would have him feeling right as rain. Or at least, physically right.

His day with Clay was going to be excruciating, and somehow, he'd have to make things up to Minnie.

Maybe it would be a relief if he had drunkenly told her the truth about Van. It would make everything so much easier.

His phone buzzed as he pulled back out into traffic, and Bryant was tempted to see who had returned his text. God, his heart beat in loud, hard thrums in his chest as he contemplated Minnie saying no, she wouldn't see him. That she never wanted to see him again. He wasn't sure he would survive.

He just had to make it two more weeks. One more week until he left for L.A., then the week he would spend there, then he would come back and everything would work itself out. Bryant could tell Minnie about his arrangement with Van (and cross his fingers she would understand), then he could tell Clay that Bryant and Van had decided to break up and it had nothing at all to do with Bryant cheating. Then Bryant could slowly introduce Minnie into his public life, and they would be free to see where the world would take them.

He just had to make it that far.

Clay was already inside the house when Bryant pulled up at the jobsite. The last of the custom cabinets they were installing sat in the back of Clay's truck, and Clay would need Bryant's help to unload them.

Bryant scarfed the last of his hash brown and pulled his phone up. The message hadn't been from Clay or Minnie but from Van.

Clay CALLED me last night. He's convinced you're seeing some dude on the side and wanted to warn me. I told him to mind his own damn business. But HELLO. Why don't I know about your new beau yet?

Bryant tapped his reply as he saw Clay clomp down the stoop in his peripheral vision. *She might be someone special.*

When he looked up, Clay wasn't smiling. Bryant took a deep breath and tucked his phone back in his pocket, steeling himself for dealing with grumpy Clay all day.

"You doing okay?" Clay asked as Bryant slammed his truck door shut.

"I will be," Bryant said.

"I was a little afraid to send you home by yourself."

"I wasn't that bad."

Clay's response was a skeptical crinkle of his brow. But Clay didn't drink more than a couple beers every now and then. He didn't understand how much of a tolerance Bryant had developed.

"I wasn't drunk enough that I couldn't call for a ride. Then I just needed to sleep it off, but I appreciate your concern."

"I called Van," Clay said.

"To tell her I was drunk?"

"To tattle on you."

Bryant nodded. "She told me about that."

"So you've talked?"

"We talk every day. I tell her everything, so when she told you to mind your own business, it was what she meant."

"I know," Clay crossed his arms and shook his head. Bryant thought he saw some pink rise under his freckles. "I'm sorry. Yours and Van's relationship is none of my business. And I shouldn't meddle."

"It's fine," Bryant said, placing a hand on Clay's shoulder. "You don't have to explain. I get it."

Clay's face twitched into a grimace before he shuddered his expression down and looked back at Bryant blank faced. "I'm trying to understand," he said.

"I know." Then Bryant pulled him into a quick, one-armed hug. "Let's move these cabinets inside so we can work where it's warm."

Clay was quiet that morning, but the tension was no longer there. That was a relief, because Van had been texting him all morning, asking about who he'd been seeing and how they'd met, what was her name, when was her birthday? What did she look like, and what about it had gotten Clay all riled up?

When Bryant had texted, *I'll tell you all about it when I get to L.A.*

But that's ages away!

It'll be worth the wait, I promise. You can tell me about what's going on with Bishop.

There's nothing going on with Bishop.

YET had been Bryant's final reply. Van had texted him an emoji with crossed eyes, and he took that for as much of a confirmation as he was going to get.

He should have talked to Van about this sooner. He would have to call her in the next couple of days, once he had things worked out with Minnie. He hadn't heard from her by noon and was starting to worry that whatever he'd told her had scared her away for good.

Bryant was trying to concentrate on *The Leavers* by Lisa Ko as he ate his lunch when his phone finally buzzed with a notification from Minnie. All it said was, *I'm working late.*

That was not a good sign.

Anything I could help out with?

Her grand opening was in a week. Surely she needed a hand with something.

The track lights need positioning. Could you bring your big ladder?

Bryant tapped back, *Anything you want* as quickly as he could. Because he would give anything not to mess this up right now.

Her response didn't come until three o'clock, and the intervening three hours nearly killed him with anxiety. Bryant had never worried about his cardiovascular health before, but he could feel his pulse in his left arm and knew that if he stuck his arm in the supermarket blood pressure cuff, it would probably automatically dial the emergency room.

When her response did come, all it said was *Thanks. See you at 8.*

Bryant had been routinely showing up at her place at 6 p.m. It gave him just enough time to shower and grab whatever he needed for that night's cocktails. If he hadn't already realized that something was wrong, this signal really would have driven it home.

If he could only remember what he'd said the night before. He'd talked about Clay and he'd talked about Van, and he vaguely remembered saying the word boyfriend, but he couldn't remember if he said Clay thought Bryant had a boyfriend, if he said he did have a boyfriend, or maybe he'd had boyfriends. Either way, he hadn't planned on coming out to his girlfriend in quite that fashion.

He'd learned early on that partners who weren't bisexual often became insecure about his affections—as if his bisexuality made him more likely to cheat than a partner who was attracted to only one gender.

When Bryant went home to shower after work, he did not turn his heat back down like he had been doing. If he did come home, he didn't want to come home to a cold and empty house. The empty house would be sad enough.

He thought for the millionth time about getting a cat— or two. He'd always wanted one to sit on his lap while he read or follow him up to bed at night and sleep on the second pillow he never used. It would probably be a black cat; he didn't know why, but that was what he'd always pictured himself with.

Was it possible to miss a cat he hadn't even met yet?

Probably about as possible as being heartsick over a woman he'd only been sleeping with for a few weeks and had never had a serious conversation about their relationship with before he'd gotten drunk and spilled his darkest secrets as he'd probably drooled all over her chest.

He grew hard just thinking about Minnie's chest and relieved himself down the shower drain before feeling ashamed. He was already acting like he'd lost her, and that wasn't necessarily the truth.

But he did have a shot of whiskey for courage before he left the house.

Then he brushed his teeth, because he did remember Minnie tossing his flask onto his kitchen counter like she was fed up with him. She probably didn't approve of excessive drunkenness. Hell, she was a twenty-three year old who was about to open her own bookstore; of course she didn't.

Bryant's hands sweated as he knocked on the front door of Revival. He was so nervous, he'd donned one of the pairs of designer jeans Van had forced on him, and one of his nicer flannels over an unblemished gray T-shirt, topped with his usual leather jacket. It wasn't exactly his finest clothes, and Van would never let him out in public in L.A. dressed like this, but it was his version of nice—he still felt like himself and not the character of Bryant Wilder he played on *Pop Star*.

The inside of the shop smelled like old books and sugar and chocolate when one of Minnie's employees let him in. He had to hide his grimace. Bryant had known she'd hired a staff, but they were usually gone by the time he showed up. He wasn't sure what Minnie had said about him, if she'd said anything, but the cheery brunette seemed to be expecting him.

"Minnie's in the kitchen," she said. "She wanted to make sure you brought the ladder."

"Yup," Bryant said and grabbed the twelve-foot ladder he'd leaned against the side of the building and eased it inside. He propped it against the wall just to the right of the window display and did his best not to storm into the kitchen. He still crashed through the swinging stainless steel door too quickly, and Minnie, who was frosting a three-layer chocolate cake at her prep table, glared at him.

His body didn't care. It sighed in relief just to be in her presence, even as he sensed he needed to be careful.

"Hey," he said. He'd meant to keep his voice soft, but it came out as more of a croak.

"Hi," she kept her eyes on her cake.

"So, I think I need to apologize to you about last night?"

Her eyes flicked up to him, latent with scathing accusation, and then were back on the plate that rotated beneath her frosting knife. "Do you even remember last night?" she asked.

"Enough to know that you probably have some questions."

She lifted one shoulder, then let it fall. "One or two."

"Ask me anything," he said and hated himself for the lie. "I'm an open book."

She set down her knife. "Why do you need to keep our relationship a secret?"

Bryant stumbled back a step, as if she'd physically shoved him. That was not a question he'd expected to come out of her mouth. "What?"

"You told me last night that you needed to keep our relationship a secret for just a little while longer. Is that why we never go anywhere? Why you had me park in the alley last night?"

"I'm only trying to protect you from the paparazzi. They can be relentless, and sometimes they follow me everywhere because I'm friends with Van, and I don't want people speculating about you. I'm hoping to talk to Van and Phoenix—that's Van's business partner—when I'm in L.A. for a few days so I can figure out how to present our relationship to the public without them jumping down your throat too much."

"You think they'd be interested in who I am because you're friends with Van Birch?"

"It's a distinct possibility." Minnie bit her lip at that, like she wasn't happy about that either.

"So, then you do think we have a relationship?"

"Of course we do."

"Because you also said last night that you have hook-ups, not relationships."

"Historically," he said and chanced a few steps toward her prep table, secretly glad her knife was dull. "But, Minnie, you're different."

"Well you also said you usually have hook-ups with men, so yeah," She gestured toward her figure, "Yeah, I'd say I'm different."

There it was, the only thing he feared more was her actually knowing about Van. He'd prayed he hadn't given that away. Not yet.

"Not—not exclusively. I like men and women."

She stared at him then and said. "Oh."

"Yeah," he said.

"I should have figured that out already."

"It's okay," he shrugged. "It's confusing to a lot of people."

She wiped her hands on her apron and came around the prep table to stand by Bryant. He wanted to pull her into his side and never let her go, but he held back and tucked his hands into his pockets so that he wouldn't touch her.

She leaned against the steel table. "I guess there's a lot we still don't know about each other."

"I'd like to change that," he said.

"Did you know it's my birthday tomorrow?" she asked.

"No," he said, and his eyes alighted on the cake behind her. "Is that what the cake is for?"

"That and it sounded amazing," she said with a small grin.

"My birthday is August seventeenth," he said, by way of offering equal exchange, and her grin widened just slightly.

"You'll be twenty-six?"

He nodded.

She grinned and said, "Then I should confess that I'll actually be turning twenty-three tomorrow."

He nodded again. It made sense that she'd been rounding up only a few weeks before her birthday. "Are you doing anything special?"

"I was going to call in some take-out and have cake with the girls," she waved toward the employees who were cleaning on the other side of the kitchen door, "And Rocco is coming over before he goes in to work. I told you about him, remember?"

"The guy you grew up with?" Bryant frowned as he remembered the story. She'd called him her cousin, then explained that they weren't related at all and that she'd moved here to be near him. A pang of jealousy sounded in Bryant's chest, but he pushed it back.

"Yeah, I'd like you to meet him, if that's okay with you."

"Sure," he said. "I'd like that." And he would. That Minnie wanted him to meet someone she considered family did please him. It meant that she had real feelings for him, but there was also a huge possibility that Rocco knew exactly who Bryant was. The women outside probably knew exactly who he was to Van Birch too.

And that would only spell disaster.

Bryant's entire life felt like a trap sometimes. No matter what he did, he was going to be found out, and he was going to be flayed by the media, and he was going to lose this woman.

Bryant couldn't lose Minnie.

He offered her a hand, and she took it. He pulled her into his arms and held her close. "I'm sorry about last night," he said.

"Will you tell me what happened later?" she asked, looking up at him with hope and hesitation in her eyes.

He placed a soft kiss on her lips. "I will," he said. And then he did something that his body protested but that he knew would be safest for him. He pushed back and said, "I think we should slow things down a little bit."

Minnie flinched, and Bryant pulled both her hands into his. "Not because I don't want to be with you, but because I do. If that makes any sense."

"Sort of." She squinted up at him, and he knew he wasn't helping her confusion.

"I want to be with you," he said. "Just you, for as long as you'll have me, but we just jumped into this so quickly, and I've known all day that you might not want me anymore because I surprised you with my sexuality, and I don't want to do that. I don't want to lose you because I didn't have the chance to tell you the truth."

She cocked her head. "Is there more to tell?" She asked.

"I have twenty-five and a half years of friendships and discovering who I was. I want to tell you all of it."

"Oh," she said.

"And I want to know everything about you too, if you'll take the time to share with me."

"What does that look like for us going forward then?"

"Regrettably, probably less sex, more talking. More cooking and less drinking."

Minnie smiled at that, like he'd known she would. "I think that's a good idea." She entwined her fingers with his.

"We can pretend we don't know how awesome it is to sleep together and start at the beginning. Get to know each other before diving into a long-term relationship."

"But that's what you want?" Minnie asked. "A long-term relationship?"

Clarity broke through the fog of the night before, and Bryant remembered one of the most important things he'd said to her. He cupped her chin with one hand, focusing deep into her eyes. "I meant it when I said that you are my destiny, Minneapolis, and I'm desperate not to mess this up."

Finally a genuine smile broke across her lips like waves at sunset, and Bryant felt his heart rate calm to a soothing, satisfied rhythm. "No more secrets," she said.

He nodded. "I promise, after the next few weeks, I'll have told you all of my secrets."

CHAPTER 8

*B*ryant had explained why he'd been so upset after hanging out with Clay that he'd drunk himself into a stupor. His answer hadn't exactly satisfied Minnie. Bryant had said that Clay tended to think Bryant's relationships weren't healthy, and Clay was trying to protect Bryant from himself. "And I am so in love with you that I didn't want to think of us as anything but pure and healthy, but..." He'd shrugged. "Maybe he was right."

Minnie had glowed at the confession. He was in love with her, and he didn't want to lose her. That was positive. She figured there were a few other things that he still needed to work through before they could be in a real, honest-to-goodness relationship. She didn't give a damn that he'd had relationships with men in the past. And she'd told him that. She'd been a little shocked, and not sure what to believe because of his drunkenness, but as long as he was attracted to her and wanted to be with her, that was all Minnie could ask for from a potential partner.

The drinking was another issue. Minnie had seen the

flask in his toolbox when he'd fished out his wrench to adjust the light—and it hadn't been the same flask she'd taken from him the night before. How many did he have? How many times a day did he sneak a nip? And why?

He hadn't drunk anything all evening, and when the girls had left, he'd kept on diligently positioning the can lights so they lit up every bookshelf just so. And when he finished, he kissed Minnie goodbye, said he'd see her the next day, like the gentlemen he'd promised to be.

But Minnie couldn't quite shake the feeling that she was missing something. That Bryant hadn't told her everything. Not yet.

She had almost told him about her past. About what had really driven her from New York. Because yes, she had been bullied. But not, you know, for no reason. Minnie had done the unthinkable and accused Rick Drury, star lacrosse player and Renee Culpeper's boyfriend, of sexual assault. Publicly. She'd filed a complaint with the school; she'd filed a report with the police. He'd been suspended from the team, and the team had lost the championship and all of that had been more important than the fact that Rick had had sex with a drunk and uncooperative Minnie who had told him no repeatedly.

The story had blown up, even made some national outlets, but locally, Minnie had become infamous. She had been harassed on the street; paparazzi had followed her everywhere. Renee, who Minnie once considered her best friend, had slapped her across the cheek and accused her of trying to ruin Rick's life. Minnie's enraged response, that Rick had ruined his own life when he'd raped her, had not gone over well.

Minnie had called Rocco crying one night after she'd been cornered by a mob of drunk guys yelling at her, spitting at her, taking swings at her on her way home from the campus library. Even if they were missing on purpose, she had been backed into a corner with nothing on either side but stone walls and six men twice as big as she was. So what if they'd not been connecting on purpose; all it would take was one of them to decide hitting her was a good idea for the rest of them to join in. Minnie had actually feared for her life when two campus police officers had broken it up and shoved her into the back of their patrol car. She'd thanked them for the rescue, but the one in the passenger side had only sneered at her and told her that the campus didn't need any more bad publicity.

Rocco had listened to the whole thing as Minnie hyperventilated into the phone. She lived alone in a decent apartment near campus that Jonas paid for, but it had big windows, and she'd had to pull the curtains over every one of them. She'd made the phone call to Rocco after she'd bolted her front door, then her bedroom door, then pulled her comforter over her head.

"Come to Kansas, Mins," Rocco had said. "I just bought a house; I have three bedrooms. No one will know you here in Wellville. You won't be in the paper. You won't be harassed. You'll be safe, and you can get back on your feet, and you can start over without all of the trauma."

"What about school?" When Minnie had first told Rocco she wanted to leave, he'd told her to stick it out. It was only one semester. She couldn't just walk away from an Ivy League education, so Minnie had been trying. But now she was afraid to even get out of bed.

"Fuck that school," Rocco said. "If you want to finish

your degree, you can do it anywhere. Right now, you need to get out."

Minnie had been on the first plane to Kansas the next morning. She'd left everything but her comfiest clothes behind in New York. No schoolbooks, no designer dresses; maybe she'd brought a couple of her favorite pairs of shoes, but other than that, Minnie had traveled light.

She'd camped out in Rocco's guest room for almost three months before she'd emerged with her plan for Revival Books and Coffee. "Revival" because that would be the project that brought Minnie back to life.

And it had, to some extent. Revival had given Minnie something to work toward, a purpose, but Bryant had made Minnie feel alive for the first time in almost a year. He had made her feel safe and daring all at the same time, and until the night before, Minnie had trusted him with all of her. But the paparazzi on his front lawn? Even if it had just been a handful of them, they had reminded her of what it had been like to be hounded and degraded.

That was not the life she'd chosen for herself when she'd moved here. And she wasn't exactly sure what that meant moving forward with someone who was friends with a super star.

Her birthday celebration had gone well. Rocco hadn't let her do much of anything, and her new employees had given her a gift certificate for a massage. Bryant had brought a bottle of wine with a bow on it. Minnie had kept the introductions with Rocco simple. They'd been missing each other a lot lately, but her long-time friend could be protective of her, especially after New York. He was the older brother she hadn't been born with but was thankful for none-the-less. She'd introduced Bryant to Rocco as "Bryant Wilder, he was originally the contractor, but now he's a friend, and he's been helping me get the place ready."

Bryant had offered Rocco his hand as Rocco's eyebrows rose. "Wow. Like Van Birch's Bryant Wilder?"

Bryant had blushed and ducked his head. "Yeah."

"Thanks for helping Minnie out when I couldn't be here. I told her she was being too ambitious with her opening date. No chance you can convince Van Birch to come to town for the grand opening? The publicity would be off the charts."

"Sorry, but she'll be in town next month. We can probably convince her to stop by then."

"Do," Rocco said with a nod.

Bryant had been shier in the crowd than he usually was with just Minnie, but she'd forgiven him that when he pulled her into a corner before he left, kissed her, and pressed a small box into her palm.

"Happy birthday."

"Thanks." She moved to open it, but he closed her fingers over the parcel. "Open it later, in private."

She let a mischievous grin spread over her lips and saw his eyes light with heat. "It's not like that, but now I have plenty of ideas for Christmas," he said and kissed her again.

Then he hunched his shoulders and slid his hands into his pockets and said, "I know the next couple of days are busy for you. Clay and I are planning to stop by your grand opening, but then we have to fly out to California for business. I'd like to see you as soon as I'm back. Like, come straight here from the airport."

"I look forward to it." Especially if it meant sex. They hadn't made love in days, and Minnie was growing antsy with want for him. And knowing it would be another week? She was glad she was going to be too busy to dwell on it.

"I will be counting down the seconds until I come back to you," Bryant said. His lips covered hers, and Minnie surged onto her toes. He wrapped her in his arms, and Minnie didn't want to let him go. She wanted to hold on to him forever. His tongue met hers, once, then twice and heat surged between Minnie's legs. She was contemplating if she had time to drag him upstairs for just a few minutes when, with a nip of her lower lip, Bryant pulled away.

"Can I come see you later?" he asked. "In a couple hours, once everyone is gone?"

"I'd be pissed if you didn't."

Bryant gave her a bashful grin as he stepped back, holding her fingers between his until the distance between them was too wide for them to reach. "I'll see you soon," he said. Then he was gone.

Rocco helped Minnie clean up after the celebration. He seemed like he wanted to say something but kept his mouth shut, which was fine. Minnie knew he'd find a way to phrase what he wanted to say eventually. He'd never been able to keep his thoughts to himself. If not today, she was sure she'd hear about whatever was bothering him soon.

When Bryant arrived, it was almost midnight. Minnie had been drowsing on her sofa. She'd left the door open for him, and she was only partially aware of him letting himself in until his body covered hers. The moment Bryant's lips connected with Minnie's she was awake.

She'd been aching for his touch, and it had taken her

about three second to undo his fly enough to have her hand down his pants.

Bryant cursed and indulged in her three long, slow strokes before he had them unclothed. Minnie rolled the condom on, and when Bryant sank inside her, it was like heaven.

Being inside Minnie was like losing himself. All the noise in Bryant's head shut down, and the only thing he had to concentrate on was the feel of her skin on his, the heat of her core wrapped around him, the silken slide of them together. Their bodies together were a benediction, the granting of amnesty for the unending complications that had become his life.

Making love to Minnie was simple and good, and Bryant never wanted to stop. He pulled her up to sitting, positioning her legs on either side of his hips so her breasts pressed fully into his chest. "God, I love you," he said.

Minnie let out a sound that was half laugh, half sob and fastened her lips to his with the ferocity he was beginning to see she used in everything she tackled. He admired her ambition, her quiet tenacity. He knew he had to work to keep himself from getting swept away by her, but here, now, tonight, Bryant only wanted to revel in the blessing that she wanted him.

He wanted to go all night, but his desire to bring Minnie pleasure was stronger. His hand roved down her shoulder as he shifted so he could guide one of her nipples into his mouth. Then he caressed down her stomach and lower until his thumb pressed against her clit. Minnie moaned and ground against him. He sucked harder at her tit, circling with his thumb at the same time.

"Jesus, Bryant," she breathed, and Bryant bit down just hard enough on her nipple to make her curse. Minnie fell over the edge into her pleasure with Bryant chasing right after her.

They lay together on the sofa for hours afterward. Minnie dozed on top of him, and he lay awake, staring at her ceiling as he stroked her hair and reveled in the feel of her silky-smooth skin. This would be the last time they'd have in private before Bryant left for California, and he didn't want to leave. He couldn't shake the feeling that if he did, he'd be leaving for the last time.

CHAPTER 9

*B*ryant was gone when Minnie woke the next morning, but he'd pulled the duvet off her bed and tucked her in on the sofa. He'd also left her a note telling her how much he'd miss her over the next few days and to expect to see him at the grand opening.

Minnie kissed the paper and stretched under the heavy blanket, relishing in pleasant soreness between her legs. She would have stayed there, languishing for hours, but Rocco was due by any moment, and she didn't want him to find her naked and all sex-disheveled, so she hauled herself into the shower.

Rocco had taken some time off work so he could help her with the grand opening, and she really appreciated it, despite her telling him that he shouldn't use his vacation time to work for her for free, but per usual, Rocco hadn't listened. By opening day, he still hadn't told Minnie what was on his mind, and Minnie didn't have the time to speculate about what it could be.

Minnie wore her birthday present from Bryant for luck.

The delicate gold chain with a dainty heart charm was the perfect accessory for a Valentine's Day opening. Bryant had inscribed their initials on the back in miniscule script. Minnie felt like her heart was swelling to bursting when she thought of him, despite the low level of nausea that had been plaguing her the last few days. Her nerves were threatening to overwhelm her, but touching the heart around her neck helped to center her. Everything was only going to get better from here, even if she'd barely heard from Bryant in the last few days. Her store would be open, she'd have a daily routine, and in a week, Bryant would be back, and they'd keep working on their relationship. They'd worked past this little awkward hump that they'd been riding since the night Bryant had had too much to drink.

Clay and Bryant had shown up to the opening, just as Bryant had promised. When they arrived near the end of the day, they looked dusty and cold, like they came straight from the jobsite. Rocco was already talking to them by the time Minnie spotted them, but it took her another few minutes to make her way over. When she did arrive, Rocco slung his arm around Minnie's shoulder, tugging his arm tight like he was about to pull her into a headlock.

"The place looks fantastic," Clay said. "Congratulations, Minnie."

Minnie had attempted to thank him, but Rocco had spoken over her, "My girl has put in a lot of work, but we can't thank you two enough for the bookshelves."

Clay broke into a genuine smile. "I've been meaning to ask. Do you mind if I come in sometime and take photographs for our business portfolio?"

"Whenever you like," Minnie said. "It would be an honor."

Clay flashed her a sideways grin, and Bryant elbowed him in the ribs, and Minnie thought it was a cute exchange. Bryant had told her about Clay's sideways grin and how he used it to slay women. She appreciated being a part of their teasing.

It made her feel included. Like maybe someday she could be one of them.

An alert went off on Clay's phone. He puffed out his cheeks and let out a long-suffering sigh as he flipped it off. "We have to get going, or we're going to miss our plane," he said by way of apology.

Bryant only grinned at her, still not saying anything, and Minnie was beginning to understand that he didn't do well in groups. She understood. She'd been much worse when she was younger, and she still hid sometimes when she needed a moment to herself. But she wanted him to be as effusive as he was with her in private. She wanted him to wrap his arms around her and kiss her and tell her how amazing her party was, because she'd worked so hard on it.

But he didn't, and Minnie didn't understand why. There were no paparazzi around. And the reporters who had been there had left hours before.

Clay shook her hand, and when Bryant stepped forward to do the same thing, he bent as if he meant to kiss her cheek, but Rocco pulled her into his chest and out of Bryant's reach.

"Have fun in California," Rocco said.

Bryant frowned before his face turned to stone.

"Yes, good luck," Minnie said. "Stop by when you get back."

When they were gone, Minnie wrenched herself out of

her cousin's arms and whispered, "What the fuck was that about?" low enough that none of the customers heard her.

Rocco still watched the door where Bryant and Clay had just exited. "How much do you know about that guy?" he asked.

"Who, Bryant?"

Rocco gave her a look that told her not to play stupid. "We're getting to know each other."

"And how much do you know about Van Birch?"

Minnie shrugged. "She's from here. She and Bryant went to high school together. She's Clay's sister, and I know a few of her songs."

"You've never watched the show?" Rocco asked.

"No, have you?"

Rocco shrugged, and though his face remained somber, color rose to his dusky cheeks. "Everyone around here watches the show, Mins."

"Okay. What are you trying to say?"

"I'm saying that those two look like home-grown Kansas, and maybe they really have construction business in California, but they're probably also going to film the next episode of *Pop Star*."

"Sure," Minnie said, not sure what she was missing.

"I don't trust the Hollywood types," Rocky said. "And I don't think you should either."

"Bryant's not going to hurt me," Minnie said.

Rocco's eyebrows disappeared beneath his hairline. "How well have you gotten to know him?" he asked. Then his eyes narrowed as his expression tightened into a scowl. "Have you slept with him?"

Minnie felt herself go scarlet. She and Rocco had never really talked about their sex lives. She'd introduced him to one or two of her boyfriends over the years, and she'd met some of the women he'd dated, but that was about as far as it had ever gone.

Rocco sighed and pulled her into a hug, finishing with a kiss on her cheek. "Watch the show, Mins."

Bryant really had stopped to look at one of the books on the display table by the window, but what had kept him rooted to the spot long enough to keep staring was the way Minnie's *cousin* kept hugging her, touching her, talking in her ear, and then kissing her. Sure it was just a kiss on the cheek, but he knew Minnie's body language, and she was not acting affronted by the other man's affection. She even watched after him, as if what he'd said had left her in a daze, and Bryant hated him for it.

He'd seen Minnie dazed too, and it had taken him three orgasms to get her there. All this guy had to do was whisper in her ear, and she was gone. Suspicion gave rise to jealousy. What kind of relationship did they have really? Bryant had spent the last few days spilling his guts about himself, but he really didn't know anything about her. She'd asked for no secrets, but what secrets was she keeping from him, he wondered.

Bryant spent the entire flight to L.A. (minus the time it took to shower and change into the clothes Phoenix had left in the private jet's closet for him) digging up everything he could about Minneapolis Halvarson. There wasn't anything incriminating, exactly, but that her father was a well-known developer in Colorado. She'd gone to Columbia for school, which Bryant had known. But from all the gossip articles he'd found, it looked like she'd spent her most of her college career as a socialite, attending every high-end or red-carpet event in New York rather than studying. There had been a couple other guys in the photos, but more often than not, Minnie had been escorted by Rocco Mendez. The speculation about their relationship ran from sweet to salacious.

But the elaborate hair and makeup, the designer dresses? The posing for the camera? That wasn't the Minnie Bryant knew. His Minnie was sweet and fierce and a little shy but driven. Where had the New York socialite gone?

But that was when Bryant had found the worst of the articles. The nasty ones. The shots of her attempting to avoid being photographed, the article accusing her of lying, the police report of when she'd filed charges against the athlete who had raped her and the backlash she'd experienced.

This was why she'd dropped out of Columbia.

He hadn't been able to figure it out, why someone so smart and so driven would give up an Ivy League education. Even if she had partied her way through school. And even knowing that, Bryant was stuck on the photos of Minnie with Rocco. She'd moved away from that to live in the same place Rocco lived. That said something. Bryant didn't want to believe what it meant. And maybe the two were on a break or something, but the sickening feeling that he was a rebound or a revenge fuck was something Bryant couldn't shake.

In a desperate attempt to feel connected to the Minnie he knew, his humble, Kansas Minnie, Bryant texted her when he landed. A simple *I'm going to miss you like crazy while I'm gone.*

Her response came a while later, and while the words *I'll*

miss you too. Thanks for the necklace. I love it. Hurry back, had been what he'd been hoping to hear, they fell flat. She'd had to add *Hurry back* at the end, closing down the end of the discussion like she didn't want to text him while he was away when he'd planned hours of teasing and sexting each night.

It stung, but Bryant tucked his phone away, and when the limo brought them to Van's place, where the cameras were already rolling, Van greeted him by jumping into his arms and kissing him like she really had missed him. Bryant pretended that this was the way Minnie would greet him when he got back to Wellville and only stopped when Phoenix and Bishop booed in the background.

"We just broke out the whiskey," Van said. "You game?"

The little black-haired pixie still had her legs wrapped around his waist, and not for the first time, Bryant wished he felt toward her the way he'd always pretended to. He pecked her lips and smacked her bottom. "You know it," he said.

She pulled him toward the breakfast bar where Phoenix was pouring shots. Van shoved one into Bryant's hand and said, "Happy Valentine's Day." Her smile was bright and besotted for the cameras.

He tapped his glass against hers. "Happy Valentine's Day, Van."

CHAPTER 10

*B*ryant always slept in Van's bed when he was in L.A. It helped with the illusion, sure, but mostly it was just a comfort thing. Van was his best friend, and they always stayed up half the night catching up and enjoying the company of one of the only people on earth they could each be honest with.

It had been in this position, cuddled up to Van in her bed in the wee hours of the morning that Bryant had imagined himself telling Van about Minnie, about how hard and fast he'd fallen for her, and then asking Van's advice for getting over the last rocky days—and what to do about Rocco.

But they had collapsed into bed completely wasted the last two nights, and the more Bryant looked at the pictures of Minnie and Rocco on his phone, the more he wanted to do the same every night. There was one photo in particular from last spring. Minnie had worn a nearly sheer, sparkling silver and white dress to some charity gala or other, and Rocco, in a bespoke black suit, held her on his arm. His head was tilted down to hers, and love and mischief sparkled up at him through her eyes. There was a joy so complete in her expression, Bryant wondered how he'd ever thought to compete with a love like that.

Maybe something had happened. Maybe they'd been on a break. Bryant didn't know, but he knew there was something going on there, and of course he had to find out about it while he was out of town when asking Minnie about it would sound jealous and accusatory.

Hell, he was feeling jealous and accusatory. Rocco had been supposed to be her cousin, not her off-again, on-again lover. Thinking about it made Bryant want to hit something.

As he lay in bed, not yet feeling the full extent of the hangover he knew was waiting for him, he texted Minnie. *How's the shop doing?*

Her response back was quick but said, *Busy. I don't even have time to eat.*

Okay. Bryant didn't know how to take that. *I can have Skittle's deliver a pizza, even from California.*

Minnie sent him back a green-faced emoji. *Thanks for the offer, but I've still got first-week butterflies. I'll try solid food next week.*

Take care of yourself, Bryant typed out, then debated deleting it. He hit send before he could change his mind.

It sounded like a farewell, but Minnie didn't need him slowing her down right now, especially if she wasn't feeling well, even if it had been good to talk to her.

Van stirred and scooted so her head was on his shoulder, her arm draped over his stomach.

"Who you talking to?" she asked.

"Nobody," he said.

"Does your nobody happen to be the reason why Clay wanted to beat you into a pulp last week?"

Bryant sighed and threw an arm over his face. "Yeah, but he doesn't know who she is."

"Considering he still thinks you're hooking up with a dude behind my back, no, he doesn't know who she is." Bryant sighed again, and Van poked him in the ribs. "I'm joking, you know Clay doesn't talk to me if he can help it. Tell me about her."

But instead of telling Van about Minnie and what he felt for her, he told her about Minnie and Rocco, and how sure he was that it wasn't going to work out like he'd thought it was going to.

"But you thought it was going to work out?" Van asked in awe. "Like long term?"

"I was going to talk to you about ending the charade, for good," Bryant said, hiding behind his arm again.

"But now you're thinking that it's already over?"

"You tell me what you see," Bryant said, and reached for his phone to show Van the red carpet picture of Minnie and Rocco.

"This is what they looked like together before you left?" Van asked.

"I mean, that was the way he was looking at her, and she looked post-orgasmic."

"And you've seen her post-O face enough to recognize it at a distance?"

"Yes."

Van's eyebrows rose at Bryant's emphatic confirmation. "No wonder Clay effing called me. You've been screwing this chick's brains out, haven't you?"

Bryant only shrugged. "I just hope it isn't over by the time I get back."

"Have you been texting her at least?" Van asked.

"Some. She's busy; she just opened her own bookstore."

Van snorted a giggle. "She was obviously made for you. If you mess this up, I might have to kill you."

He only nodded, a lump forming in his throat. There was nothing left to do but hope that Minnie and Rocco weren't a thing by the time he made it back to Kansas.

"Well, let me know what happens when you get back to Wellville," Van said. "I'm cool to end it. Just say the word."

Bryant leaned over and kissed Van on the cheek. "Thanks."

"Anytime."

"What do you think about telling Clay, either way?" Bryant asked.

Van stiffened so thoroughly, Bryant was pretty sure he felt the mattress go rigid too. "No," she said too quickly. "I don't want Clay to know. Ever."

Bryant stroked her hair and sighed. "It's difficult to lie to him every day."

Van snuggled into him more closely, "I know," she said. "I'm sorry. I ask too much of you, but as long as we keep the charade going, I need for Clay to think it's real."

Bryant stroked her hair as his world spun a little around the edges.

"Are you still mad at him for what he said way back when?" Bryant asked. It was on the tip of his tongue to tell Van that the only thing that she was in danger from with Clay was that he was going to lose patience with waiting for her to notice him one of these days and ask if he could kiss her.

She only shook her head where it lay on his shoulder. "I've had enough shaming from Clay on my sexuality during high school. It keeps things more even if he thinks we're together, and he's not sniping on my possible Hollywood paramours."

Bryant rolled his eyes. It was bullshit. He knew the real reason was because Van had been denying her feelings for her stepbrother since her dad married Clay's mom. Bryant had vowed long ago not to become involved in Clay and Van's tug of war. If Van was still set on pretending Clay didn't feel exactly the same way about her, then that was none of his business. He was just her beard.

"Have there been any Hollywood paramours?" Bryant asked. "You've been awfully quiet on that front lately."

Van rolled onto her back and covered her face with her hands. "It has been so long, you don't even know."

"Surely there's been opportunity?" Bryant asked.

"If you mean creepy dudes that stalk the tour bus and dirty roadies," Van said with derision in her voice, "then there's plenty of opportunity for a quick fuck against a green room door, but I want something more than that. I want a relationship, you know, like you want with the bookstore chick."

"Then why are we still doing this?" he asked, rolling onto his side to face her.

Van's lips twitched, and then she gave him a sad smile. "Because I'm not ready to give you up either," she said.

"I'm not going anywhere. I will always be here for you. You know that."

"Yeah, but the second we break up on TV, you're not going to be on the show anymore, and then I won't have the excuse to fly you out here once a month and let Phoenix dress you up like her own personal Ken doll, and we'd lose touch."

Bryant pulled her up against his chest. "You know, I'd still be on the show if we broke up on TV; I'd have to be around to make your new on-screen interest uncomfortable."

"Okay, that's what we'll do. Maybe we could pair you with Phoenix. She's never had a love interest on the show."

"No," Bryant said. "No more fake boyfriends. And no offense to Phoenix, I think she's fantastic, but I'm pretty sure she'd eat me alive in private."

"She eats most men alive. I'm pretty sure that's how nobody finds out about her lovers. She literally eats them."

"Right," Bryant said. He knew Van was joking, but Phoenix definitely gave off that man-eater vibe. And she had zero energy for anybody's bullshit. He couldn't think of a man off the top of his head that he'd actually seen Phoenix say yes to.

Van snickered. "It's so cute that you're, like, twice her size, and you're still afraid of her."

"I'm fairly certain she has very, very sharp claws," Bryant said.

Van *hmmm*-ed. "Most definitely." She was quiet for a minute, then said, "How shitty are we going to feel when we get out of bed, do you think?" Van asked.

"Pretty awful," he said. He was already starting to feel the headache and the upset stomach.

"Yeah," she said. "Let's just stay in bed and pretend the rest of the world doesn't exist for a little while."

Bryant didn't argue.

CHAPTER 11

The butterflies in Minnie's stomach had not gone away. In fact, they'd developed into full-on nausea. Revival was closed on Sundays, so Minnie had slept in, had taken her time drinking half a pot of coffee and choked down two bites of oatmeal. Now she was at the grocery store stocking up on the essentials so she could eat more than cinnamon rolls and turkey sandwiches this week.

Except almost everything in the store made her stomach turn. She'd been going to make chicken noodle soup, but the sight of the raw chicken made her gag, and even the salty smell she associated with canned soup had her turning green. By the time she'd reached the dairy aisle at the back of the store, the only thing she had in her cart were the fixings for macaroni and cheese. All she needed was milk. Then she spied the yogurt, and the nausea ebbed, so she stocked up on strawberry yogurt, because that sounded so good, Minnie considered shooting back a few cups of it like they were Jell-O shots.

That was how Minnie knew. This wasn't nerves left over from opening Revival. This was something else. Minnie recalled that first night with Bryant, how charged and explosive it had been and how utterly unprotected they'd been. Minnie still hadn't been to see a doctor about her birth control, and even though they'd been more careful after that, they'd still had a ton of sex. And really, just the one time would have been enough.

Minnie swung by the pharmacy. Her heart pounded as she tossed two boxes of pregnancy tests into her cart. Despite the explosive birthday sex, things with Bryant hadn't exactly been great when he'd left. He'd been a little distant, and she'd been half too busy to text, half afraid to bother him. At the same time, she looked forward to his return, and Minnie had been hopeful they could work through whatever this awkward patch was. But now?

She didn't even know where to start. Panic rose, travelling up her spine and back and settling across her shoulders. Her breath came in sharp pants as she joined the queue at the register.

She knew how to deal with this. Breathe. Take one deep breath in and one deep breath out. Being pregnant wasn't the end of the world. She didn't have to go through with it if she didn't want to. She could terminate it and not even think about it again. Then she wouldn't even have to tell Bryant—or anybody. Except maybe Rocco. He's who she'd want to go with her, but even as she thought it, Minnie knew she wouldn't go that route. If the tests said she was pregnant, she would keep the baby.

That was something that she hadn't known was true about her until this exact moment. She'd always suspected she'd have no trouble walking into a clinic. She didn't have the cognizance to figure out why it was that she wanted to keep the baby right now. Her head spun with all the separate implications.

Should she call Bryant now or wait until he got back? Probably wait until he got back so he could work without having his life overturned when he was halfway across the country. Yes. She would take the tests. Find a doctor and have dinner ready for Bryant when he returned to Wellville. She'd give him a kiss, feed him, then tell him he was going to become a father.

Minnie's heart rate quieted now that she had a plan. To distract herself until she could get home and use the pregnancy tests, she let her eyes wander over the tabloids. Minnie had never paid much attention to them before, but since learning that Van Birch was a friend of Bryant's, Minnie's curiosity had been piqued. Van was always leaving a coffee shop in a black t-shirt and leggings or dancing with her red-haired friend at a club or posing on the red carpet with someone glamorous. But on the cover of the nearest magazine, Van was pictured with a tall man with dark, messy hair and chunky black glasses wearing a light gray suit with his shirt open at the collar. Minnie knew that chest. Knew that man.

Minnie touched the clean-shaven face on the glossy cover. She'd never seen Bryant so shiny. He always had a bit of dirt under his fingernails or a few days worth of stubble on his chin. He wore flannel and steel-toed boots, not fawn brogues and bespoke suits. In the photo, Van, petite and sleek, pressed against his side in a slinky black dress as she stared up at him with adoration. He smiled down at her, and Minnie's stomach swooped and rolled.

Then her eyes travelled to the black and white background image of Van and someone who looked an awful lot like Bryant dancing in a dark club. The headline read *Sweetest Gesture this Year! Van Birch's Hometown Honey Flies to L.A. For a Valentine's Day Surprise*, and Minnie thought she was going to lose her breakfast right then and there in the checkout line.

She tossed the magazine, face down, into her cart. She had pulled out her phone to google Van and Bryant's names together, but then it was her turn to check out, and she decided it was best to wait until she got home.

Bryant wasn't Van's boyfriend. They were friends. That was all. But as Minnie went through the motions of checking out and driving back to her apartment, she couldn't remember a time that Bryant had actually defined his relationship with Van. He'd been honest about knowing her and that she was Clay's stepsister. That they'd gone to high school together, that they kept in touch these days, but there had never been anything about how they were romantically involved. Because of course he wouldn't, not when he was trying to sleep with stupid, naive Minneapolis every chance he got.

No wonder Clay had been giving him a hard time. He didn't dislike the fact that his best friend was bi, he disliked the fact that his best friend regularly cheated on his sister.

After Minnie shakingly placed her positive pregnancy test on the bathroom counter, she settled in on her sofa with her laptop and most of the yogurt and googled every-thing she could find about what was apparently the epic Hollywood-style #goals relationship between Van Birch and Bryant Wilder.

Minnie should have let him freeze to death that night she'd gone over to his house. It would have served him right, because not only had he been cheating on his girl-friend of four years, he'd left Minnie, who had worked so hard to prove that she was mature and worldly and over the drama, looking stupid and used and pregnant.

Her searching led her to a website that streamed every episode of *Pop Star* up through the current season. Minnie didn't think twice about pressing play. She was halfway through the first season, watching Van rise to fame, when Rocco knocked on her door, then let himself in. Minnie glanced over her shoulder, not bothering to hide her tears as the camera zoomed in on Bryant and Van dancing together at some super swanky club. The camera swooped around them like the moves had been choreographed for a movie, but it caught every place they touched. Minnie could feel the chemistry between them through the screen.

"You knew?" Minnie asked as Rocco plopped onto the sofa next to her and automatically wrapped his arms around her. "Why didn't you tell me?"

On screen, Bryant had pulled Van into a long, lingering kiss, after which she arched an eyebrow at him and pulled him off the dance floor. He followed her, panting like a dog, until she blew a kiss at the camera and shut them into the limousine and into privacy. Rocco leaned forward and shut the lid on the laptop.

"I didn't want to ruin your big day," he said. "You've worked so hard, and I was hoping he was as decent of a guy as they make him look like on TV, and maybe he would tell you himself that he was just fooling around, but I guess not."

"He told me I was his destiny," Minnie tried and failed to hold back a sob. "And I thought I could be."

"I'm sorry," Rocco said as he rubbed comforting circles

over Minnie's back. "I'm really sorry, Mins. This isn't what I wanted for you."

This wasn't what she'd wanted for herself either. It had taken her almost a year in New York to stop feeling like sheltered bumpkin. She hadn't known she'd worn Jimmy Choos until Renee had complimented her on them; they'd just been the shoes the stylist her father had hired had picked out for her. When she'd finally found friends, Minnie had never really felt like she'd fit in. It was why she asked Rocco to visit as often as he could, why she dragged him to all their social events. Her college friends had mooned over him, and Rocco had hated every single one of them. Minnie knew he hadn't approved of her lifestyle in New York, but growing up with so little and suddenly finding herself surrounded by luxury, she had convinced herself she deserved it.

In the months since she'd been in Wellville, Minnie had figured out that she wanted a quieter, simpler life. She'd been happy living with her mother and working to help keep them afloat. She was proud of herself for only accepting her father's money on her terms and for creating the kind of life in which she knew she could grow and find happiness. From the moment Revival had occurred to her, Minnie had seen a future for herself in Wellville. The last few weeks, Minnie had seen herself building that future with Bryant. A kind, simple, handsome Kansas contractor to live a simple Kansas life with.

She sniffled as she calmed a few minutes later. It had all been a lie. Bryant had just been bored between visits with his actual girlfriend. But had he? He'd seemed so sincere, and sure there had been a lot of sex, but sex that good couldn't be a lie, could it? Plus, Minnie had never felt a connection like that with another person. Perhaps Bryant was unhappy with Van. Maybe he'd grown disillusioned with the long-distance love affair with a famous woman.

But really, did it matter if Bryant had been thinking about leaving Van? No, because he was in L.A. with her now, and Minnie was in Wellville, pregnant with his baby. She sniffled again. He was choosing Van, and from everything Minnie had seen, Van might be a little wild, but she seemed like a genuinely good person. Minnie wasn't going to ruin Van's happiness for her own gain. Especially since Minnie didn't want to be with Bryant anymore. Not after seeing him with Van and knowing he'd been with her this whole time.

Minnie sniffled a third time, and Rocco disentangled himself from her. "Let me grab you some tissues."

She nodded dumbly. Minnie didn't want to be the woman who wrecked Van Birch's perfect relationship. Bryant's cheating would come out, and when it did, Minnie would be cast as the villain. The paparazzi would come back. They would hound her; random people on the street would harass her. This was Van's hometown, the entire population could turn against Minnie. Her business would go under, and then where would she go? Wellville was supposed to have been her haven. Her revival.

And the baby. For her child's entire life, they would be the baby that broke up America's golden couple. Every time they did something important, their name would be followed by, "better known as the reason Van Birch dumped Bryant Wilder's stupid ass and found someone who didn't impregnate other women behind her back." Okay, so maybe that was her broken heart talking, but if she let it happen, that could be her child's legacy.

"Goddam, motherfucking motherfucker!" Rocco roared from the bathroom. More curses followed as he stomped back down the hallway. "Please tell me this isn't what I think it is?" he asked, his eyes wild as he held up the pregnancy test.

A new wave of tears spilled down Minnie's cheeks. "It's exactly what it looks like."

"I am going to kill him," Rocco said, fighting to get the words out around his heaving chest. "When he gets back from L.A., I am going to track him down and kill him with one of his own goddam screwdrivers."

"No, you won't," Minnie said, standing and wiping her eyes. She took the pregnancy test from Rocky's hand and stared at the two pink lines. "Because we're not going to tell him."

"Don't be ridiculous," Rocco said. "Wilder is going to take responsibility for this mess. I don't care how much it humiliates him."

"What about how much it humiliates me?" Minnie said. "And think about the baby. It will be an object of ridicule before it's even born. Think about how Revival will suffer, the hate mail. The news articles. I can't go through that again."

"You're going to keep the baby?" he asked.

Minnie nodded, swiping at her eyes. "Yeah."

Rocco sighed and pulled Minnie into his embrace, just holding her for a few minutes. "I would never ask you to relive what you went through in New York, Mins."

They were quiet for a minute as they both remembered the last year. Minnie's mind lingered on the dark room, Rick's distinctive tattoo. The ridicule that had come with filing her report. The defeat of leaving Columbia. Her father's cruel words when he'd heard what had happened, and Rocco's invitation to Wellville to recover in peace.

"There's a plus side to all of this too," he said after a few minutes.

"What's that?" Minnie hated how pathetic her voice sounded as she spoke shakily into his shoulder.

"How mad is your dad going to be when he finds out we're having a baby together?"

Minnie huffed a disbelieving laugh and started crying all over again. Her father would be furious about the baby to begin with. It would be testing the limits of their relationship if she pretended Rocco was the father, but Minnie relished the idea of making Jonas squirm. She and Rocco had pretended to be a couple off and on for years, just to get a rise out of her dad. He'd never approved of Rocco, preferring Minnie to meet a rich man from Columbia whose New York connections Jonas could use to expand his business empire. That Rocco was willing to support her even now made Minnie feel like she didn't deserve him in her life.

She lived the next few days believing her life was going to be okay. She still felt hollow on the inside, and she was still sick to her stomach most of the time, but she wasn't going to have to do this alone, and she was growing used to the idea of telling everyone that she and Rocco were going to have a baby, used to the idea of leaving Bryant behind entirely.

Then, on Thursday, when she looked up from setting out a new display of hardbacks she found Bryant standing in the window, watching her with nervous hope.

Minnie's heart jumped into her throat, and she felt her stomach churn a little extra hard. He was adorably disheveled, wearing his usual worn jeans paired with his leather jacket. She wanted to hold the tabloid cover up next to his face and make sure he was even the same person as the manicured Hollywood heartthrob in the photo, but she knew better. This was his humble Kansas contractor costume, and she would not be fooled by it.

Minnie motioned for him to follow her to the hallway that connected the store to her apartment.

Her heart pounded in her ears. And she didn't even feel her feet touch the floor as they exited the store and climbed the stairs to her apartment.

When they were at her door, Bryant flipped her around and pressed her into the door as he molded his body against hers. He captured her lips in a starved, insatiable kiss. It took him a few seconds to realize she wasn't responding, but when he did, he pulled back, brows furrowed and lips pressed together.

"Is everything okay?"

Minnie shook her head. "I know about Van."

Bryant's brows folded together, though she could hear the panic creep into his voice as he asked, "What about Van?"

Minnie pulled her shoulders back and stood as straight as she could with Bryant still boxing her in. "I know about you and Van."

Bryant deflated. "What do you think you know?" he asked so quietly that Minnie barely heard him, even though his mouth was next to her ear.

She could barely hear herself over the thudding of her heart. "Th-That you're high school sweethearts. That you've been together forever and that you've been on the cover of numerous magazines together. That you went to L.A. on Valentine's Day to be with her and film your reality show because you haven't seen her in a month. Sometimes there's rumors that two of you aren't monogamous, but I am. I won't be a part of breaking up America's favorite couple."

Bryant's fists knotted on either side of Minnie's head and with a growl he pushed off the wall. He whirled and slammed a fist through the sheetrock on the opposite side of the hallway. Minnie jumped and tears streamed down her cheeks, startled out of her numbness by his reaction.

"I'm not with Van, Minnie," he said, facing her, dropping to his knees in front of her. "I never have been; you have to believe me. It has always been for show, to protect her, but she's like a sister to me. Nothing more."

"I've seen the show, Bryant. I've read all of the articles. I don't believe you."

Bryant's head dropped to his chest, and he tossed his glasses down the hall. His arms wrapped around her legs as he pressed his forehead into her knees. "What if I got Van on the phone? She'd corroborate everything. So would Phoenix."

A week before, Minnie wouldn't have known who Phoenix Lambert was, but now Minnie could probably recognize the sharp-tongued redhead a football field away. "But why didn't you tell me from the beginning, if that was true?"

A single sobbed wracked through Bryant's body. "Because I made promises to Van a long time ago, and I keep my word, but I love you, Minnie. You." He looked up at her, face drawn tight and naked looking without his glasses. He clenched his arms tighter around her legs, and Minnie couldn't help herself when a single tear stole down his cheek, she had to reach out and catch it. He was so beautiful, even in his despair.

"Nothing you say is going to change how I feel," Minnie said. "It's over. It has to be."

Bryant shook his head and pushed back on his heels like she'd struck him.

"I will not stop fighting for you," Bryant said. "I will do whatever it takes to convince you that you are the one that I want."

He reached for his back pocket, like he really would take out his phone and call Van. Like a simple phone call was enough to put everything to rights. She wished all of this was that simple.

Minnie shook her head, and opened the door behind her, then motioned to the room beyond. "Look around, Bryant. It's already too late."

He peeked around her legs and into the open living room door. The space was littered with boxes, some closed, some open, some half-packed. Her bookshelves were bare. The art she'd hung on the walls was gone. The little pieces of her that had been spread around the apartment had disappeared. It was mostly furniture and the one red throw blanket that had always lived on the back of her couch.

"You're leaving?" he asked. "But Revival—"

"I'm not leaving," she said. "I'm moving in with Rocco."

That had Bryant on his feet, his face morphing from distraught to outraged in less time than it took Minnie to blink.

"So you're back together?" Bryant asked.

Minnie scrunched her brows together. "What do you mean, 'back together?'"

Bryant faced her square, standing too close. "You aren't the only one who did some digging while we were apart. I looked you up. I've seen the photos. I've read the gossip articles. I know why you left Columbia, who you father is." The way he said it, made it sound like a threat.

"Yes, well, it's not exactly the same scale that you and Van are on, but I was followed in New York. I dealt with the paparazzi. The harassment. And I refuse to do it again. I will not go through that for anyone. Not for you, not for my father, not for anything."

That was such an understatement, but Minnie didn't know how to explain succinctly that Rocco was the one unchanging part of her life as everything else had shifted and moved around her almost too swiftly for her to process over that last five years. And now it was happening again. Minnie would not apologize for clinging to him when she didn't know how she'd keep standing otherwise.

But Rocco had never been more than a friend, a substitute brother. "Cousin" had always seemed like the perfect description. The idea of sleeping with him was incestuous, though Minnie wouldn't deny that there were times she had hammed up their intimacy for the cameras, just to annoy her father and ramp up his disdain for Rocco's "common origins" and his "illegal immigrant mother."

It was the least she could do after the way he'd treated her and her mother for the first eighteen years of Minnie's life.

But right now, Bryant had hurt her so deeply and the pain was still so sharp and fresh that Minnie didn't want to explain any of that to him. She wanted him to hurt just like she did, and she wanted him to go away. Telling him that she was with another man was the most sure-fire way to get him to leave her alone.

So, she laid a hand on Bryant's chest, took a deep breath, and said, "Yes, Rocco and I are back together."

Bryant stole a hand around her wrist, clutching her hand to his heart. "Is it because of Van?" he asked. "You don't have to use him as a shield. I promise, I can end things with Van with a text message, and she will understand. I told her all about you, and she'd ready. It's a farce, Minnie, please."

Minnie's heart broke. He would do it, she knew. He would leave Van Birch, whether the relationship was real or fake, just to be with her, but Minnie wouldn't let him. She wouldn't do that to him or to Van or to their child. Because even if it was fake, it didn't mean there wouldn't be a tabloid scandal that Van Birch might weather in a matter of months but which could haunt Minnie and her child for the rest of their lives.

"If you and Van break up, it shouldn't have anything to do with me." Minnie heard footsteps on the stairs and knew it was Rocco coming back with the pho she'd been craving. "But for my part, moving in with Rocco, being with him, it's what I want."

Bryant's head dropped again, and his fingers dug into her wrist in desperation as his face crumpled.

"I think we could have had something special," Minnie said. "But it wasn't meant to be."

And when his grip loosened at her words, Minnie pulled back and swirled back into her apartment, unable to take any more of the open heartbreak on his face.

Maybe there was some truth to his words. Maybe he really had fallen in love with her. But the fact remained that he'd never been hers to have and that this baby deserved more.

There came two pounds on the door, a pathetic murmur of "Minneapolis," and then nothing.

CHAPTER 12

*B*ryant rested his forehead against Minnie's door, trying to wrap his head around all that had happened. Minnie had found out Bryant's secret, and she had abandoned him. She'd jumped right back into her relationship with her old boyfriend. She hadn't even waited for him to come back and to talk to him about it, to let him explain about Van.

It was as if all his worst fears had played out in his absence, and he had never felt so powerless.

A hand clenched on his bicep and wrenched him around. He found himself facing the broad, stocky presence that was Minnie's boyfriend. He dropped a bag of takeout at his feet and tightened his fingers around Bryant's arm in a bruising grip. Rocco might be a head shorter than Bryant, but he was not a weak man.

Challenge gleamed in Rocco's eyes as he growled, "You are not welcome here."

"I see you didn't waste any time making me look bad the second I left," Bryant spat.

"You and your lies didn't need much help. One magazine cover and Minnie knew you weren't worth her time."

"That was my secret to tell," Bryant said, advancing so that he pushed Rocco into the wall next to the hole he'd punched.

"Then you should have told it sooner," Rocco said. "It's not my fault you screwed up."

"No," Bryant snapped. "You just get to reap the rewards."

Rocky's grip tightened further, and Bryant knew he'd have bruises, but he didn't care. If Rocco let go, Bryant would definitely hit him.

"I will always protect Minnie," Rocco said. "From you, from her bastard of a father, from the press and everyone who wants to hurt her. I will always be there for her."

Rocco pushed Bryant into the wall then released him. He rolled his shoulders, then ducked to pick up the takeout. Rocco used a key to let himself into Minnie's apartment and left Bryant standing by himself in the hallway.

CHAPTER 13

*B*ryant lived in a fog for months. He had no memory of how he got from place to place, from job to job. Nothing in his life had changed. He still worked with Clay every day. He still flew to L.A. every few weeks to film, he still slept in Van's bed, but she'd never asked him about Minnie again, and as she started touring for her latest album, she didn't have much time for anything else.

Nothing seemed to matter to Bryant all that much. He avoided going into Revival. Clay bought coffee from there for the crew sometimes, but Bryant hadn't been back at all since the day he'd begged Minnie to understand in the hallway, then let her new boyfriend mark his territory.

He didn't find out that Minnie was pregnant until July when pictures of her arm-in-arm with Rocco at someone's fancy rooftop party showed up on a Denver website . She wore a white lace dress that showed off her tiny baby bump. Bryant had been on a plane when he read the article and was glad the most he could do was close his laptop and toss it to the seat across from him. He'd known it had been over in February, but he hadn't realized how committed Minnie and Rocco were. They were going to have a baby together. They certainly hadn't wasted any time making one.

Bryant had opened the computer again five minutes later to read all about how excited Minnie was for her baby to be born later that fall, and Bryant decided he was done. He couldn't do it anymore. He turned off all his alerts, he unsubscribed from all the gossip sites. Bryant was going to forget about Minnie and what might have been. He rose from his seat, grabbed three of the tiny bottles of whiskey from the minibar, and started trying to erase the feel of her skin, the sound of her voice, and the future he'd always seen when he'd looked into her eyes.

CHAPTER 14

*M*innie didn't have a difficult pregnancy, though she was tired all the time and she felt like a hole had been drilled through her heart. Little by little, the pain of being separated from Bryant lessened. Partially it was a comfort to come home to Rocco every day. He was as excited about the baby as if it were his, and he relished attending the required functions in Denver just to rub the fact that Minnie was going to have a child with him, out of wedlock, in her father's face.

They hadn't told Jonas that she was going to have a baby before they showed up at the Fourth of July party his company always threw, one of her yearly required events. She'd told him she was bringing Rocco, and he'd grumbled, but just as Minnie had expected, when she arrived, Jonas had a whole line-up of single colleagues ready and waiting to greet her, including some younger ones this time. It seemed he was growing desperate. Minnie shared a smile with Rocco before he helped her out of the limo.

She'd chosen her dress explicitly to show off her

growing bump. Her father's jaw fell open, and so did the jaws of the men all around her. Her father recovered quickly, introducing her and Rocco to his assembled friends, then whisking her inside the building and out of earshot from any of the gossip columnists who were there that night.

"Is that real?" he asked.

Minnie gaped. "You think I'd fake a pregnancy?"

"You have a history of needling me and making light of my expectations for you."

"Yes, well, expectations are difficult to bear when you let my mother die."

It was the same argument they had every time they were together. Her father reminded her that he was her benefactor, and Minnie reminded him that his money and his regard for her had come far too late.

They stared at each other in silence for a solid minute before her father nodded toward the plate glass windows that looked out onto the patio where the cocktail hour was happening. "It's Rocco's, I assume."

Minnie gave him a demure smile. "It's his name that will be on the birth certificate."

A breath of annoyance snuffed its way through Jonas's nose. "At least you're constant. I'll give you that."

That was all her father had said about the subject for most of the night. It wasn't until after the fireworks, when it was only a few of his favored guests left splitting one last bottle of champagne, that her father cornered Minnie and Rocco on a swinging bench that looked toward the mountains. Rocco had draped his jacket over Minnie's shoulders, and she was drowsing on his shoulder, exhausted by the late hour and the tension of being with her father.

He handed her a glass of water and said, with three of his friends just behind him, "You'll be announcing a wedding date this summer."

Minnie snorted into her drink, and Rocco actually laughed. When her father glowered, Minnie said, "We're not getting married."

"You will if you want to keep receiving your allowance," her father said.

Minnie shrugged. "I have enough." It wasn't strictly true. She had saved as much money as she could, living with Rocco and renting out the apartment over Revival meant she actually had income. While the bookstore was doing well, it wasn't even close to turning a profit and probably wouldn't until the third year. But that was fine. She could manage, and when she turned twenty-five in a year and a half, she'd have her trust fund. She'd like nothing more than to be out from under her father's thumb.

"Don't test me, Minneapolis."

She shrugged. "I'm not getting married, Jonas."

"You're going to let your child be born a bastard?" he asked Rocco.

Rocco only reclined his head against the back of the swing. "It was good enough for the two of us," he said, and laid a protective hand over Minnie's bump. "And personally, I'm not a fan of marriage."

Jonas's face clouded over in fury, and he turned and walked away without a word.

"For a man who's never been married, he sure has some strong opinions."

Minnie had rolled her eyes and said, "Let's go home."

Minnie hadn't heard from her father since, though once a month the money still arrived in her account. In

September, she got a call from Midge, her father's assistant, informing her of when her baby shower was to be.

The only person there Minnie knew was Midge, but there were certainly a lot of reporters and the most expensive baby gifts she could imagine.

When it was over, Minnie went back to her humble life of baking and shelving and selling books. She liked her life, she decided. The only problem was that she lived in fear of Bryant coming into Revival.

But he never did. Clay brought in a photographer to take pictures of the bookshelves and stopped in for coffee most mornings, but he never said a word about his business partner. Sometimes he asked about her pregnancy, but nothing about Bryant or Van or any hint that any of them had a life outside of Wellville.

Then, a few days after Thanksgiving, Malcolm Arturo Halvarson was born. And Minnie's life changed completely. Bryant would always be a part of her, but her instinct to protect her son from Bryant's duplicitousness and his fame multiplied tenfold. She would protect her precious child with everything she had. And if she had to choose a father for her child, in a completely non-sexual way, Rocco was the perfect person for the role.

She fell a little bit in love with Rocco those first few weeks after Malcolm was born. He treated the baby like he was his own. He'd take over baby duty when he got home from work at two in the morning so Minnie could get some sleep, and he carried the baby around the house during the day in a sling. Malcolm had been born with a head full of thick black hair that made him look like he really was Rocco's child, and Minnie was thankful for her choice of partner, even if they weren't romantically involved.

Minnie couldn't regret her affair with Bryant, as much as she still had no desire to see him. As Malcolm grew every day, Minnie found herself not just satisfied with her life, but happy. For the first time, possibly, since her mother had died.

Then three things happened all at once to turn her world on its head all over again.

A date night, a tornado, and The Van Birch Incident.

CHAPTER 15

JULY 2019

*B*ryant counted back in his head. It had been months since he'd been out on his own. The last time he'd gone without Van—with the idea of finding a partner for the night—had been just about a year ago, not long after he'd found out Minnie was pregnant. Bryant hadn't had the heart to go through with it, and he hadn't been with anyone at all in the intervening months. Though he'd tried not to think about her, he still yearned for Minnie's forgiveness. He hadn't let himself check in on her since then. Hadn't been to Revival, hadn't read one news article, hadn't googled her. Clay had mentioned that she'd had her baby around Christmastime last year, and that's all that Bryant needed to know.

He'd still been pining over her then.

He wouldn't say he was anymore. Bryant was over it —mostly.

He missed Minnie. Bryant thought a part of his pathetic soul would always love her, or at least, he would love the thought of what they could have been. Jealousy burned every time he remembered that she'd had a baby with another man, especially when Bryant remembered that one time they hadn't used protection. How easily that could have been him.

There had been times over the last year and a half when Bryant had wished that he had been the father of Minnie's baby. When he was laying alone in bed at night—the bed he'd never had a chance to share with Minnie—he was especially susceptible to fantasies of what it would have been like to live with her, marry her, have children with her.

Bryant was officially pathetic. He needed to get a life of his own. Minnie had moved on like their affair hadn't even been a rock in stuck in the sole of her Toms. She'd started a family with someone else, and Bryant could tell that Van was close to breaking off their arrangement. She'd been sleeping with Bishop for a year now, and he knew that it had been blossoming into something more these last few months. Something serious.

And Bryant was happy for her. She deserved it, even if Bishop rubbed him the wrong way sometimes.

But Bryant was still stuck hanging between genuine heartbreak and a charade that had defined his life for five years now.

That was why he was going out tonight.

He needed to get his head out of his ass, get laid, and get some new perspective.

He parked at the back of the lot at Tessa's, so far having evaded the paparazzi for the evening. They were more interested in figuring out if Van had officially left him for Bishop yet. Only a few stragglers cared what he got up to on his own time anymore.

The inside of the club was packed for a Thursday night.

Good. That meant that there were more people to blend in with and more people to act as possible partners for the night.

His heart might still be a mess, but physically, Bryant was ready to move on. He needed to sleep with someone who wasn't his fantasy of Minneapolis Halvarson.

He started out at the bar and was two whiskeys in when a man across the room caught his eye. He stood by himself, shorter than Bryant, but still probably about six feet tall with dark hair. He hadn't seen Bryant yet, but Bryant could imagine what the man would feel like beneath his palms, the way he would expose his neck at his climax, and the way Bryant would bite his chin, the man's scruff spiky and rough against Bryant's lips. He drained the last of his drink and plunked the glass on the bar, about to cross the dance floor to ask the potential hook-up if he could buy him a drink, when another man snagged his attention.

Motherfucking Rocco. On the dance floor, grinding with a brunette who most definitely wasn't Minnie.

Rage flared, and Bryant forgot all about the possibility of hooking up. He was out on the dance floor, ripping Rocco away from the woman. Bryant spun him so Rocco's arm was pinned behind his back. Bryant pulled Rocco's arm so tight that if Rocco moved the wrong way, Bryant could snap his wrist. Bryant hadn't needed the move since he'd finished his deployment, but he'd relish the crack of bone breaking when it came.

It took a minute for Bryant to realize that the brunette was screaming, and they'd caused a scene on the dance floor, a ring forming around them. Bryant realized where he was and that he didn't actually want to hurt Rocco, because hurting Rocco would hurt Minnie, so he released his hold.

Rocco immediately whirled around and shoved Bryant hard in the chest, pushing him back a step. "What the fuck is wrong with you?" he shouted over the music.

Bryant stepped forward toward Rocco again, pulling himself up to his full height. His whole body felt tight with rage, and Bryant could feel his heartbeat in every muscle.

Rocco didn't back down; though he was shorter, he hadn't lost any of his muscle mass in the last year and a half. "What the fuck is wrong with *you?*" Bryant asked. "What the fuck are you doing here with her?" He motioned toward the brunette. "Where's Minnie?"

Rocco's face morphed from a frown into a scowl. "Minnie is none of your fucking business. Don't you dare think of messing with her head just because your girlfriend is publicly cheating on you, you pathetic piece of shit."

That's when Bryant lost it. He didn't care anymore. He'd wanted to take his anger about what happened with Minnie out on someone for more than a year. Rocco was the perfect target. The bastard had everything Bryant wanted, and he was here screwing around on the best woman Bryant had ever met.

Bryant threw the first punch. Rocco threw the second. Bryant had just tackled him to the floor and was gearing up to pummel the bastard when two sets of beefy hands closed around his arms and hauled him back to his feet. Two more bouncers descended on Rocco, and the two of them were pulled off the dance floor and thrown into the alley behind Tessa's.

Rocco yelled about pressing charges, and the bouncer who still held Bryant back said, "One of the bartenders already called the cops. Take it up with them when they get here."

Two minutes later, two squad cars pulled up behind the club, and Bryant lost all his fight. He hadn't been arrested since he was nineteen. That had been for fighting too. He'd thought he'd learned to keep his impulses under better control since then. He'd thought he'd been doing better, but as Bryant called Robin Birch, Van's dad, a man Bryant himself thought of as a father , from the police station, he was ashamed to explain that at twenty-seven, he was still the same dumb kid.

Three hours later, Robin picked Bryant up. It turned out Rocco hadn't pressed charges, but Robin, who was one of the few people who knew about Bryant and Van's public farce said, "The last time you got into a fight like this it was because a kid who wasn't worth your time called you 'fag.' Is that what this was?"

Usually, Bryant liked it that Robin didn't shy away from hard truths, but hearing that word made Bryant cringe even now. He hadn't let words like that bother him in a long time, but tonight, Bryant felt every one his vulnerabilities. Bryant hurt everywhere, and he didn't know what to do about it.

"We were fighting over a woman," Bryant said.

"The woman who was with Rocco at the club?" Robin asked as he let Bryant into the car.

"The one who wasn't at the club," Bryant said as he fished his wallet and phone out of the sack of his belongings they'd given him upon his release.

"You mean Minnie?" Robin asked, his voice so level Bryant couldn't tell what the other man was thinking.

"How do you know Minnie?" Bryant asked.

It was a stupid question. Robin's law office was only a few buildings down from Revival. He was probably in there all the time. "I think the better question is, how do you know Minnie?"

"We had a thing for a few weeks. Ages ago. When I put in the shelves for the bookstore. I went to film in L.A., and when I came back she'd already moved on with Rocco and then there was the baby and—"

"Ah." Bryant could hear Robin's quick mind filling in all the gaps.

"Not that it's any of your business," Robin said. "But Minnie and Rocco aren't together. They're raising Malcolm together, but they're not a couple."

Now Bryant felt completely miserable. "He still should have been at home with his kid," Bryant mumbled, and Robin, thankfully, kept silent.

It didn't even matter to him that Rocco and Minnie had broken up. They were still living together. They still had a child together. And Bryant was still in the same situation he'd been in before, except tomorrow he'd be at the top of all the gossip sites when news of his arrest got out.

When Bryant's phone finally came to life, he tapped on the unread text message.

It was from Minnie.

I convinced Rocco not to press charges because I don't want to make trouble for Van, but I will not be so kind a second time.

Bryant spent the next day feeling sorry for himself and spiraling toward self-destruction. He was already half wasted from sipping on his flask all day long as he pulled into his garage after work. The skies had turned purple, then green, on his way home from the jobsite, and he could hear the wind roaring even before he'd switched off the engine. He couldn't hear the sirens, but hail pelted his back as he ran for his cellar door, and Bryant knew what was coming.

He just hoped Clay had made it home on time.

Bryant woke stiff and cold. He'd slept in an old armchair that he'd inherited along with the house. His basement was made of damp concrete and spiders, and the chair that sat next to the furnace was the only place he could stay mostly dry.

He shivered and cracked his neck as he noticed sunlight peeking through the egress window on the other side of the room. He didn't know how long the storm had raged after the tornado had passed through, but he had no doubt there had been a tornado. He'd decided it was safer to stay in the basement until the storm had blown over, but now that morning was here, he was afraid to go upstairs and see what the damage was.

The noise had been horrific. He half expected his house to be in splinters when he pushed the basement door open, but his kitchen was still there. Quiet and serene in the pale morning sun. He padded through his house, trying the light switches, plugging in his dead phone. No power.

His stomach growled, and he made himself a sandwich with lukewarm ingredients out of his dead refrigerator and went upstairs to his bedroom for fresh clothes and to splash his face with cold water. At least there was water.

Who knew if it was currently potable.

When Bryant had found no broken windows, no shattered walls, he held his breath and stepped out onto his front porch, allowing himself to see the destruction around him for the first time. The houses on either side of him stood intact, but the massive oak in his neighbor's yard now lay across the sidewalk, having brought down a power pole with it, and the houses across the street were nothing but splinters.

Panic swelled in his heart. He was the only single person on his block. Directly across the way was an elderly couple who always brought him apple pie at Christmas. Next door to them was a family with four kids under the age of ten.

His neighbors next door, newlyweds with an infant, also stood on their porch. The husband had wrapped his arms around his wife who held their baby. Both were white-faced as Bryant approached.

"Has there been any movement?" he asked.

She shook her head. He said, "We just got up the courage to come outside. They've all got to be trapped in their basements."

"Is the whole town like this?" she asked.

Bryant turned in a circle. Wellville was relatively flat, and without obstructions, you could see for miles, but all he saw was a handful of houses among chaos.

"It's possible," he said, then asked the neighbor, "Help me check on the Richards?"

Bryant spent the whole day digging out his neighbors. More people came by to help eventually. By sunset, everyone was accounted for. No one in his immediate neighborhood was injured, but the police officer who drove through mentioned that not everyone had been so lucky, that they were still accounting for all the casualties.

He and his neighbors who still had kitchens fed as many people as they could, and another police officer stopped through with bottled water and more food. Bryant had entire families camped out in his living room and had finally had a chance to charge his phone in his truck.

He'd spent the day staving off fears about his family, about Clay, about Robin, about Minnie. How many of them had been as lucky as he'd been? Already, the things that had consumed him these last couple of years seemed like petty bullshit. Why had he been so angry and not taken the initiative to take care of himself? Why hadn't he had the nerve to tell Van it didn't matter that he didn't have a relationship to go into? He needed their charade to be over so that he could figure out what his life was supposed to be on his own.

Then his signal finally loaded, and his messages buzzed into existence one right after another.

Texts from Clay and Robin saying that they were all right. Texts from his crew with varying degrees of mostly all right. Some were in shelters because their homes were damaged or gone. One had a broken arm. There were three texts from Phoenix asking him to call her, which he ignored. His bar brawl wasn't important right now.

There was one from Van, asking him to call her, that she'd heard from everyone else, but she needed to know he was safe.

He called her back immediately. He didn't even finish reading her text all the way. She answered on the third ring and Bryant knew something was wrong. Her voice was hoarse, too quiet, when she said. "Thank god you're alive."

"I'm fine. The house is fine. You do not sound fine. What happened?"

Silence.

"Van, what happened? Are you okay?"

"No." It was such a short, small answer and not the one

Bryant had been expecting. Van was always okay. Even if she was sick, she pushed through, she performed, she made it happen. Van never gave up. On anything.

"What's happened. Where are you? Are you safe?" She'd had a stalker last summer. One that had actually broken into her house while she'd been on tour. They'd arrested him eventually, but so many scenarios were running through his head too quickly.

He was about to ask whether Butch, her head of security, was with her, but her too quiet voice said, "I'm at Phoenix's."

That was good. Phoenix's house was a fucking fortress unless you had an armada and could come at it from the sea. "What happened?" he asked again.

He heard Van's deep inhale. Then she said, strong and clear, "Bishop raped me last night."

And Bryant was pretty sure the world stopped spinning.

CHAPTER 16

*R*occo's house hadn't been in the direct path of the tornado. But she, Malcolm, and Rocco had still spent a restless night in the basement bedroom waiting out the storm. They knew there was damage. They could hear the water pouring in, but they didn't dare leave the safety of being underground until morning. Not with the power, the radio, everything going out.

At dawn, when they stepped into the serene, quiet sunlight at the same time as the rest of the newer neighborhood, they were greeted by downed limbs and debris everywhere. The neighbors across the street used to have a privacy fence, now it looked like a pile of matches. Shingles and trash littered the street. There were trees down, including the ash tree that used to be in Rocco's front yard. Now it lay where the roof over the living room used to be.

"The bookstore," Minnie said. "We have to check on the bookstore."

Rocco agreed; he couldn't call his insurance company until the phones were back on anyway, and they picked their way across the city to Revival. The devastation they witnessed was unlike anything Minnie had ever seen. Entire neighborhoods were nothing but rubble. Police officers manned the intersections; fire trucks wound through abandoned streets.

Downtown was destroyed. They had to drive a mile out of their way to get back to the street Revival was on, and then they had to park two blocks away and walk. An officer warned them that he couldn't guarantee that none of the buildings were damaged as he eyed Malcolm dubiously. Rocco took the baby from Minnie's arms and said, "You go. We'll be right here."

The officer kindly escorted her to Revival, which was miraculously still standing. There was a broken window on the back side of the building and the old-fashioned sign hanging from the front had been wrapped in on itself, but the shop itself was untouched. Minnie wanted to fall to her knees in relief. That they'd survived with a broken window and a tree in the living room seemed like such a blessing.

Rocco had to go into work that night, the factory was outside of town and one of the only fully operational spaces in the county.

Minnie wasn't proud of it, but after Rocco left, she loaded Malcolm into her car and drove straight to Bryant's street. He was the only missing piece. She might not want him in her life, but he was still Malcolm's father. No matter how much he had hurt her, Minnie didn't want him to be squashed by a tornado. Her heart pounded as she neared his neighborhood. It had been destroyed. There was hardly anything left but splintered wood. But there, in the middle of the street stood three almost perfectly intact small Victorian houses. Bryant's house in the middle was dark but whole.

Minnie blew a kiss as she passed by, because she didn't know how else to thank the universe for this miracle.

Her father called her first thing the next morning. He hadn't called to make sure she was alive the day before, but Minnie hadn't even started coffee yet when he called and asked her if she had any ins with Van Birch.

"Rumor is she's calling in the cavalry to help rebuild Wellville before winter," Jonas said. "And I want in. Tell me how to contact her people."

Minnie was silent as too many thoughts flew through her head. She could call Bryant. It was for a good cause, but did Van Birch really deserve to have Jonas Halvarson released on her? And did Minnie want to call Bryant? It would be an excuse to check in after the tornado, but no. She couldn't confront him knowing she had his child and was keeping Malcolm from him. She didn't think she would be able to keep Malcolm from him if he ever began to suspect, and it was better this way. They didn't need the fame in their lives.

"I've never met her," Minnie said.

"In the two years you've lived there, you've never met anyone who had anything to do with Van Birch or her family?" her father sounded skeptical.

"Not knowingly."

"It's not that big of a town, Minneapolis, and you're practically a celebrity yourself."

"People only know who I am if they know who you are or happen to follow New York gossip sites, and thankfully, most people in Wellville don't. Here, I'm just the woman who owns the bookstore."

Her father grumbled something about news of Malcolm's birth making the papers in New York, and Minnie rolled her eyes. That someone had picked up on Minnie's small-town exploits and written an article about what a strange creature she was wasn't exactly something she was proud of. Let her so-called peers think her an oddity. Minnie was happy here.

Or she had been for a while anyway. Rocco's increasingly divided attention as his new girlfriend took up more of his time left less time for Minnie to pretend they were their own unconventional family. She remembered the fight with Bryant at Tessa's, which had had Minnie fuming until the tornado happened. Now there were more important things to worry about than Bryant being an idiot, but Minnie's life felt no less on the precipice. Like all of it could change at any moment, and she'd find herself frightened and truly alone this time.

The power and the internet came back on later on that second day. And that's when Minnie saw the news. The big story wasn't the tornado, though it was trending on Twitter. The big story wasn't even Bryant getting into a fight at the nightclub like it had been before the tornado. The big story with non-stop coverage was Van Birch accusing her manager of sexual assault.

Minnie broke down in tears as she stared at her phone. She was nursing Malcolm, and he broke away to look at her, but Minnie couldn't stop crying. Minnie's own experience, the dark room, that distinctive tattoo, the school athletic director threatening her, the way her friends had turned on her, the decision to leave school. To hide. To heal. Even though it had been years, even thinking about it made Minnie feel small and out of control.

Van Birch had been attacked by someone she knew, someone the show—because yes, Minnie had continued to watch it as a form of penance for never telling Bryant about his child— had been framing as a rival for Van's affections. Someone, it was rumored, she was already sleeping with. Someone people loved. Henry Bishop had his own fan sites and a huge social media following. He had one of those Instagram accounts that was all abs and man buns, and Minnie would be lying if she claimed not to have been distracted by a photo or two over the last few months.

Van Birch was going to be skewered on the level of Christine Blasey Ford—or possibly worse. People felt like they knew Van Birch. Hell, Minnie felt like she knew her, and they'd never met. Minnie wasn't sure she wanted to meet her. She half expected the first words out of her mouth would be, "Oh my God, I slept with your boyfriend two years ago and I am so, so, so, so sorry. I didn't know."

But Minnie didn't want to hurt this brave woman any more than she'd already been hurt. And to go public, to press charges, that was the bravest thing Minnie could think of. She didn't blame Bryant for loving Van. She hadn't blamed him for a long time, she just wished there would have been truth behind what Bryant had felt for her.

Minnie's father hadn't given up on getting his company involved in Van's rebuilding efforts. As celebrities descended on the town along with hordes of paparazzi and cameras of every type, Minnie saw her father's logo splashed across the signs of people who were donating to the rebuilding effort. Minnie tried not to cringe. It was good that her father was helping. It was a good cause. So many of her regular customers had been left homeless that she was glad that her family was making a contribution, but it rankled that she knew her father had ulterior motives. Because it was just to bolster his national reputation, Minnie didn't trust him.

And then, once the rebuilding had started and most of the famous people had left town and life was finally starting to return to normal, Phoenix Lambert walked into Revival. She came straight up to the bakery counter and said, "I need a place to work where I can't be bothered, but also has excellent Wi-Fi. I will pay you six hundred dollars a week to rent a table."

Minnie had cocked her head and held out her hand. "Minnie Halvarson."

"Phoenix," she said, no last name given.

Minnie smiled. "Nice to meet you, Phoenix. I have just the space, and all it will cost you is a cup of coffee a day."

She led Phoenix to the conference table in the stacks that almost no one used except for the knitting group on Tuesday nights and the women's Bible study on Thursdays.

Phoenix babbled the whole way through the stacks about how she insisted on paying, even as she unloaded device after device onto the surface of the conference table. A laptop, two phones, two tablets, and a wireless keyboard.

"It's not necessary, really," Minnie said.

"Nonsense. Your business has to be suffering. Coffee and books are luxuries when you don't have a place to live. I have money and a place to sleep. Let me pay you."

"What if I told you to donate the money back to the rebuilding effort instead," Minnie said, and Phoenix looked at her for the first time. Really looked at her as a person instead of someone who was a means to an end.

"You own a used bookstore in a miniscule town in the middle-of-nowhere Kansas, and you don't need money?" Phoenix asked, perplexed, and Minnie huffed out an annoyed snort. "Forgive me if I'm wrong," Phoenix said. "I'm sure you have loyal customers, but when your average transaction is what, five dollars, you have to be always struggling."

"The business does well enough," Minnie said, not thinking it was any of Phoenix's business what was in Revival's ledgers. "But I don't need six hundred dollars a week for the table. I only charge a forty-dollar tab to reserve it for groups, nothing for individual use."

"Then charge me forty dollars a day," Phoenix said. "Whatever your rate is, I'll pay it. I don't take things for free when I can just as easily pay my way."

Minnie sighed. She hated bringing her dad's name into it, but Jonas would have absolutely found a way to hype his company by getting in with the rebuilding effort. And with Phoenix coming to her, Minnie had to move into damage control or her dad would find out she had connections to Van Birch, and he'd bother her even more than he already did. "I get it. Really, I do. I'm the same way, which is why I'd rather your money go to the rebuilding effort. And frankly, I'd pay you not to mention to my father that we've met."

Phoenix's eyes narrowed with interest, and a little bit of offense. "Should I be insulted, or is your father the asshole?"

Minnie cringed, she hadn't meant for it to come out that way. "My father is Jonas Halvarson, from Halvarson Developments," she said, hoping the name was on her radar.

"Holy shit," Phoenix said. "The sanctimonious almost-billionaire from Denver?"

"That's him," Minnie said.

Phoenix made an aggrieved sound in the back of her throat. "His people were such a bitch to work with. Even now, he's giving the historical society a headache about luxury apartments downtown. I almost turned down his money, but how do you turn that kind of money, you know?" Phoenix said.

"I get it," Minnie said. "That's basically been my entire life."

"I bet," Phoenix said as she pulled out a chair and picked up the larger of the two tablets. "It's decided then. Six hundred dollars a week to the rebuilding effort and one coffee a day for the indefinite use of this table between nine and four on weekdays, and two hours of your time every week during that time in exchange for my not telling your father that we're friends."

Minnie knew her confusion showed on her face. Because Phoenix laughed, "I like you. I don't meet a lot of people I like immediately. And when I do, I keep them close. What do you say? Be my friend?"

"I could use a friend," Minnie said. She saw a lot of people every day and was friendly with a good portion of her clientele but nothing that ever left the bounds of business. Minnie had a feeling that friendship with Phoenix was a fierce affair. "Deal." Minnie offered Phoenix her hand for a shake again.

Phoenix smiled. "So, Minnie. Can you make me a forty-ounce coconut milk latte? Because that is the level of caffeination I'm at these days."

Minnie understood the feeling. "I'll see what I can do."

"Wonderful." And as Minnie turned to leave, Phoenix said, "If you have a minute, you should make something for yourself too. Come back and tell me how an heiress wound up owning a bookstore in Van Birch's hometown."

All that was waiting for Minnie back up front was paperwork and cleaning the kitchen, and all of that could wait until later. "One has nothing to do with the other, I promise,"

Phoenix just smirked and plunked her bags down on the conference table.

CHAPTER 17

*V*an had stayed with Bryant almost every night since she'd been back in town, and he decided that she had an unhealthy obsession with her phone. She was on it all the time. It would be one thing if she were reading books or playing Candy Crush, but she was seriously on Twitter reading about how everyone thought the charges against Bishop were made up for publicity's sake. She read the death threats, she read the rape threats, she read all the ways the internet didn't believe her or believe in her worth, and then read more and more and more.

Bryant had to pry her phone away from her to make her go to sleep some nights, and he could feel her laying beside him awake, reliving the worst of everything.

There was nothing Bryant could do to stop her. She listened to him talk but only heard what she wanted to hear.

When Van had returned from California, she had looked so fragile, like a broken bowl that had been glued back together, and Bryant had been willing to do anything he could to help her heal. And he was so desperate to fix her world for her that he would do anything for her. If she wanted to actually pursue a relationship with him, he had been game to try, for her. Because he loved her. As much as he'd tried to get himself excited for beginning a sexual relationship with Van, it had been Minnie he had been thinking of. It was still always only ever Minnie.

Thankfully, Van and Clay had realized they were meant for each other and were still only fighting it a little bit. Bryant was relieved they'd started finding one another.

He was about three seconds away from deciding he was going to be celibate for the rest of his life until he found out that Phoenix was using Revival as her central office, and that she wanted to meet Bryant and Clay there to sign some paperwork regarding the special segments of *Pop Star* they were filming for the rebuilding in Wellville.

Bryant had been so busy with the rebuilding that he hadn't had much thought to spare for anything other than work and Van, but still, there was always that niggling question of how Minnie was doing. Was she happy now? Was she enjoying herself? Was Rocco treating her right? Despite what Robin had said, Bryant didn't believe that Minnie and Rocco weren't together anymore. They still lived together. They still were raising their child together.

It had been easy to avoid going into Revival. Bryant hadn't wanted to see Minnie happy with someone else, and even when he'd driven past the building to make sure it hadn't been part of the destruction the tornado had wrought in downtown Wellville, Bryant hadn't been inclined to go inside. The thought of doing so now made him so anxious that none of his coping strategies worked, and he couldn't focus on anything the entire day before. He mislaid plans, lost three boxes of nails, and had to reframe a doorway twice before he eventually dipped into his flask and calmed his nerves enough to just get it done.

He hadn't stopped once the flask was empty. He went through his second flask once he was home and collapsed into bed, useless and frustrated. The next morning, he refilled his flasks, put on the usual clothes he would wear to work, didn't think twice about his hair, didn't bother shaving, and didn't bother hiding the measure of whiskey he poured into his coffee when he sat down for his meeting.

Phoenix pretended she didn't notice, and Clay cocked his head to the side. He didn't approve of Bryant's flasks but didn't usually say anything if Bryant had a pull after the workday was over. Drinking at nine o'clock in the morning was something new, but it was the only thing that would help the hangover from the night before. Bryant didn't know any other way to keep his hands from trembling. Every second he sat in Revival, the chances of having to interact with Minnie grew exponentially.

Minnie hadn't served him, though he'd seen her through the window in the kitchen door, rolling out some sort of dough. She probably hadn't even noticed him, and that was fine. It was for the best. Just knowing that he occupied the same space with her and that she wanted nothing to do with him when he couldn't even get over her made him feel awful.

He behaved badly. He snapped at Clay, was surly to Phoenix, and left sooner than he should have, but being in Revival made his skin crawl. The fact that he still wanted Minnie, still felt that sick jolt of attraction, desire, and the heart-melting pull of belonging from just that quick glance of Minnie made his stomach clench.

Bryant rescheduled his appointments, went back home,

and went to bed. Nobody bothered him for the rest of the day. He thought that was probably for the best.

Minnie had been putting in more than the mandatory two hours a week with Phoenix. She'd started plopping herself down at Phoenix's table with two cups of coffee and a plate of pastries. The pastries Phoenix usually ignored, but the two of them would both take an hour—or some days, two—out of their days to just talk.

It was the perfect solution for the mornings Minnie had Malcolm with her, because he was getting old enough that it was nearly impossible to get anything done while he was at the shop anyway. They would let him play on the floor at their feet while they talked. Phoenix seemed to like him, and though Minnie was slightly afraid that she might realize how much Malcolm looked like his dad, Phoenix seemed mostly happy with Minnie's explanation of her arrangement with Rocco. She'd even made Rocco blush the day he'd come to pick Malcolm up early.

"Oh, wow," Phoenix had said when Minnie had introduced her. "You are just as gorgeous as your red-carpet photos."

Rocco didn't usually like being reminded of the few times he'd donned a tux for Minnie, and he'd turned shy and bashful with a pink tinge to his cheeks as he murmured a quiet, "It's nice to meet you."

Minnie and Phoenix had giggled together after he'd left, and for the first time in a long time, Minnie felt like she had a friend. A real friend who wasn't Rocco. Minnie hadn't realized how badly she'd needed a girlfriend.

They talked about everything. About their jobs, about Malcolm, about their pasts. Phoenix had looked Minnie up directly after their first meeting. When she'd arrived the next day, she'd walked right up to Minnie and said, "I'm not usually much of a touchy-feely person, but I'm going to hug you now."

And then she had. It had been stilted and a little awkward, but Minnie had appreciated the gesture. Phoenix had shared her experience with her stepbrother from her childhood, and of course, they'd discussed the similarities between what had happened to Minnie and Van. Until she'd sat down with Phoenix, Minnie hadn't realized how much she *needed* to talk about it. How that one night had framed so many of the decisions Minnie had made in the last few years, from moving to Wellville to taking a chance on Bryant and ultimately, the decision to not tell Bryant about Malcolm, to let Rocco be his father instead.

Minnie didn't tell Phoenix the full story, of course, and she was fairly certain Phoenix wasn't telling Minnie the entirety of hers either. Which was fine, they'd only known one another for a few weeks, but Minnie had suspected Phoenix was keeping a few secrets. She was pretty certain none of Phoenix's other friends knew that Robin Birch joined her for lunch most days and that they were more than friendly acquaintances.

The only other man Minnie had seen watch a woman so adoringly had been Rocco with his new girlfriend, Erin. And maybe Bryant on TV when he was looking at Van. Minnie hadn't seen the two of them together since Van's return to Wellville, and that was just fine with Minnie.

She sympathized with what Van was going through. Minnie had wanted to wrap the woman in a tight hug and simultaneously stay at least five hundred yards away from her, lest she suspect the ways Minnie had unwittingly betrayed her.

She'd known she'd run into Van at Revival eventually, but the day Phoenix had introduced them, Van had seemed like she'd been ready to accept any friend of Phoenix's as her own.

Now Phoenix and Van wanted her to come over to their place for a movie night.

A movie night.

Minnie didn't know if she'd ever had good enough girl-friends to be invited for a movie night. She'd been too busy trying to survive as a child, and too busy trying to prove she was worth a damn to her father and to society since her mother had died, that things like movie nights with girl-friends seemed like a luxury.

But oh God, going to Van Birch's house? Who even was Minnie anymore? She was going to go hang out, as friends, with the girlfriend of the man she'd fallen in love with. The man whom she'd glanced through the kitchen door at Revival looking sexily disheveled and full of ridiculous angst. God, he still looked delicious to her, even when he was bedraggled and surly.

Despite the pull, there was no way Minnie could face Bryant. The thought of looking into his eyes and not confessing all about Malcolm was too much for her. She would feel too guilty about a decision she couldn't afford to feel guilty about.

They'd had to hire an out-of-town contractor to fix the house, which was still ongoing. They'd cordoned off the living room with plastic, but it had made the house feel less like the home it had been for the last year. Minnie found herself reminiscing about her old apartment more and more. It was currently empty. She could move back in just to avoid the hassle of construction and the disruption to their schedules, but it didn't feel fair to leave Rocco on his own to deal with the construction.

There was the chance that he might invite Erin over more if Minnie did move out.

They had moved into an awkward new territory for them. Neither of them had been in a serious relationship since Malcolm had been conceived. They'd been too focused on the baby to pursue a relationship outside their little makeshift family. Rocco hadn't exactly been looking for a girlfriend, but Erin was a regular at Revival, and they'd started talking as Malcolm had played with her daughter, who was two, on the rug in the corner where Minnie kept some blocks and bead mazes for kids. It had become a popular spot for moms to meet during the day and proved handy for when she needed to have Malcolm with her in the shop.

Rocco and Erin had chatted for months before he'd asked Minnie if she minded if he took Erin out to dinner. Minnie had been nothing but encouraging. It was unrealistic to think that the two of them wouldn't need a deeper connection eventually. Their parental partnership would only get them so far. Minnie hadn't counted on how lonely it would feel to have Rocco out of the house so often. Her evenings had been full of restless cleaning and bad reality TV after Malcolm was in bed. Sometimes, she even hoped Malcolm would wake up crying, just so she'd have another opportunity to snuggle him.

Rocco had assured Minnie she could date, that he'd always watch Malcolm for her so she could get a night out.

Minnie had wanted nothing to do with men, but she had called in the favor for movie night at Van's.

Minnie had been shaky with nerves all day, despite Phoenix's assurances that no men, not even Van's dad, would bother them.

Only when Minnie arrived, it was Robin who let her in the door. Phoenix had run upstairs to fetch Van, who had been writing a song with Clay, and Bryant was due by any minute to pick Clay up for their "man date," as Phoenix put it when she returned to the main level of the house. She pulled Minnie into the kitchen, away from Robin, and poured them both glasses of wine. Minnie wanted to ask Phoenix if she was okay, because the environment in the house felt charged, ready to pop, but Minnie couldn't put her finger on why.

When Bryant arrived, Minnie felt like everyone could see exactly the ways in which she'd betrayed both Van and Bryant. As if all of her insides were playing on the television in front of them instead of the movie Phoenix had queued up.

But Bryant only scowled in her direction once, and Minnie held back, noticing how they all seemed to be a part of a family. She felt like an outsider and the worst kind of home-wrecker.

And she spent the entire movie missing Malcolm in her arms and crawling all over her lap or pawing at her chest in his still clumsy attempts to ask for milk.

It was almost a relief when Robin interrupted them near the end of *Jurassic Park* to say that the boys had gotten into some trouble. Minnie took the opportunity to bail, even as Van and Phoenix rushed to the jail to see what they could do.

When Minnie got home, she was able to find video of the altercation that had landed Clay and Bryant in a cell for the night. They'd been at one of the dive bars on the edge of town when Henry Bishop had come in with an entourage. Bryant had hit him first, and Minnie saw some of the rage that had given Rocco his black eye the day before the tornado. It was a side of Bryant Minnie had never seen before.

Clay had never been anything but sweet with a side of cranky, but the way he'd slammed Bishop into the wall had her remembering that both Bryant and Clay had been in the Army. They knew how to fight, and they would protect Van with everything they had.

Rocco found her an hour later. He'd fallen asleep in Malcolm's room after putting him to bed. Minnie sat in the rocking chair they'd pulled into the dining room during construction, watching the video on repeat as she wept. She couldn't even tell Rocco why when he'd asked, except that here was real, unscripted truth that Bryant loved Van unconditionally, and Minnie, despite everything, still wanted him to love her.

CHAPTER 18

*E*ven though they hadn't even finished their movie night, Van had seemed to adopt Minnie right along with Phoenix after that night. The two were in Revival all the time; the paparazzi swarmed on the sidewalk outside, hoping to gain a glimpse of the starlet. Locals had caught on and Revival had never been so busy. Van was a good sport and signed endless autographs while her security guards scowled over her shoulders. And wherever Van went, Bryant and Clay weren't far behind. Like puppies. Or ducklings.

It was obvious how much both men loved Van, and when Minnie wasn't fending off the sheer shock of being in the same room as Bryant, she was able to appreciate the loyalty Van inspired. The mega star had never been anything but kind to Minnie, and Minnie found herself genuinely liking the woman and all she was doing to use her own sexual assault as an avenue to give voices to other survivors. Minnie couldn't help but respect her.

Minnie couldn't even hang on to her old jealousy about Bryant. The day after the guys had been arrested, pictures went live of Van and Clay kissing. Not just kissing, but Van straddling Clay's lap on a concrete stoop, the house behind it having been demolished by the tornado. The way the two of them held one another—the desperation on Clay's face, the contentment on Van's—they were clearly in love.

The entire nation was in shock. Especially Minnie. She understood that Clay had probably been in love with Van for a long time, but she didn't understand what that meant for Van's relationship with Bryant. Phoenix had released a statement claiming that Van and Bryant had privately broken off their romantic relationship some time ago, but they remained such good friends that not much had changed.

Minnie had been repeating the phrase, "broken off their romantic relationship some time ago," to herself for two days before Van called her as she was closing up the kitchen one night.

"I bet you've got some questions for me," Van said, and Minnie blushed. Was the woman a mind reader? Minnie had been trying to figure out how to ask Van about her relationship with Bryant once Van and Phoenix returned from their trip to L.A. The trick was not sounding like she was in it for the gossip—or for Bryant—neither of which Minnie was sure she could pull off.

"I don't know what you mean," Minnie said instead. Because she wasn't going to be the one who told Van that Bryant had cheated on her, even if their relationship was over. And that was absolutely the only thing that Minnie had questions about.

"Nothing about Bryant you want to ask me?" Van asked, a lilt to her voice that implied she'd been wiggling her eyebrows as she'd said it.

"Should I have questions?" Minnie didn't like the way the question squeaked out.

"Oh girl, don't even pretend. Like, a year and a half ago, Bryant was all about you. He told me everything."

"He did?" Minnie was pretty sure her brain flat-lined.

"Bryant and I tell each other everything. He told me about you back in the day, about how he thought it could be something special, then nadda until after the tornado and he tells me how he's been pining for some girl who broke his heart by having a baby with another guy. Didn't take much sleuthing to figure it out."

"He told you he had an affair with me?" Minnie asked, but she couldn't feel her lips, so she wasn't sure how clear the words had been.

"Of course—well, it's not *really* an affair when you're in a fake relationship—but I was really happy for him, and I don't know what happened between you two, but if there's still a chance for you guys, I don't want you to think you have to stay away on my account."

Fake. Van had just said fake relationship, hadn't she?

"I don't understand," Minnie said.

She could practically feel Van's grin. "Bryant and I have never been in a romantic relationship. We're friends—best friends—but that's it, I promise."

"But—"

"But you have to keep it a secret," Van said, cutting Minnie off. "It's my biggest secret—well, my biggest secret used to be that I was in love with my stepbrother, but since the cat's out of the bag on that one, you are now the keeper of my next biggest secret."

"I—wow."

"I know," Van said. "I'm a freaking scandal waiting to happen. I'm thinking if I can drop a bomb about once a month, my name will never leave the headlines, you know?"

Minnie was pretty sure Van was joking, but she was also pretty sure her brain was broken.

"Anyway, I just wanted to clear the air, just so you didn't think you had to keep any secrets from me or anything. And you know, if you ever want the tea about everything Bryant's ever done, I'm your girl."

"I appreciate that," Minnie said. "But Bryant and I happened a long time ago."

"The offer still stands," Van said.

When the call was over, Minnie couldn't remember what else she'd said—or what Van's sign off had been. But it was a lot harder to ignore Bryant's frequent presence after that phone call, and she did feel more like she could count on Van as a friend after that.

Van had started joining Phoenix and Minnie for their 10 a.m. coffee breaks. A lot of the conversation had centered around the organizations that helped sexual assault victims they were featuring on their social media, which had led to Minnie sharing her story with Van.

Van had risen from her chair and pulled Minnie and Malcolm, who was on Minnie's lap, into a smothering hug. "You must have felt so alone."

Minnie had teared up a little and let Van rock her side to side as she swayed the hug. She had felt alone. Isolated in a place that even Rocco hadn't been able to touch at first. It had been that yearning for making a connection that had lead Minnie to giving in to her attraction to Bryant so quickly.

Minnie hadn't even had a chance to respond to Van, as the other woman squeezed Minnie so hard that Malcolm squirmed between them. "You are not alone, anymore," Van said. "You're completely stuck with us."

Minnie hadn't been sure whether to laugh or cry as Phoenix had grinned at her over Van's shoulder.

The very next day, as Minnie was keeping an eye out for Van to arrive—Phoenix was already in back—she saw someone familiar enter the shop out of the corner of her eye. She'd just finished cleaning the kitchen from the morning's baking sessions and had been headed back to her office. She liked to grab book catalogs to bring with her when she joined Van and Phoenix, so at least she could pretend she was working. But no. Henry Bishop had just walked into her store.

Adrenaline spiked, and she was around the counter and in his face before she even realized what she was doing. "You aren't welcome here," she said. Zero politeness. None of the cajoling sweetness she used with customers when it was time for them to move on for whatever reason.

Henry Bishop flashed her a stunner of a smile, all white teeth and auburn beard and grace. "I heard you have some of the best coffee and cinnamon rolls in town."

The cinnamon rolls only made Minnie think of Bryant, and even if Bryant had hurt her, he had also helped her feel safe and secure and worthy for the first time in a long, so Minnie repeated. "You aren't welcome here."

Bishop's smile tightened. "I'm prepared to spend money here today. Possibly a lot of money."

Minnie flashed him as menacing a grin as she could

muster. "Then it's a good thing I don't need your money." Then she set her hands on his chest, and he was so shocked, that he took a step back. "I wouldn't take your money if I hadn't made a sale in weeks. As it is? I'm doing just fine." Minnie crowded him again, poking him in the chest right above where his stupid vest buttoned. "And I don't serve rapists, so you, and anybody who works for you or who is travelling with you or anybody that supports you, I don't serve them either."

Every poke of Minnie's finger was accompanied by a backward step on Bishop's part, until Minnie had crowded him up against the door.

"Hey now, those allegations are—"

"Absolutely fucking true," Minnie said.

Bishop's eyes flicked up behind her, and Minnie was vaguely aware that a crowd had gathered behind her.

"Jesus, you're a bold one," Bishop said.

"I don't have patience for assholes like you. Now are you going to leave, or do I need to get the police involved?"

"I didn't do anything wrong."

"You were asked to leave an establishment and exhibited belligerent behavior. They'd be here in a heartbeat. I serve them all their coffee, you see."

"I'm not being belligerent."

"Or I could call in Van's security team. I'm sure they'd be happy to help."

Bishop narrowed his eyes at her, as if he wasn't sure if she was bluffing, but Minnie was almost certain Phoenix was hiding in the stacks, relaying everything that was going on to Van's personal bodyguard.

"You wouldn't know how," he said.

Minnie pulled her phone out and dialed Phoenix's number. "Phoenix?" she said into the phone, and Bishop's face paled. "Yeah, Bishop's here." She paused. "Call whoever you like. I was trying to kick him out, but I could detain him instead."

That had seemed to be the ticket. Bishop ducked out the front door, cutting through the sea of paparazzi who had followed him in the front door. Minnie stuck her head out the door as Bishop tried to pretend she hadn't just run him out of her store.

"You see that asshole?" she asked not just the photographers, but everyone on the street. "He is not welcome here. You hear that, you fucking bastard?" Minnie shouted after him. "Don't you ever dare come back here."

Minnie was aware of the sounds of a dozen cameras snapping photos of her, and she didn't even care; she watched until Bishop disappeared around the street corner. Then she went back into her store and faced the half-circle of customers who had gathered near the front displays to watch the show. "Any of you have a problem with that?" she asked.

All of them shook their heads no. "Good," she said. Then beelined herself for Phoenix's table and succumbed to the pressure and the tears that were the aftermath of the adrenaline. All while Phoenix held her and told her what a badass she was.

Minnie, however, was not enough of a badass to keep Van from being kidnapped. Just a week later, Van had been grabbed from the alley behind Revival during a photoshoot, and though she'd been found quickly, Minnie still felt like she was at least partly at fault.

Even after they'd recovered Van and were gathered at the hospital, Minnie was still reeling. She sat in the waiting room, partly afraid for her new friend's health, partly afraid she was going to lose her new friendships because of the whole thing had happened behind her shop, and partly because she didn't want to be anywhere else.

The gossip sites were all wondering if Van had left Bryant for Clay now, and how devastating it must have been for Bryant to find out that his girlfriend had been cheating on him with her own stepbrother, but Minnie studied him from where he sat on the other side of the hospital waiting room, his head in his hands, his fingers curled through his hair.

He looked distraught, but that was to be expected. If what Van said was true, Bryant cared for Van very much, but not in a romantic way.

Minnie remembered the words Bryant had said to her the day he'd come back from California. He'd told her that he and Van were just friends, that they didn't have the sort of relationship Minnie thought they had. She'd never thought that he'd been telling the truth then. The show, the pictures, the way the two of them behaved in public—they put on a good farce. But knowing the truth now? Should Minnie have listened to him then?

Maybe.

It didn't change anything. Minnie still didn't want Malcolm to have anything to do with Van's and Bryant's charade, and it was too late to go back now.

When they finally allowed the family in to see Van, her father went first and was gone for a long time. Phoenix, who had been pretending Van's dad wasn't there, went next. While Bryant was gone, Minnie stared at his empty seat, feeling the urge to speak to him, but not certain what there was to say.

When Bryant returned, he mumbled something about Van wanting to see Minnie. So Minnie went. She wanted to see for herself that Van, despite her concussion, was going to be alright.

Van smiled when Minnie walked into the room, though her eyes were bright and unfocused. "Phoenix told me you were here. Where's Malcolm?"

"He's with Rocco."

"I like Rocco," Van said, closing her eyes. She'd only met him once when he'd picked Malcolm up from the shop.

"Me too," Minnie said. "He's been my best friend my entire life."

"But he's not Malcolm's father, is he." It wasn't a question, despite the breathy, dreamy way Van delivered it. She must have been on some good drugs.

Minnie didn't want to lie anymore. Not to this brave woman. "No, he's not his biological father."

Van nodded, then brought an IV-ed hand to her forehead as if the motion had caused her pain. "You know you broke Bryant's heart, right?"

"I—" Minnie didn't know what to say to that. "It—I mean —No. I never knew."

"He has been devastated over you."

"He wasn't mine to love."

"He can be," Van said, reaching her hand out for Minnie's, and Minnie squeezed her fingers and shook her head minutely. "I won't tell him he's Malcolm's father," Van said, and Minnie's heart stuttered that Van would actually say it aloud. "But you should. He'd want to know."

"No offense, but I don't want my child to be blamed for

breaking you and Bryant up. If I tell Bryant, it will come out, and people will trace it back and—."

"Stop worrying about that," Van said with a drunken wave of her hand. "Because as soon as Clay shows up, I'm going to propose. That'll shock the hell out of everyone. You'll be the sweet girl who helped Bryant pick up the pieces after I cheated on him with his best friend. You'll be the hero."

Van closed her eyes then, and Minnie knew the conversation was over, but Minnie didn't stop thinking about it for weeks.

Van and Clay started playing up their relationship, and just days after her release from the hospital, there were rumors they were getting married. The world couldn't have cared less about Minnie. Not that they had a reason to yet. Not that she had even talked to Bryant. But Phoenix was still always around, and Van and Clay visited the shop daily.

Things had turned around for the pop star. The amount of hate mail and death threats she received had started to drop now that there was undeniable evidence that Bishop had attempted to harm her. But she still traveled with her security guards, and Clay never let her out of his sight— rarely out of his reach, even.

For a while the amount of paparazzi in town was worse than ever. The roads were a mess. Minnie had to shoo them from the front window of Revival every morning when Phoenix showed to do her work, and as summer turned into fall, it seemed like none of the Van Birch group were going to leave Wellville. Speculation began to circulate that they'd all permanently relocated to Kansas. Certainly businesses did well. The paparazzi still had to eat and drink and sleep, and Minnie was happy to serve them, as long as they left their cameras outside.

As construction wrapped up on the house, Minnie found herself spending more and more of her evenings alone with Malcolm as Rocco spent more and more nights with Erin. Minnie couldn't help but look up how the media was portraying Bryant from day to day. None of her new friends ever mentioned Bryant to her, and he still never visited. It was as if, with his and Van's public break-up, they had simply stopped being friends. Like they'd divorced him from their family, but Minnie knew that wasn't true.

She saw pictures of them together out and about town. Clay and Bryant and Van or some variation thereof. They all appeared to be just as great of friends as they had been before. Better even, because Clay and Van had always seemed uneasy together before. Turned out it was the crazy sexual tension between them.

But Bryant. He smiled for the cameras. More often than not it was that goofy smile Minnie had come to associate with him having one too many drinks.

And she worried about him.

She asked Van about it one blustery October afternoon when Van had sought refuge from the paparazzi in the kitchen with Minnie. She'd been telling Minnie about how her security detail now shut down the local YMCA every morning so she could exercise without them having a heart attack.

"I made Bryant come with me so I wouldn't feel like I was putting on a show for Butch and his goons. It was nice having him there."

Minnie's heart pounded at the mention of Bryant, but she kept her eyes on the cinnamon she was sprinkling over the giant batch of cinnamon rolls. They still reminded her of Bryant and the night they'd conceived Malcolm, which was unfortunate because she couldn't stomach them anymore, but they were her most popular item on the menu. This particular batch was a special order for the bank next door for their board meeting that afternoon.

"How did that go?" Minnie asked, feigning serenity she did not feel.

Van was silent for a long minute, then said, "It would have been better if he wasn't hung over."

"He's been hung over a lot lately, hasn't he?"

She caught Van's nod out of the corner of her eye. "I mean, he's always been a big drinker. Hell, we all are—except Clay—" a slow, goofy smile spread over Van's lips as she thought about him. She shook herself out of it a moment later and continued, "But these last couple of years, I think it's turned into something more."

Minnie nodded as she started rolling the dough into a long, tight tube. "I've been worried about him since we were together. Especially after I found his flask."

"He has three flasks," Van said.

Minnie gaped. That was waaay too many flasks. Even one flask was concerning, because who needed alcohol on them at all times? But three?

"I know," Van said, nodding as she took another sip of her latte, then ticked them off on her fingers. "One in his jacket pocket, one in his toolbox, and one in the glove compartment."

"That's not even legal!" Minnie said.

Van slumped against the cabinet behind her back and shrugged. "I've always known that he was self-medicating to some degree, but I've been thinking of asking him to speak to my therapist, see if she can get him on some actual medication instead."

Minnie scrunched her brows. "Like anti-depressants?"

"Maybe," Van said. "But he was diagnosed with ADHD when he was in the Army. And they gave him a lot of ways to manage, but he hasn't been on meds since he got out. He's always claimed he's got a routine, and I haven't had much reason to doubt him, but these last few months, since I've actually been with him all the time, I am a little worried."

That was new information. Bryant had never mentioned anything to her—but then again, he'd never told her anything personal about himself outside of the usual get-to-know-you talk. She knew he'd grown up with a single mom. That she rarely came back to Wellville to visit him outside of major holidays, that his father had left when he was too young to remember him. He'd told Minnie he read almost obsessively, and he'd seemed almost obsessed with her, but she didn't know enough about ADHD to know if those were symptoms or how he really felt.

Minnie did know that self-medicating with alcohol was never a good idea. Rocco's dad had been an alcoholic, and he would show up at Rocco's mom's apartment, which was next door to Minnie and her mom's apartment growing up. He would yell and throw things around and Rocco and Aunt Ivette would escape into Minnie's room, and Minnie would sleep with her mom. Only none of them would sleep until he went away again. That happened every few months until he finally never came back.

Minnie had been terrified whenever she'd heard Rocco's dad's boots on the stairs, and that was definitely not what she wanted for herself or for her son.

She knew Rocco was a good father to Malcolm, but she'd

barely seen him for weeks. He'd been there for Malcolm during the day, but he'd also been spending his nights off at Erin's, where they had privacy. While Minnie was happy for him, she'd grown lonely. She loved spending her evenings with her son, but she left Revival at five. Malcolm was in bed by 7:30. She spent an hour or two doing chores around the house. She listened to music or an audiobook, but once she was done, she tried to read or watch TV but found she couldn't concentrate. Most of the time she got her computer out and worked on answering emails or checking sales reports and researching new books to buy.

She'd hardly read since Malcolm had been born and started to feel like an imposter bookstore owner for her inability to finish a book, but her doctor had assured her that it was normal for a new mother to be distracted. As Malcolm neared his first birthday, Minnie worried she would never return to her former self.

So when Van and Phoenix insisted that she come out with them to Tessa's upon their return from L.A. to celebrate Van and Clay wrapping up recording on their new album the week before Thanksgiving, Minnie was excited for the opportunity for a night out. Rocco encouraged her to go and promised he'd be home for the night with Malcolm.

Phoenix and Van picked her up in a limo, mostly for the novelty of it, they claimed. Clay and Bryant were also present, and while Van sat draped around her fiancé, who didn't seem to be able to take his hands off her, Bryant sat huddled in the corner away from all of them. His knee bounced to a rhythm that was faster than 90s drum and bass. He actually twiddled his thumbs as he looked out the tinted window. His shoulders were stiff and his jaw clenched. His overlong hair fell into his eyes behind his glasses. Bryant looked uncomfortable as hell, and Minnie couldn't understand why everyone was just ignoring him.

They passed around a bottle of whiskey, and while Minnie took the barest sip, she watched Bryant's throat bob as he swallowed two mouthfuls like it was water before Clay pulled the bottle from him, telling him not to hog it all.

Clay corked the bottle before Van could pass it around a second time. "Oh, you are so not any fun," Van said.

Clay tucked the bottle beneath his seat. "There will be plenty to drink once we get there. You don't need to show up blitzed."

"I don't want to be blitzed," she said, "Just pleasantly buzzed."

Clay leaned in close and placed a kiss on Van's neck. "Like I said, there will be plenty of time to get pleasantly buzzed once we're in the club." Then he kissed her neck again, and Minnie had to avert her eyes. Their love was too bare. Too exposed, it made Minnie feel raw, like she'd stayed in the sun too long and then had a fall.

Minnie wished she had Phoenix's excuse for not paying them any mind, but as much work as Minnie had any given day, it hadn't compounded into the need for a screen in front of her face at all times. Phoenix was already coordinating their arrival, because she tapped her screen and said, "Butch has already set up security. We're a go as soon as we pull up."

"Thank god," Bryant said, and Van nudged him with her foot.

"You should hook up with someone tonight."

He shot her an annoyed glare, like they'd had this conversation before.

"What?" Van said, feigning innocence, "I'm serious. You need to get out of this funk you've been in for, like, forever."

Bryant's expression didn't change, though his eyes met Minnie's for the barest second before he shot a look back to Van. "I'm here, aren't I?" he asked, and Van seemed to take that as as much of a concession as she was going to get.

Minnie wondered how much time Van had spent convincing Bryant to come at all. Had it been days of begging? Had deals been struck? Had they all cajoled Bryant out of the house. And if they were concerned about his drinking, why were they all going to a club? They could have just as easily come over to Revival for hot chocolate and cinnamon rolls and board games. As Butch opened the door to the limo and a gust of cold November air swept in, Minnie thought it would definitely be warmer at Revival.

Minnie fought past the goose pimples that crept up over her legs and accepted Phoenix's proffered arm as they made their way past the line and straight into the club. Van and Clay paused in front them, posing for the cameras like they'd been the Hollywood golden couple the whole time. Bryant followed behind, head up and smiling. He even high-fived some girl wearing far too little clothing for the freezing temperatures, but the second the club door shut behind them, Minnie saw his shoulders droop and his hands go into his pockets as he ambled his way over to the bar. If he'd been a lonely kid in an alley, he'd just need a crushed soda can to kick to complete the image of being dejected and alone.

Minnie wanted to go to him, but Phoenix had already procured her a drink and was dragging her to their reserved table while Bryant struck up a conversation with a man at the bar. Had Bryant met him there? Had he been dating? Minnie had been under the impression he'd been moping around his house and the only time he ever got out was when Van forced him out of his shell, but what did Minnie know? That was probably wishful thinking on her part.

"He's not seeing anyone," Phoenix said, following Minnie's gaze.

He leaned over the man he'd been talking to, Bryant standing with a whiskey in his hand while his new companion sat, sipping beer from a bottle at the bar.

"It's none of my business," Minnie said.

"It could be," Phoenix said, already pulling her phone out of her purse, "If you wanted it to be. He's besotted with you."

Minnie shook her head. "He was besotted with me, but that was almost two years ago."

Phoenix nodded. "I'm pretty sure you broke him."

Minnie frowned as she watched Bryant flirt with the man at the bar some more. He didn't look broken, though he was already signaling for a second glass of whiskey, and Minnie was still barely sipping at her first Old Fashioned.

"What about you?" she asked Phoenix. "Have you done anything but work lately? I haven't seen you with anyone. Not even a certain silver fox."

Phoenix took a sip of her Manhattan. "That is because I am extremely discreet about my liaisons. I prefer to keep my love life out of the tabloids."

"So, have you broken anyone's heart recently?" Minnie asked, her meaning clear.

Phoenix set down her phone and shot Minnie the intense kind of sharp stare Minnie had seen her level at Clay when she thought he was being annoying or, more recently, at Bryant whenever he took a drink, but which Minnie had never received. "Why would you ask me that?"

Minnie shook her head and sipped her drink to buy some time. "Just because you said I'd broken Bryant..." Minnie trailed off, not sure how to take the sharp focus that was Phoenix's full attention. She was like a hawk, or a full-on raptor; you got the feeling that if she wanted to, she could pull the flesh from your bones, and she wouldn't even be sorry.

Then she seemed to realize that Minnie's question had been innocent, a jest even, and reined herself back in. "No one who matters," she said and took another sip from her martini glass. "I haven't had a serious relationship in years. I don't have time for one," she said.

Minnie nodded and wondered how much of that was true. How much was Phoenix glossing over with her casual take on her sex life? Because the piercing stare and feeling of foreboding that came along with it told Minnie that there was a lot more going on than Phoenix was willing to talk about. Specifically, that a lot more had been going on between Phoenix and Van's father than Phoenix wanted to admit to.

Minnie tried not to take offense. They'd only been friends for a couple of months. It took time to build that kind of intimacy. They would get there, and to help, Minnie said, "I haven't slept with anyone since Bryant." It was a regretful sigh that escaped her lips. She didn't like thinking that it had been almost two years. That was unthinkable. She'd used to be just a little bit slutty, before the lacrosse player. But life and motherhood changed a lot.

Minnie wouldn't trade a whole showroom of strangers in her bed for her life with Malcolm.

"You should change that," Phoenix said, nodding toward the bar.

Bryant stood by himself now, his companion having begged off somewhere. "What do you mean?" Minnie asked.

Phoenix raised one manicured, flame-red eyebrow. "You two are stuck on each other. You should just sleep together and get over it."

"It's not that simple," Minnie said.

"Oh, he's going to be pissed," Phoenix said. "But Bryant is too kind to hold you keeping him from his son against you for too long."

That got Minnie's attention. "You know?" she asked in a whisper. "About Malcolm?"

Phoenix rolled her eyes. "I'm pretty sure that the only person who thinks Malcolm is Rocco's biological child is Bryant."

Minnie sat up straight and could feel sweat breaking out on her palms. "Even Clay? Do you think he'll say anything?"

Phoenix shrugged. "Clay has his own sense of honor, but at the moment, he probably considers it none of his business. Plus, Van is keeping him preoccupied. He doesn't have the same time for gossiping with his buddy that he used to."

Phoenix found Clay and Van on the dancefloor, oblivious to everyone but each other. And glancing at the bar, Bryant was still alone, still drinking. Minnie wanted to go to him. She wanted to pull him onto the dance floor and make him smile, make him think about something that made him happy for just a little while.

So she knocked back the rest of her drink and stood. Her green dress had felt Christmassy and festive when she'd donned it earlier in the evening, now it felt skimpy and too much like a slip. Minnie was conscious of the way her breasts looked gigantic in comparison to her waist, which was generally a good thing, since it had taken her a minute to return to the size she'd been before Malcolm, but as Bryant felt her approach and turned around to watch her, she remembered that her breasts were not and had never been small. Bryant's eyes were glued to them.

He didn't smile at her when she stepped up to the bar beside him, only followed her with his body, never turning his back to her, and cocked his head to the side.

He said nothing, so Minnie squeezed her way onto the stool next to him, placing her so close to him, she could feel his body heat through his gray button-up. "I'd like an Old Fashioned," she told the bartender, who was also staring at her breasts.

"Put it on my tab," Bryant said, which helped snap the bartender out of his stupor and made him hop to.

Minnie donned a smile and craned her neck to look up at him, "Thanks."

"What do you want, Minneapolis?"

His tone reminded her of her father, and she rolled her eyes. His sullenness was not the same thing as her father's entitlement, but she knew how to handle men who didn't want to be handled.

"I thought maybe we could dance," she said.

"Why would we do that?" He took a sip of his nearly empty whiskey glass. Was that his second or third? Minnie had lost track. She wondered if Bryant even counted anymore.

"Because it's fun," Minnie said, and let her shoulder graze his stomach as she crossed her legs and repositioned herself on the stool. She rested her elbows on the bar, and she knew he could see right down her dress.

Her whole body went on alert, as she could feel the path his eyes made down her dress, over satin clad hips and down her legs, to her three-inch-tall heels, and back up.

"Your husband won't mind?" he asked, with bitterness in his voice.

Minnie wrinkled her nose and accepted her drink from the bartender. She took a sip, this one was sweeter than the last, to delay answering his question, just because he was being purposefully annoying.

"I don't have a husband, but if you mean Rocco, he's at home with Malcolm and his girlfriend and his girlfriend's daughter, so no, I don't think he'd mind if I danced with someone at a club."

"He's threatened me, you know." Bryant said.

"And you gave him a black eye, so I feel like the playing field has evened out."

"He still won't like it."

"Then it's a good thing it's not his choice," Minnie said, wanting to get him out of this mood, she slid the toe of her shoe over his calf. His head jerked toward her, and he finally met her eyes. Steely determination was replaced with vulnerability before transforming into desire. "I'm a big girl," Minnie said. "I can make my own decisions."

"And you want to dance with me, now. After all this time?"

Minnie shrugged and took another sip of her drink. "There's nothing standing in our way anymore. We could give it a shot."

Minnie was surprised at her own audacity. Had she thought these things in the last few weeks? Absolutely, but only in a deep, secret place inside herself that she liked to pretend didn't exist. To make herself vulnerable to Bryant again, to take him in and face telling him about Malcolm, it was big and scary and should not be something she did on a whim.

But she had been lonely. And she might have stopped sleeping in Bryant's old undershirt when she grew big enough that her belly would have stretched it, but that didn't mean she'd stopped missing him.

Bryant stood silent. She could see his jaw clench and release as he processed what she was saying, but he unconsciously shifted closer so that his body was almost pressing against her side.

"Let's just dance," Minnie said. "It doesn't have to be anything more than that. Maybe we can be friends."

A sad sort of smile broke over Bryant's lips then, and he bent to whisper in her ear, sending shivers up and down Minnie's spine. "We can't be friends, Minneapolis, because I will always want you too much for that." Then he placed a dry, lingering kiss just below her ear and stood, pulling her from her stool and onto the floor.

He pulled her close, a gleam in his eyes as if he didn't quite take her seriously, as if he was going to prove her wrong—that this whole scheme was a bad idea. That not only could they not just not be friends, but they couldn't be —shouldn't be—lovers either.

But as Bryant wrapped his arms around Minnie's waist, as he pressed her chest against his stomach, her head against his chest, swaying well out of time with the music, Minnie felt herself surrender completely. If her only choice to be near him, to fix the rift between them, was to let their bodies talk, then that's what Minnie would do. She would dance with him, take him home and make love to him until her soul healed over and maybe his did too.

Minnie didn't know if their differences were insurmountable, but she knew how tired denying her feelings for this man had made her, and as Bryant stepped back, twirled her, and started dancing in time with the heavy club music, Minnie hadn't felt more invigorated about a decision in a long time.

She wanted this man, and perhaps he wanted her as well.

CHAPTER 19

*B*ryant never wanted to stop touching Minnie. They'd been dancing for an hour, and every second he couldn't feel some part of her body against his was like torture. Her dress was like torture. He hadn't been able to even look at her in the limo without feeling himself come to life with arousal. Slinky, strappy, satin dresses should be illegal to wear in public. Her dress looked like little more than a slip, and the way it slid over her skin, under his palm, only called to mind the way she felt underneath him, laid out on his bed.

But they'd never slept in his bed. Something he was ready to rectify right this second.

He wasn't sure he trusted the impulse. He definitely didn't trust her. So what if she wasn't with Rocco anymore? They still lived together, still had a son together. One that they'd conceived while he'd been out of town trying to convince himself that she wasn't cheating on him with her "cousin."

But acknowledging that he'd never stopped wanting her,

that he'd never want anyone else but her, not really? That had him panicking on the inside. Holding her in his arms now, imagining that she might slip away, that the reprieve from the misery he'd been feeling these last couple of years might be temporary and fleeting, made him want her even more. If he was going to have to live his entire life without her, he wanted to have as much of her as he could while he had the chance. And if Minnie was offering, Bryant was taking.

Because he was a mess.

He knew it. He had been a mess for years.

Everyone could blame it on how hard it must be for him to come to terms with the love of his life falling in love with his best friend. But that had never been an issue for Bryant. He was so happy for Van and Clay that he wasn't sure how to articulate it other than to shove them together whatever chance he got.

That gave him more time to wallow in his misery away from prying eyes.

But he was touching Minnie. She had her hands on his hips and was swaying hers in a mesmerizing back and forth motion that had his fingers twisting in the fabric at her waist and pulling her against him. He ducked his knees and moved with her so that her hips brushed his with every sway.

He reached down, resting his hand over the curve of ass, then down to the bare skin on her thigh. He wanted to brush his fingers up, under her skirt, pull the material to her waist and let his hand skim over her mound, then down, between her lips and inside her, all while he held her against his growing erection. He could make her come like that, and he wanted to, but not here in front of everyone.

"Let's go," he said, his voice hoarse, and barely audible over the music.

Minnie didn't need to actually hear him to know what he was asking. She nodded and pulled him toward the front of the club. He grabbed their coats and asked about an Uber.

Minnie shook her head and pulled his lips to hers, using the lapels of his leather jacket, the same one he'd worn last year when they'd left from this same club and slept together for the first time.

"Revival is just down the street."

It was sleeting as they stepped out the front door, and they ran, hand in hand, past the line of people waiting to get in, past the paparazzi, and into Revival. The inside was dark and quiet but warm. He could feel Minnie shivering though her coat and with her skimpy dress and bare legs, he knew she had to be freezing.

"Come here," he said and tucked her into his jacket, wrapping it around her. The ice that had collected on her front melted against his shirt, but he didn't care. He wouldn't be wearing it much longer. The first flash came only seconds later, and while Bryant cursed, Minnie giggled. Of course they'd followed them.

"You're going to be all over the gossip pages," Bryant said.

Minnie only giggled as she tugged him toward the books. "Wouldn't be the first time."

She dragged him deep into the stacks to Phoenix's conference table where there was no view of the front windows. She turned on one of the reading lamps, and Bryant was able to see more than the pale outline of the table and the edges of the bookshelves. He was able to see

Minnie as she stepped out of her shoes and dropped her coat to the floor.

His mouth went dry as she approached him, shoving his coat over his shoulders like he was a toddler who wasn't able to do it himself yet. He couldn't. He was too busy watching her, marveling. He'd almost forgotten how beautiful she was. How delicate her features, how high the arch of her brow, how dainty her wrists.

She tugged his belt open, then started on his shirt tails, and the only word Bryant could form was, "Here?"

"Here," Minnie said, and then her hand was in his pants, wrapping around his length and squeezing. He moaned and forgot everything but the feel of her as she pumped him once, twice, then let go. "Please tell me you have a condom," Minnie said.

He did. He'd shoved a couple in his wallet out of sheer determination that he was going to find a hookup and screw them senseless in an attempt to not notice who Minnie might be with these days. To forget her.

Bryant pulled them out to show her, and she grinned wickedly.

Then she reached for the hem of her dress and pulled it over her head. She wore a white lace thong and a white strapless bra that barely contained her ample breasts. He remembered the taste and feel of them in his hands, his mouth. When she noticed him staring, she reached behind her back and with a shimmy, the bra fell away and she was bared to him.

Her breasts were fuller than he remembered, he thanked motherhood for that as she yanked his shirt over his head and he toed off his shoes. He knelt in front of her in nothing but the designer jeans Van had picked out for him and skimmed his hands up her magnificent legs.

His nose was level with the bottom of her ribs, and he licked at the stretch marks that crossed over and under her belly button. The skin wasn't as taut as it used to be, but Bryant felt himself flooded with awe at remembering that she'd created a person since they'd last been together.

His only regret was that that person hadn't been created with him.

Minnie guided his hands up her sides and closed them over her tits, squeezing his fingers beneath hers. Every piece of him surged with need as he tested their weight in his palms, then rolled his palms over them. They were heavier than he remembered. He rocked up onto his toes, capturing one of her nipples in his mouth. She moaned as he rolled it between his teeth then lathed it with his tongue. Then to test his theory, he gave a suck and a sweet, freshness flooded his mouth.

"Bryant," she gasped, and he lapped at her other nipple, which had started to drip. God, he'd never thought he'd find this sexy, but her body amazed him.

"You are the most delicious woman," he said, rising all the way and guiding her back until her backside hit the top of the conference table. "Everything you do, everything you make, the way you move." He pushed the chairs aside and laid her back on the table. "It was like you were made to tempt me."

He kicked his pants off and retrieved the condoms, while Minnie snort-laughed. "I forgot how flowery you get when you're aroused."

Bryant hovered over her, his cock teasing her covered opening as he set his glasses aside and grinned down at her.

"Don't pretend that you don't like it," he said and pressed his cockhead against the silk lace that separated them.

She moaned and pushed against him. He could feel her wet heat through the flimsy material, and he was tempted to pull them aside and press into her, but with a teasing kiss full of tongue and heat, he pulled back. He rolled the condom on before he hooked his fingers into the straps on her thong, pulled them down, and tossed it into the darkness behind them.

Bryant parted her legs, and positioned himself between them, angling her hips upward. Then he thrust inside Minnie with one quick push of his hips into hers. She let out a cry that was half pleasure, half surprise. Bryant had to still for just a moment and collect himself. The feel of her surrounding him was better than he remembered. It had been too long since he'd been with anyone. Too long since he'd been with her, and he wanted her with a mania that he didn't think one night was going to satiate.

He said her name, "Minnie," like a broken prayer as he started to move on her. She wrapped her legs around his hips as if she was afraid he was going to pull away and not come back. She squeezed her thighs, pulling him even closer at the same time as her hands scrambled for purchase on any part of him she could reach. His forearms, his chest, his shoulders, reaching up behind his neck and digging into the hair at the base of his skull and pulling.

Bryant was lost then. There was nothing but sensation. Nothing but this woman who needed her pleasure. Nothing but the feel of her body against his. Nothing in the universe mattered but this moment, and Bryant was determined to make it last as long as possible.

He felt her shudder on him, felt her inner muscles

pulling at him as her body went taught, and she moaned as she went pliant a moment later with her release. Not giving her a chance to recover, Bryant pulled her up against his chest and wrapped her legs more firmly around his hips, then he pulled her off the table and sank to his knees. He held her with one hand wrapped around her back, the other snaked between them to press against her clit as he pushed her down onto his cock, rocking his hips up into her.

She found the new rhythm even as she whimpered with the aftershocks of her last orgasm and used her thighs to angle herself just so. It only took three thrusts for her to moan in ecstasy again, and Bryant felt as if they were in the same body. Her pleasure was his own as his release descended violently and completely.

He murmured her name again, and again before collapsed backward onto the floor.

CHAPTER 20

*M*innie panted on top of Bryant. She'd come into this room shivering, but now she was covered in sweat, and she'd never felt better. Minnie had almost forgotten how good sex could be. She was limp and invigorated all at the same time, and it was possible that Minnie didn't ever want to lose this feeling. The hot, satisfied bliss so complete, it left no room for doubt or guilt.

Minnie kissed Bryant's sweaty chest. His hands never stopped roaming over her.

"That did just happen," Bryant said, his voice a whisper in the quiet shop. "I'm not dreaming it this time?"

Minnie kissed his chest again. "It was real." She nipped at him, and he squeezed his arms around her, clamping her to his side. "I can't believe we had sex on the conference table," she said.

He chuckled. "That was one of my fantasies," he said; the "before" was implied.

Minnie shimmied to the side so she could cuddle her head against his chest with her shoulder on the hardwood floor. "Do you think Phoenix will know?" she asked. "I have a feeling she'll take one look at it and ask for a bucket of sanitizer."

Minnie could hear the grin in Bryant's voice as he said, "I wouldn't be surprised."

"Do you know what's going on with her?" Minnie asked. "We used to talk about things, but now she's being cagey."

"Things like sex?"

"And men."

Bryant's fingers traced up and down the length of her spine. "You've finally got me naked again and you want to talk about *Phoenix's* love life? I'm disappointed."

Minnie playfully slapped at his side. "She's my friend, and she's really good at avoiding talking about herself though, and you don't even realize it half the time."

Bryant kissed the top of Minnie's head. "Last I knew, she and Robin were hooking up, but I hear he's in the doghouse right now, so who knows."

The tenor of his voice, a little gravelly, a little sleepy had almost distracted her from the words he spoke. He hadn't said anything Minnie didn't already know. "She's refused to talk about him or anyone for months, and normally I'd be grossed out by such a huge age gap, but it's so obvious how much he loves her."

Bryant's hand skimmed down her shoulder, then traced over her breast and down until it settled on her hip. "I'm surprised she talked to you about him at all."

"She offered it. I barely even had to push."

"Huh," Bryant said. "She usually doesn't talk about personal stuff to anyone but Van."

She shook out her hands and huddled her shoulders. "She seemed lonely at the time. She still seems lonely."

"Do you think she loves him?" Bryant said, "Because he's basically my father too, and he doesn't deserve to be treated like dirt."

"Yeah, I think she does." Minnie ran her hand through Bryant's hair, pushing it back out of his eyes. He'd never expressed familial affection for anyone but Clay or his mother to her before. "But she'd never admit it out loud."

"I have trouble thinking about it too long," Bryant said, pulling her back down beside him. "I'd rather think about us instead."

Minnie rejoined him on the floor, but reality was starting to flood back in. The floor was cold and hard, and Minnie needed to go to the bathroom. And how was she going to explain this to Rocco? He was not going to be happy. Minnie reminded herself that she didn't need his permission. If she and Bryant could fix things between them, could start over and put the past behind them, then Rocco would have to be happy for her.

"I'm a little afraid of that," she said as she struggled to get comfortable on the hard floor.

"Why?" he asked.

She sighed and sat up wrapping her arms around herself as the cold started to settle into her skin again.

Bryant followed her to sitting. "You're cold," he said. Then looked around him like he just realized they were on the floor in a bookshop instead of luxuriating in a bed. "Let's get cleaned up and dressed." He pushed to his feet and offered Minnie a hand to help her to hers. "Then we can pretend we're civilized while we raid the cinnamon roll stash."

"You want cinnamon rolls?"

Bryant pulled her into his side, and his arms and chest

were ten degrees warmer than she was, and Minnie pressed closer into him. "I've never stopped wanting your cinnamon rolls. I've been dreaming about them for almost two years."

He kissed her so tenderly then that she knew he was talking about more than cinnamon rolls. He meant he'd never stopped wanting *her*. He'd been dreaming about *her*.

Minnie wasn't cold anymore. The heat of his words warmed her from the inside, but she needed to use the bathroom, and she worried it was already getting too late.

She ran a hand down his chest and noticed for the first time that he was thinner than he'd been before. Leaner. His long, ropey muscles stood out more starkly against his skin, and she thought it was more a sign of neglect, rather than improved health. She would feed him all the cinnamon rolls he wanted.

"Meet me in the kitchen in five minutes?" she asked. "And try to keep to the shadows in case there are still any photographers outside?"

Bryant kissed her forehead and stepped away to retrieve his clothes. "You ashamed of me?" he asked.

"No," Minnie said. "But I'd rather have you all to myself for a little while longer."

"You do know we're going to be all over the internet come morning? Maybe we even already are."

Minnie shrugged. "Then let me at least pretend until morning." She smiled at Bryant over her shoulder and disappeared into the bathroom.

Once she had donned her dress and her coat, because she was still chilled, she dug her phone out of the inner coat pocket and found three text messages.

The first from Phoenix:

Hope you're having fun. Let me know if you need a ride, I can send a car that isn't an obnoxious Uber driver who will sell photos of you to online gossip rags.

Minnie checked the time. It was already past midnight. Getting up at five in the morning to start the baking was going to suck. Minnie would have Malcolm with her all day, because Rocco was on day shifts this week. As Malcolm got older, it was getting more difficult to keep him happy while she worked. Perhaps it was time to put him in day care. She made a mental note to think about it later.

She asked Phoenix to send someone her way in an hour.

The next text was from Van. *I hope the fact that you and Bryant both disappeared means that you disappeared together. Get it girl, he is so in love. Just be careful.*

The last message was a photo from Rocco, which she pulled up as she entered the kitchen. The photo showed a sleeping Malcolm in his crib, dressed in Santa footie pajamas. His pacifier had fallen from his mouth, and he slept with one hand over his head. His hair had lightened over the last few months. Instead of the shock of black hair he'd had at birth, he now had the same rich chocolate brown hair as Bryant. You could see Bryant through his nose and and eyes, and Minnie suspected that as he grew older, Malcolm would develop the same square chin and perhaps his father's height as well. He was tall for his age.

She was still admiring the photo of Malcolm when Bryant entered the kitchen behind her. He pulled her back against his front as he wrapped his arms around her from behind. Back in his clothes, he smelled like whiskey, and Minnie sighed as much in frustration as she did in comfort. How often was he still using his flasks? Had he taken a sip just now, before coming out to meet her?

She didn't think so, his breath didn't have the overwhelming fresh alcohol stench on it as he bent forward and kissed her neck, then rested his chin on her shoulder. "This is your son?" he asked.

"Yes. Malcolm."

"He looks cozy," Bryant said, but she couldn't figure out what he was thinking as he said, "I wish I could get away with those kind of pajamas, but I roast in them these days."

"And you'd look ridiculous."

He chuckled and angled the phone so he could see the picture more clearly. Minnie's heart rate ticked up. Was he seeing the same things she'd just been admiring in her son? Was he recognizing the resemblance to himself? "What color are his eyes?" Bryant asked, his voice soft, and not at all suspicious.

"Blue," Minnie said on an exhale, hoping that didn't give the whole thing away on its own. Anyone who was paying attention would realize that Minnie's green eyes and Rocco's brown eyes would not equal blue eyes. But the combination of Bryant's blue gray eyes and hers? The options were either blue or green, and Malcolm's eyes were so dark blue, that sometimes when she looked into them as he nursed, she could convince herself that they were violet.

Bryant didn't say anything, just stared at the photo for a moment, and said, "He looks like you." Minnie didn't think Malcolm looked like her at all, but he did have her pale skin tone, the same pink hue of her skin was mirrored in his round cheeks, and his chubby little toes were similarly round to hers. Whenever Minnie looked at Malcolm though, all she saw was Bryant.

Minnie tucked her phone away, afraid that the more opportunity she gave him to examine her son, the more chance he would have to develop suspicions about

Malcolm's true parentage. Minnie would tell him, she promised herself right then and there that she would, just not yet.

She stole from Bryant's embrace and pulled two water glasses from the rack next to the dishwasher and filled them. She set them on the counter before she pulled the leftover cinnamon rolls from the day out of her cooler and popped them into the microwave to warm them up.

"I'd like to meet him," Bryant said. "Whenever you think we're ready for that step."

Minnie's heart melted a little bit more. He wanted to know how her son—his son. And Minnie wanted him to know him as well; she just also knew that introducing Bryant to Malcolm would bring the inherent risk of losing Bryant. Because he would figure it out quickly. Bryant was an intelligent man. He would recognize himself in the child.

"I'd like that," she said, though she didn't turn to look at him until the cinnamon rolls were out of the microwave. He stood on the other side of the prep table and had pulled up two stools. Minnie joined him in their makeshift midnight snack and said, "We have a lot to talk about."

He nodded and sunk his fork into his cinnamon roll. "I should have told you about me and Van from the beginning," he said. "It just felt so complicated back then, and I'd made a promise to Van that I wouldn't tell anyone. I couldn't even talk to Clay about it."

Minnie nodded. "It must have felt like drowning," she said.

"Yes." He took a bit of his pastry and washed it down with most of his glass of water. "That's exactly what it's been like. I'm sorry I hurt you," he said. "I'm sorry I drove you into Rocco's arms."

Minnie opened her mouth to protest, but Bryant kept speaking as if the words had been waiting to pour out of him all this time. "I was in love with you, and I never told you the truth. And then you had Rocco and Malcolm, and I tried to forget you. I told myself that you were better off without me, but I couldn't keep you out of my head. Since the first time we were together, you have been the only person I have wanted to be with. You were my missing piece, and I have been making myself miserable trying to move on, but I just can't."

Minnie's cinnamon roll sat untouched. The words, the break in his voice as he admitted how much she'd hurt him, broke her. If he knew the whole story, would he feel the same way about her? Because it was as if Bryant was speaking the words from her own heart.

"These past couple of years haven't been horrible," Minnie said. "I enjoyed being pregnant, and I enjoyed annoying my dad by refusing to marry Rocco and refusing to sell the shop and move home with him so he could try to control me all the time. And there have been times when Rocco, Malcolm, and I have been very happy together." Bryant hung his head, and Minnie paused and squeezed his shoulder, begging him to look at her. When he did, she could see the pain, the despondency in his eyes, so she offered him a small, shy smile. "But Rocco and I were only ever together for Malcolm. We've always been friends, and that's all we are. He will always be a part of my family, but it's you I want," she said, and something that looked like hope crept back into his expression.

"It's you I've been yearning for, missing so much that some days my stomach hurt so bad, it was all I could think about. It's you I thought I could never have, because you weren't mine to keep, but I think I started falling in love with you the first day you and Clay came to measure for the bookshelves. And I never wanted to let you go."

Bryant pulled her into his arms then, crushing her to him with the quiet desperation she suspected he'd been living with since Van's first single blew up and he'd agreed to live a lie.

"I will be nothing but honest with you from now on," he said. "I promise. No secrets."

"No secrets," Minnie echoed, even as a small part of her died a little at the promise. She vowed that she would tell Bryant soon, when the time was right, that Malcolm was his biological son, and that Minnie would like to have more children with him.

"So, when do we get to tell Rocco?" Bryant asked.

Minnie grimaced. "Give me a couple of days to set it up," she said.

But she didn't. Because she was a coward. And she knew what Rocco would say, even though the fact that Van's and Bryant's relationship had been a farce wasn't common knowledge, there was enough gossip that it was now a circulating theory. And Minnie and Rocco had discussed it. Minnie said Van had confirmed it, but Rocco didn't care.

"He still put the needs of another woman before you. When you're in a relationship with someone, you don't do that."

"It's more complicated than that," Minnie said. When Rocco shook his head, Minnie had said, "So if Erin asked you to do something that was in direct defiance of something I had asked of you, you wouldn't even hesitate to hurt me?"

"Erin wouldn't do that," Rocky said. "She understands our situation. She's okay with it."

"So if you guys get married and end up having to move away someday, you're going to what?" Minnie asked. "Abandon Malcolm and I? Try to take Malcolm with you?"

Rocco's mouth had dropped open, then shut again without him saying anything. He ran his hands through his short black hair so that it spiked straight up. "I hadn't thought that far ahead, but I wouldn't ever do either of those things. Malcolm is my son, and you are his mother. We would figure something out."

"Malcolm is his son too," Minnie had said, and Rocco had pounded the side of his fist into the coffee table so hard the floor beneath it had rattled. Minnie jumped and Malcolm, who had been napping on a blanket on the floor, whimpered in his sleep.

"I am his dad," Rocco said. "Would you try to take him away from me?"

Minnie shook her head. "Of course not, but I'm just saying that someday, we'll have to tell Malcolm the truth, and now that Bryant isn't attached to Van anymore, and Malcolm's very existence won't cause a scandal, maybe it's time to tell Bryant that he has a child."

"No," Rocco said. "Nothing good would come of it, Minnie. It's just another opening to let him hurt you. He could sue for custody. He could reject you and take Malcolm away from us. He'd have Robin Birch and all of Van Birch's money on his side. If he decided he wanted Malcolm, he could take him like that," Rocco snapped, "And the fact that they share DNA would make my name on his birth certificate irrelevant."

Minnie had dropped it after that. She hadn't thought

that Bryant might want to take Malcolm away from her. The only scenario in her head had been them being together. Or them co-parenting him here, with Rocco, if she and Bryant couldn't work things out.

But the lingering fear of that conversation, the reverberation of Rocco's fist on the coffee table as he staked his claim on Malcolm. Minnie knew it would tear Rocco's heart out if Bryant denied Rocco's right to Malcolm. He had been Malcolm's father since the beginning, but now that Minnie was on the other side, now that Bryant was free to be hers, she wondered if she'd made the right decision in keeping Malcolm's true parentage a secret all this time.

Maybe the scandal would have been worth it to avoid the twisted mess she found herself in now.

It was easier to ignore it, to tell herself that this thing between Bryant and herself was so new and so fragile that she needed to take the time to enjoy it, let it mature, before she did anything. And Bryant was so amorous, it was easy to do.

He stopped in at Revival every morning for coffee before work. He visited her after Malcolm was in bed on nights that Rocco was out at work or staying at Erin's. Their time together was short and precious enough that they didn't take time to ask many questions. They relished in their physical proximity so thoroughly that there wasn't space for anything else yet.

The photographers still followed Bryant everywhere, and Minnie knew it was only a matter of time before Rocco noticed the photos of the two of them together. They had been popping up everywhere.

But still, Minnie didn't say anything.

CHAPTER 21

*B*ryant had spent the last three weeks worshipping Minnie's body, and it had been heaven. It felt so good not to have to worry about dodging paparazzi to see his lover, so nice to go out with someone in public without getting phone calls and texts from a stressed-out Phoenix about how what he was doing could negatively affect Van. And best of all, it was amazing to not have to lie to Clay anymore.

Clay was so blissed out from spending his every spare moment with Van, that he was a lot more pleasant to be around these days. Not that Bryant had ever disliked spending time with his friend, but he hadn't realized how grumpy the man he considered his brother had become until he was suddenly smiling and joking and ready to have conversations that were more than grunts and scowls.

Now that Bryant was done wallowing in his own misery, he was able to enjoy all the positive changes that came along with no longer living a life shrouded in secrets and deception.

Times like now, when he'd been holding Minnie in his arms for hours, had made love to her until she was limp and sleepy and curled into him, Bryant had never felt more satisfied. His hand skimmed down her side, tracing the soft skin from her sharp shoulder, down to the dip of her waist, then over the curve of her hip and back. He never wanted to be anywhere else.

The reality show had wrapped for the season; they'd even filmed the Christmas episode already. The rebuilding work from the tornado was winding back down to manageable levels, and Van and Clay were gearing up to build his house this spring, before touring together over the summer to promote their new album, and Bryant was feeling gloriously free.

Gloriously in love. Gloriously whole for the first time in a long time. He was sleeping, he'd gained about fifteen pounds in cinnamon rolls, and he was so, so happy. The only thing he wanted more of was Minnie. He could tell that she was still cautious with her trust, that she wanted to let him in all the way but that she was afraid.

He understood. He wasn't entirely pleased that she still lived with her former lover, and though Bryant had never been in the house at the same time as Rocco, it was obvious that they weren't intimate in that way anymore. They maintained separate bedrooms and separate bathrooms, with Malcolm's room between theirs in the long hallway. Bryant was trying to be understanding, but he wanted more than fitting into each other's lives in whatever ways they could. Bryant wanted to structure his whole life around Minnie and Malcolm. He was prepared to make allowances for Malcolm's father, but Bryant wanted them both in his life all the time. He wanted to move them into his house, marry Minnie, and start his own family with her.

Bryant traced circles over the swell of Minnie's hip as he recalled the few encounters he'd had with Minnie's son in the last three weeks. He'd been napping in a playpen in a corner of the kitchen one afternoon. He'd been playing with Minnie on one of the sofas in the main seating area in Revival. Malcolm had buried his face in Minnie's shoulder when Bryant had tried to introduce himself. Bryant came to Minnie's house most nights, but Malcolm was always asleep by the time he arrived. Minnie had to rock him back to sleep one night, and Bryant had peeked through the crack in the bedroom door, his yearning to see Minnie as a mother too strong to disregard. Malcolm had shot Bryant an annoyed glance over his shoulder, as if Bryant were intruding, before cuddling back into Minnie's arms.

Minnie had saved Bryant a cupcake from Malcolm's birthday party just after Thanksgiving. Bryant had burned with a mixture of longing and jealousy when Minnie had shared pictures of her helping Malcolm open his presents, of which there had been an extravagant number.

Minnie had laughed and said, "My father thinks money is a good substitute for love."

She didn't talk about her father much, but he didn't press that. He'd learned enough information about him in the time when he'd been cyber-stalking her to know that he wouldn't care much for Jonas Halvarson. He was interested in money and appearance and was one of those older men who dated women the same age as his daughter, which Bryant had never been able to get behind.

He supposed he didn't think less of Robin for having an affair with Phoenix. Bryant wouldn't pretend to understand it, but he knew that Robin was not a predator in the way Jonas Halvarson struck him as being. Robin had seen something in Phoenix; she wasn't a prize the way the women Minnie's father was photographed with were.

Minnie stirred beside him and rolled over so that her breasts pressed against his chest, and Bryant traced her hip down to cup her deliciously round bottom and gave a playful squeeze.

Her bleary voice had a hint of sleep-induced gravel as she said, "Are you still awake?"

"Maybe," he said and placed a kiss on her temple. "I was thinking about next week."

"Hmmm," she was barely awake enough for this conversation, but Bryant was going to ask anyway.

"What are your plans for Christmas?"

Minnie rolled so she could look up at him. "We're going to Denver to pretend my dad likes us at his Christmas Eve holiday party. Then we're driving back here Christmas morning so Rocco can do Christmas with Erin and her daughter, Jenna."

"How would you feel about bringing Malcolm over to my mom's house for dinner later? She'd love to meet you guys."

Minnie was silent for too long. "Can I think about it? Rocco might want to take Malcolm with him to Erin's."

"Then you should definitely come with me to have dinner with my mom. You shouldn't be alone on Christmas, and I want to see you. My mom will only be in town for the one day, so it would be nice to spend it together."

Minnie seemed to relax into him. "I'll check with Rocco and let you know. I don't know if I'd be invited to Erin's, but I'm still not sure how I feel about letting Malcolm out of my sight for even a little while on Christmas. I know it's not his first, but he was only a few weeks old last year. This year he'll be able to open presents and play with them and start learning what it's all about, you know?"

"I understand," Bryant said. And he did. But he wanted so much more, and it was taking all of his restraint not to push. "I also want to see him and get to know him, because he's yours, but I don't want to force anything you're not ready for."

"Thank you," her words were a whisper against his chest that he felt as much as he heard.

"I'm not going anywhere," he said into her hair. "I'm here for you always, Minneapolis. I'm yours. And we can take as much time as you need, but you can trust me with you, with Malcolm. You can trust me to be civil with Rocco, even though I'm jealous as hell of him."

Minnie laughed. "What are you jealous of?" she asked.

"I want to live with you," Bryant said and kissed her neck. "I want to be the man you make children with. I want to throw birthday parties and play Santa. And right now, he's the man in your life doing that, so yeah, I'm jealous as hell."

Minnie pulled him on top of her, and whispered, "Don't be," before kissing him, and they made love again.

The next day, Minnie asked Rocco as casually as she could manage, "So, what do your Christmas Day plans with Erin look like?"

He was cooking eggs and bacon for their breakfast to eat with the day-old croissants Minnie had brought home from

Revival. She'd given Bryant the cinnamon rolls before he'd left the night before. Now, Rocco looked at her sideways from where she stood, arms crossed by the coffee pot, and Minnie felt more timid than she wanted to.

"You're invited, you know. It's just dinner and presents for the kids."

Minnie nodded. "So, you are planning on taking Malcolm?"

Rocco cocked his head to the side, then turned his back on the stove top. "I was planning on bringing both of you. I know we make an unconventional family, but that's what we are. Do you have other plans?"

Minnie shifted from one foot to another. "It's just—" Why was she so nervous? It wasn't any of Rocco's business, not really. She didn't need his approval to be in a relationship with the man she loved. The more she demurred, the more annoyed Rocco looked, so Minnie made herself say it, "Bryant has invited Malcolm and I to have dinner with him and his mother that night."

Rocco's jaw ticked, but he gave her his full attention as he asked. "Oh, we're talking about him now?"

"You knew we were back together?"

"I'm not stupid, Mins. You've been completely spacy lately. You always get that way when there's a guy, and all it takes is a Google search to find pictures of the two of you together."

"Oh," she said, wondering what he meant by spacy. She hadn't been neglecting anything at work or around the house. Maybe she had been reminiscing over what Bryant's hands felt like over body during the day sometimes, but she wouldn't call that spacy, just satisfied.

"I didn't know how to tell you."

"Yeah, well, I can understand that. I'm not exactly happy about it."

"I know, but—"

Rocco turned back to his eggs and moved his bacon to a cool burner. "But nothing. You'll do what you want, but all I see waiting there is disaster, Mins."

Minnie nodded even though he couldn't see her. She felt even less confident now that she'd told him that she and Bryant were back together. "You don't know him."

"He drinks, and he's not afraid to throw the first punch. I don't need to know anything else."

"He's not like that," Minnie said, though her stomach sank as Rocco turned to her with a skeptically raised eyebrow. She was worried about Bryant's drinking, and he did get into fights. But he was so kind and gentle with her, the idea of him turning on her was so preposterous. But Rocco's mom had always said the same thing about his dad, so Minnie understood where her friend was coming from.

"I'm assuming he doesn't know that he's Malcolm's sperm donor yet then?"

Minnie rolled her eyes at the term. "No, but I have to tell him at some point."

Rocco didn't acknowledge her statement, just reached for plates out of the cabinet and started doling out portions of eggs for their breakfast. "He's not going to try to take him away from us," Minnie said. "He's kinder than that. If you got to know him a little bit you would see that."

"He makes you reckless, you know that right? You don't make good decisions where he's concerned."

That was a statement Minnie did not appreciate. Minnie had been so careful with her time these last few weeks. "I'd like to go with Bryant on Christmas," Minnie said. "And as much as I want to bring Malcolm with me, I think that would be a bad idea."

"So you're already choosing him over your son?" Rocco said.

"That's not fair," Minnie said. "How many nights have you stayed at Erin's, leaving me alone with Malcolm?"

"*That's* not fair."

"Isn't it? I've barely been away from him for more than a few hours at a time his entire life. All I'm asking is a couple of hours on Christmas to create the foundation of a stable relationship. I need to prepare Bryant for the news slowly, and if he's around Malcolm for too long, he's going to see it. There's no way he won't. And as much as I want to tell him, I'd prefer not to do it on a major holiday."

Rocco looked contrite, even as he said, "It's not going to turn out well, Minnie. He's going to resent you for keeping this from him."

Minnie knew that. She knew there was a distinct possibility that she would lose Bryant over this, but she had to tell him if they were ever going to work. "I have to take that chance."

Rocco handed her a plate filled with eggs, bacon, orange slices, and a buttered croissant. "You do what you think you need to do, but don't expect me to have any part in it."

CHAPTER 22

The Christmas Eve party in Denver was torture. Rocco had basically stopped speaking to Minnie after their discussion about Bryant, Malcolm was grouchy and coming down with a cold. Minnie's father kept her glued to his side for the photo-ops. He said it was because she looked like Elsa in her icicle dress, but Minnie knew it was because she'd been making the gossip pages with Bryant, and he wanted his name in the press. Which would have been better if Malcolm hadn't velcroed himself to her. Her arms were sore and her dress's pockets were stuffed with soggy tissues.

All anyone wanted to talk to her about was how she was dating Van Birch's ex-boyfriend and how Rocco felt about that.

Minnie didn't want to talk about it, so she told them Rocco was also seeing someone new, but they both loved Malcolm and they were trying to make sure they were all happy and well taken care of.

But then people wanted to talk to her about Bryant and

Van and what were they like? And what it was like to be around people who were so famous? And Minnie would try to extricate herself from the conversation.

The truth was, Bryant's fame hadn't affected her much. Aside from the paparazzi stalking him, there wasn't much indication that he was famous. There hadn't even been any major articles about them. Everyone was having way too much fun with Van and Clay's romance to pay them more mind than some captioned photos. Minnie hoped Bryant would be able to quietly slide from the spotlight like she had when she'd moved to Kansas after school. She found obscurity far more comfortable than wearing too tight clothes and dancing with strangers while she pretended to be drunk in public.

This life, even wiping the nose of cranky, wiggling toddler was better than the stress of that time.

And everyone asking about Bryant only made her miss him. There had been so many special orders for the bakery and so many customers for the book shop that Minnie had barely seen Bryant since their well photographed lunch date last week when she'd told him that she'd be coming for Christmas but that she'd be coming alone.

He'd just been happy she was coming.

When Minnie finally escaped her father's clutches and made it back to their hotel room, it was to find Rocco, who had left the party early, already asleep with *A Christmas Story* playing on the TV. Minnie turned it off and tried to put Malcolm to bed, but he would only sleep as long as Minnie held him, so she slept sitting up in her bed, hoping she didn't drop her son on his head.

By the time Bryant picked her up the next afternoon, all Minnie wanted, despite her shower that morning, was a bath and a nap. She'd sent Malcolm off with Rocco, and now she was feeling like she was coming down with Malcolm's cold. She had an itch in her throat, and her nose wouldn't stop running.

"You okay?" Bryant asked as he opened the truck door for Minnie.

She nodded as she climbed inside his truck. "Malcolm had a bad night at the hotel."

He circled the car and hopped in the other side, then leaned across the cab and placed a kiss on her forehead. "I'm sorry," he said. "You can go rest if you prefer."

Minnie shook her head. "No, I miss you. I want to spend some time with you."

He kissed her on the mouth then, and she could feel how much he'd missed her, just through the press of his lips against hers.

When he pulled back and started the car, he asked, "How was your dad's party?"

"Boring. All anyone wanted to ask me about was you."

"Yeah?"

"Seems like a few paparazzi photos is all it takes to announce to the world that you've moved on, and with a former East-Coast-socialite-turned-single-mom, lucky you."

"Is that what they're calling you?" he asked.

"I saw it in a tweet this morning. I guess it was also the big announcement that Rocco and I aren't together anymore, which I didn't realize anybody would care about it, but this morning it was on the gossip site that used to tag me all the time back in college."

"I used to follow that site," Bryant said.

And Minnie knew her frown wasn't attractive, but she

was so confused. "When we first got together, the last time, I googled you a few times. You were such an enigma, I had to know more about you. I stalked all the socialite pages that had ever mentioned you, especially after you broke up with me. I might have been a little obsessed."

Minnie nodded. "Like how I watched every single episode of *Pop Star*, even the new ones that came out after we broke up."

"Like that," Bryant nodded. "It's how I found out you were pregnant. I was pretty angry about that at first, that you could move on so quickly."

Minnie rested her hand on his knee as he drove. "It wasn't planned, you know. The pregnancy. I was so upset over you, and Rocco has always been there for me, so when I found out I was pregnant, it just made sense, you know?"

He squeezed her fingers. "I get it, Minnie," he said. "I'm not angry anymore. I just want to be a part of your life moving forward."

Minnie hoped he still felt that way after he learned the truth about Malcolm, because that was all she wanted as well.

Bryant pulled up to his house, which Minnie had still seen just the once, the night she tucked him in when he'd come home drunk from a man date with Clay. She'd remembered it had been clean but cluttered. Mug and cups and spoons in the kitchen. Mail covering the dining room table. Books stacked everywhere. Clothes spread over his room like he'd never learned how to fold laundry.

It was neater now, there were still stacks of books next to the sofa, but the rest had been reshelved, and the mail had been cleared off the dining room table to make room for a miniature Christmas tree. A heavenly smell wafted from the kitchen, like roasted chicken and potatoes and something sweet. Bryant had parked at the curb and led her through the front door and straight back to the kitchen, which had been cleaned at least well enough for his mom to make a mess of it with her meal preparations.

She was a middling tall woman with wispy gray hair cut in a whimsical long pixie cut. Her bangs were dyed peacock blue, and she had Bryant's blue-gray eyes. She wore a black turtleneck over a pair of Christmas leggings. Candy canes earrings swung from her ears and she wore a green apron that said "Santa's Little Helper" as she pulled a tray of sugar cookies from the oven. And that's when Minnie spotted her rainbow glasses.

This woman was her son's grandmother. And she couldn't help but feel as if the universe had picked through her brain and pulled the exact image of the type of grandmother she'd wanted for herself as a child, and gifted her this one for her son.

"You're here!" she said, plopping the tray of cookies on the last square of clear counter space and throwing her arms around Minnie's shoulders. "Bryant has told me so much about you!" She pulled back, keeping her hands on Minnie's upper arms. "My, you are gorgeous. No wonder he can't get you out of his head."

Bryant let out a quiet groan at this, and Minnie could see him rubbing the back of his neck out of the corner of her eye. "Now, where's that little one of yours?" she asked, searching the ground around their feet with her eyes.

"Malcolm isn't feeling well, so he's staying with his dad," Minnie said.

Bryant's mother frowned and pouted her lips in a costume-like way, like she was trying to hide her frown, but then pulled back. "Anyway, I'm Georgie. It's nice to finally meet you, Minneapolis."

"It's a pleasure," Minnie said.

"So, what do you know about me?" Georgie asked, and Minnie was a little mortified. Bryant hadn't spoken much about his mother in the past, just that she'd been a single mom, that she'd raised him herself after kicking out his asshole of a father and escaping their life in Ohio. Now she was a travel writer and had sold Bryant her house for a dollar before she'd taken off so it could be his. She was so busy with her career that she came back to town only a few times a year.

"That about sums it up!" Georgie said after Minnie had repeated what she knew. "I did some research into you and your family. You'll have to forgive me, the reporter in me never sleeps. Your father is a very impressive man," she said, wiggling her eyebrows. "And not too hard on the eyes either."

Minnie had to struggle not to cringe. She'd never looked at her father as anything other than the man that would do nothing to keep his mistress alive after she'd been too sick to work and too broke to afford medical treatment.

"Too bad he isn't very nice at all."

Georgie sighed with worldly disappointment. "Isn't that the way it is with successful men? Too arrogant for their own good? Oh well," she said and pulled a bottle from the fridge. "I made some eggnog. Who wants some?"

And Minnie raised her hand like she was in school—so fast, she would have thought she was having a bad time, but she decided it was more about embracing this endearingly eccentric woman in front of her.

Georgie poured them each a glass of the delicious, but deadly strong, eggnog then set about finishing dinner.

The meal was pleasant; the three of them talked about their work, and Bryant explained what was in store for Van and Clay and their wedding and their new reality show, which he would guest star on occasionally but not be a key cast member in.

Minnie told a few stories about her store and Malcolm, and it was pleasant until Georgie asked to move to the living room and see pictures of Malcolm.

Minnie didn't know why her hackles raised. It was an innocent enough question. This woman was Bryant's mother. Of course she was curious about the person who could become her step-grandchild. But Minnie suspected Georgie might be up to more than that.

To her relief, Georgie only cooed and crooned over the photos of Malcolm and asked if Minnie would send her the one of Minnie holding Malcolm at the Christmas party the night before. It had actually come out decently, despite Malcolm's foul mood. "I want to be able to show off the woman my son is dating while I'm traveling," she said.

When they left a while later, Bryant kissed the top of her head and said, "She likes you," as if there had ever been a question of her not, which gave Minnie pause, but she was so tired, and her throat had started to hurt in earnest. All she wanted was to go to bed.

CHAPTER 23

*B*ryant was so happy, he was whistling on his way home. He'd been taking things slowly with Minnie since they'd reunited. One day at a time, spending time with her after Malcolm was asleep, not pushing her too hard on a commitment. But she and his mother had gotten along. After missing her for so long, there was actually a possibility for a future with them. Bryant whistled all the way through the backyard and into the kitchen. He whistled straight up until he came across his mother, surrounded on the sofa by all their old photo albums, with her rainbow glasses perched on the tip of her nose and a frown on her lips.

He stilled when he saw her, and she looked at him over the rim of her glasses like she'd always done when he was a kid and he'd been in trouble.

"What did I do?" he asked, confused. He hadn't given her a gift; she'd said she didn't want one, and she hadn't given him one either. They hadn't for years. He *had* bought Minnie a necklace, just a simple gold chain with three pearls that rested at the dip in her collar bone, but he'd given that to her in the car before he'd dropped her off.

"That child is your son," his mother said.

All of the blood drained out of Bryant's head, and he swayed, reaching for the door frame to steady himself. "What child?" he asked, but he knew. He'd wondered once or twice if it was possible but brushed it off immediately. Minnie would have told him if that was the case. He didn't think she was capable of a lie of that magnitude.

"Minnie's child, of course," his mother said, waving her phone in the air. "Come see."

Bryant had been about to argue, but he didn't have the words. His mouth had gone dry, telling himself that Minnie would have come to him.

"Look," his mother said as he collapsed beside her on the sofa. She held up the photo Minnie had sent her next to one of Bryant from when he was one or two. She flipped to another photo, this one from a news article from the gossip site that Bryant used to follow, the one that used to follow Minnie. It was a picture of Malcolm as in infant. Bryant's mom held that photo up next to one of Bryant when he was barely able to hold his head up. She then held the phone up to his face, flipping back and forth between the pictures, comparing them to his features directly.

"That is your baby. I bet my life on it," she said.

Bryant couldn't concentrate on any of the photos long enough to confirm or deny what she was saying. "Maybe she doesn't know," he said. "Maybe she thinks he's Rocco's."

But as Bryant eyed the phone in his mom's hand, now on a new photo, a news article about Minnie's dad's annual Christmas party with a picture of Rocco posing next to Minnie, who was holding Malcom. Bryant had to admit that the baby looked nothing like Rocco. The shape of Malcolm's face and bone structure was nearly identical to what Bryant's had been as a baby. Everything about the child was long and lean. He did not have Rocco's stocky, square jaw and wide shoulders, but he did have the same look Bryant had had as a child: like he'd always been stretched too thin and his bones were too long for his skin.

"Oh my god," Bryant said after studying the photos. "Why wouldn't she tell me?" he asked his mother.

"I can think of any number of reasons," his mother said. "But you'll need to ask her to know for sure."

He'd bailed then, and his mother hadn't even said anything. She had likely expected it. Bryant wasn't able to sit still on a good day. He'd thought today had been a good day, but somehow, it had all unraveled, and his brain wasn't sure what to do with it. Like someone had handed him a tangled pile of yarn and told him to turn it into a sweater. He knew it could be done, but he didn't even know where to start.

Bryant hopped in his truck and drove for two hours. Every now and then he paused to text Minnie. They weren't eloquent texts, or even nice ones. They sounded as desperate as he felt. They were the only words he could form. He couldn't wrap his mind around the concept enough to type out *Is Malcolm my son?* Instead he sent frantic, alarming texts that, had he received them, would have thrown him straight into a panic.

We need to talk. Now.

No response.

Call me.

No response.

This isn't a conversation that can wait.

No response.

Without consciously deciding to go there, Bryant found himself pulling up outside Minnie and Rocco's house. His head was swimming as he climbed the front stoop, even though he hadn't had a drink since his single glass of eggnog before dinner. But God, did he want one now. He also wanted to do his best impression of Marlon Brando from *A Streetcar Named Desire* and pound on her door, hollering her name until she answered, but he could barely force his shaking hand to ring the doorbell instead.

He waited.

Bryant rang the doorbell a second time.

He texted her again.

He called.

Annoyed, Bryant had stepped up to the door to pound on it when it swung open, and a disheveled looking Rocco appeared, backlit in the doorway. He wore a pair of gray sweatpants and a white T-shirt, and Bryant had the fleeting thought that he wouldn't have blamed Minnie for sleeping with him if he always dressed like that when he was at home but was immediately snapped out of it when Rocco asked, "What the fuck are you doing here, Wilder? Do you have any idea what time it is?"

"I need to speak to Minnie."

"She's asleep."

"It's important," Bryant said, but Rocco stood up taller, the two men were only inches apart. Rocco lifted his chin as if in challenge, and anger and jealousy swelled in Bryant. In how many ways was this man living the life Bryant wanted? He lived with the woman Bryant loved, called her the mother of his child. He claimed the son that was Bryant's, and he looked like he wasn't sorry about it one bit.

"Whatever it is can wait until Minnie is feeling better," Rocco said.

"She's sick?" he remembered her voice sounding a little husky, but she hadn't complained.

"She caught Malcolm's cold," Rocco said, and the reality of the situation set in. Malcolm was a real, live person, one that he and Minnie had made together. And Bryant was missing out on everything. Not just today, Christmas, with his child, but his birthday, Thanksgiving, his first step, his birth, Minnie's pregnancy. Bryant was missing everything. Was he talking yet? Bryant wanted to asked what Malcolm's first word had been, but instead, he focused on the reason that had brought him to Minnie's doorstep.

"Is he mine?" Bryant asked.

Rocco took a step back as if Bryant's words had physical force behind them. "What did you just say?" The words were sharp, as if Rocco didn't really want Bryant to ask again.

"Malcolm. Is he my son?"

Rocco continued to block the door in silence, his jaw clenched, and Bryant waited. He wanted to explain about the picture, but he didn't want to appear any more pathetic than he already did, showing up here in the middle of the night on Christmas, begging.

"He's my son," Rocco said, and Bryant's stomach dropped. Had his mother been wrong? "I'm the one who was there for Minnie while she was throwing up and you were partying in L.A. I was the one who took Minnie to birthing classes, who let her use my arm as leverage when she was in labor. I was the one who went without sleep to bounce him on the damn exercise ball. I changed the diapers and made the food," Rocco paused as if he was debating stopping there, but he raised his chin so his hard, dark eyes bore into Bryant's. "You might have been the sperm donor, but Malcolm is my son. And he will always be my son, and I will always fight for what's mine."

Then he slammed the door in Bryant's face. After it stopped shaking in its frame, Bryant heard the lock slide home. Seconds later the porch light flipped off, then the living room light inside, and Bryant was left standing in the cold. Alone. And not sure what to do next.

He didn't remember the drive home. He didn't remember if his mother had waited up for him or even how he'd made it to his bedroom, but before he crawled beneath the covers, he typed out one last message to Minnie.

Were you ever going to tell me?

CHAPTER 24

*M*innie woke with a burning throat, watering eyes, and a head so congested, she could barely hear or breathe. She was only up long enough to grab a glass of orange juice and drink some chicken broth before going back to bed. She'd been vaguely aware of Rocco and Malcolm playing in the living room and had decided that was enough information. She didn't even think about calling Revival before she crawled back into bed.

It was almost dark again the next time she woke. She showered and fixed herself a proper meal, but the house was quiet. Rocco had left a note on the fridge that he and Malcolm had gone to Erin's house for dinner and that they'd be back for bedtime. He'd also left out a new box of green tea and the honey bear for Minnie. She brewed herself a cup while she waited for the Christmas leftovers Erin had sent home with Rocco to warm.

Minnie still felt groggy and tired, and her head was still stopped up, but she was cognizant enough to check in with the shop and make sure they were still on schedule for all of their orders and that they were keeping up with the bakery.

Satisfied with that, Minnie sat down to eat and checked her other messages. There were several from Bryant, and she supposed she should have checked in with him, let him know that she wasn't feeling well, but as she opened her message app, she felt her stomach roll over the bit of stuffing she'd just swallowed.

We need to talk. Now.

Call me.

This isn't a conversation that can wait.

Were you ever going to tell me?

Rocco said he was mine, Minnie. I know.

You should have told me.

You should have told me.

I can't believe this is the secret you chose to keep out of everything.

They stopped after that, and Minnie ignored the rest of her messages, the ones from Van and Phoenix, the couple of texts she'd had from Rocco that were no doubt pictures of Malcolm doing something cute at Erin's house. She dialed Bryant's number, but he didn't answer.

She checked the time. It was after six, so he definitely wasn't working. If he'd gone in to work today. Maybe he was doing some filming for Van's show?

She wasn't sure.

She texted him back. *I wanted to tell you. I didn't know how to tell you. But I was looking for the right time. I'm sorry.*

He didn't respond immediately, and Minnie was in too much of a panic to sit still and wait. She grabbed her shoes and a box of tissues, threw on her coat on her way out the door, and sped across town to Bryant's house.

His mother answered the door, looking grim, but let Minnie in. "He's upstairs," was all she said, and Minnie trudged as fast as her heavy, panting lungs would let her. She had to stop a moment at the top to cough and sneeze. She stuffed her used tissue into her coat pocket and hoped her face was clean before she knocked on Bryant's door.

It wasn't fully closed, so when there was no response, she pushed it open slowly.

The room was lit by the light of a single bedside lamp, and Bryant lay on his back on his bed, one arm over his head, asleep in the same way Malcolm always slept. Minnie, not having the heart to wake him and with her head swimming from all the activity, laid down beside him, curled into his side, still wearing her coat and boots, and fell asleep.

A sharp shake to her shoulder woke her. When she opened her eyes, the entire world spun. She had no clue where she was, only that it was dark outside. The yellow light from the lamp highlighted blue walls.

"Minneapolis," Bryant said. His voice wasn't soft, and it wasn't gentle. It wasn't hard either. If she had to describe it as anything, she would call it indifferent. Like he was resigned to her presence, but he hadn't welcomed it.

Minnie sat up, rubbing her eyes, as she tried and failed to breathe through her nose.

"What are you doing here?" he asked, and that's when Minnie noticed that the room smelled like whiskey. She couldn't smell it exactly, but she could detect its presence like she was floating in a soup made from it. Bryant didn't sound intoxicated, but she would bet everything that the reason he'd been asleep at six was because he'd spent the day emptying his flasks.

"I got your texts when I woke up, and I knew I needed to

talk to you as soon as possible," she said. "How did you find out?"

"About the son you were keeping from me?" he asked in a hard voice.

Minnie nodded, not trusting herself to make a sound.

Bryant rubbed his eyes, and Minnie wondered now if he was still drunk or starting to feel his hangover. "My mother noticed the resemblance. Malcolm looks almost exactly like I did when I was his age."

Minnie nodded; it had been what she'd feared when she sent the photo to Georgie. "So you came to the house and talked to Rocco?" she asked, cringing. That couldn't have gone well.

Bryant narrowed his eyes at her. "Well, I wanted to speak to you, but you were asleep, and he wouldn't let me in."

"I've been sick," Minnie said, and her body punctuated the statement by giving her a giant sneeze that needed two tissues to clean up.

"I see that," he said. Bryant didn't sound any more sympathetic. His voice was still flat and uninterested, and his expression was starting to mirror that. Exasperation was turning to indifference faster than she could explain herself, and Minnie was starting to panic.

"I wanted to tell you," Minnie said again, her voice shaky. "I wanted you to know that you were Malcolm's biological father, but I knew you'd be angry that I kept it from you initially, and I was just so relieved and happy to have you back, I couldn't face losing you yet."

Bryant nodded. "I suppose I understand that," he said.

Minnie felt a momentary flood of relief that he was listening to her, but next he stood, pulling up to his full height and crossed his arms as if he was barring himself from her. Protecting himself.

"What I don't understand is why you didn't tell me when you found out you were pregnant. Why didn't you tell me when he was born? Why did you pretend Rocco was Malcolm's father at all? Why did you let Rocco *become* his father?"

Bryant's voice cracked as if he was truly anguished by the fact that he hadn't been allowed to know his son. "Why would you ever think that I wouldn't want to be a part of my son's life?"

Minnie stood as well, the bed separating them like a king-sized chasm that reached to the center of the earth.

"You were with Van," Minnie said simply.

"I wasn't," Bryant said.

"But I thought you were. The whole world thought you were."

"I told you I wasn't—" he tried to interrupt.

"And I knew that if you left Van for me and it came out that I was pregnant, I would forever be marked as the whore who broke up America's golden couple, and the tabloids would always mark Malcolm as the thing that came between you and Van, and I didn't want that for him. I had just come from New York where I'd been harassed and bullied, and I couldn't knowingly put my own child through that. I did what I had to do to protect him from that life."

Bryant steamed. Minnie could almost see the anger coming off him in waves.

"You had so little regard for me that you thought I would have let that happen?" he said. "Phoenix never would have let that happen. She would have taken care of it. There might have been rumors, but no one else would have had anything to do with it. You and Malcolm would have been safe, and we could have been a family, Minnie. The three of us."

Tears brimmed over Minnie's cheeks. "You don't know that," she said. "You couldn't make me any guarantees. I've been in the spotlight; I've been part of a scandal. Maybe not on the level you and Van are, but it made my life miserable for months. I moved here to get away from that and having a baby with Van Birch's boyfriend would have brought it all back times a thousand."

"So to protect yourself, you let me think you'd slept with Rocco?" His voice was verging on a yell. "For almost two years, you let me believe that you'd left me for the man you'd introduced to me as your cousin?"

"To protect the baby!" Minnie hollered right back at him.

"I should have been given the chance to do that. I should have been given a say in the best way to protect my child."

"I found out I was pregnant on the same day I found out you'd been lying to me about Van, about why Clay was mad at you. Put that together with your drinking, I panicked."

"What about my drinking?" Bryant asked, his voice turned sharp and defensive, his fists clenched at his sides.

"You think that I didn't notice that you were always drinking?" Minnie asked. "And you haven't stopped. You're drunk right now."

He gave her a hardened look, his jaw clenched so tight she could practically hear his teeth grinding together. "I am not drunk."

"I can fucking taste the whiskey in the air, Bryant. You've practically marinated yourself in it."

"Fine, I'm a lying drunk," he said. "Any other reasons you've been keeping my son from me?"

Minnie shook her head, willing him to understand, but knowing they were too far past that now. "I didn't think you'd ever find out. When I found out I was pregnant, I thought it was over between us for good. I thought you were with Van and that there was nothing I could do about it if I didn't want to set off a scandal. So I decided to make do, and Rocco offered to help. There was no sinister plan, Bryant. I was afraid, and I'm sorry."

Bryant had crossed his arms as she'd spoken, as if they protected his heart from her words. He let silence linger as he stared at her for a solid minute before saying, "You should go."

Minnie's heart stuttered. "What?"

"You didn't want me to be a part of your life, so I won't be a part of your life. Yours or Malcolm's. Live your little fairy tale without me."

Minnie's heart crumbled like a dry scone. "You don't mean that," she said.

"I do."

"But—" Minnie bit off her own words as tears fell down her cheeks.

"But what?" She'd never experienced this part of Bryant before. The part of him that had attacked Bishop, the part of him that had punched Rocco in the face, this angry raging part of the man whom she had only known as thoughtful and gentle and intelligent. She knew those were the real parts of him, that his angry impulsiveness was defense more than anything, and her heart ached for him. Because she loved him.

Minnie loved Bryant without every ounce of her soul, and because of that, she'd known that this was what would happen when he found out about Malcolm. It's why she'd so selfishly put off revealing the truth again and again and again.

"But I love you," she said.

Bryant turned and fell backward, collapsing onto his bed, his head turned away from her, his arms over his head in the same position she had found him.

"Just go," he said. "The sooner I can start forgetting you exist, the better."

"Bryant, please," Minnie had stepped forward to sit beside him on the bed, but quicker than she could move, Bryant had reached below his pillow and pulled out a flask. He chucked it at Minnie's head and shouted, "LEAVE!"

Minnie ducked, and the flask bounced off the wall, leaving a nick in the sheetrock, but Minnie didn't want to stay anymore. Her patience with him was gone. If he was going to be a moody, violent jerk, maybe it was best if they did forget each other. Maybe she would be better off if she could forget what they'd been together. If she could figure out a way to go back to pretending.

Only Minnie couldn't pretend. Not during the days that followed. She was a hollowed out shell. Malcolm would stumble up to her in his new halting gait and offer her his favorite toys, as if that would make her feel better. The girls at Revival left her to stew in her own crankiness in the kitchen and avoided the office. And despite numerous bottles of wine and late night chats with Phoenix and sometimes Van, Minnie still couldn't make herself feel any better about the situation.

She still loved Bryant. She had still lied to him and kept him from knowing about his son. And once he'd had the truth, he'd still rejected them both.

Rocco had taken to spending most of his days at Erin's

house. He wasn't happy with her either, though he didn't say as much. He didn't say anything more to her than he needed for Malcolm's well-being. So not only had she lost Bryant, she'd lost her oldest friend and co-parent too.

Minnie hadn't felt so disconsolate since her mother had died, but at least then she'd had the promise of going off to school, of starting over, of doing something to make her mother proud. Now, Minnie felt as if she was left with nothing.

CHAPTER 25

*B*ryant had called in to work every day for a week. They had enough help these days the crew probably didn't even miss him. He hadn't done much aside from mope. He'd finished his book the first day, but he'd been so distracted by his anger and his grief that Bryant hadn't been able to pick out a new book. He was fairly certain he'd spent an entire afternoon wandering from one bookshelf to another, staring at all his titles with a bottle of whiskey in his hand.

There was a distinct possibility that he hadn't been sober since, but he was alone in the house, so there was no one to care. His mother had left on her New Year's assignment. Van and Clay had each other to keep them company. Minnie was gone. He'd never know Malcolm, so there was no one around to stay accountable to. No one to stay sober for.

It was better like this, in bed, not causing trouble, staying out of everyone's way.

Not even the prospect of Clay and Van's wedding in a

few months was motivation to get out of bed. He was happy for his friends, but Minnie would be there, maybe even with Malcolm and Rocco, and Bryant just couldn't do it. He couldn't see her and not be reminded of how angry he was with her.

Or all the ways he'd failed her.

Phone calls and texts from his friends had been consistent and concerned the first few days. He was certain Minnie had told them what had happened. Minnie had even called and texted, so much so that he'd blocked her number. But the others' interest had tapered off when he'd left their messages unanswered. That was fine. They were busy. They had important things going on.

Bryant didn't have anything.

He didn't even know who he was anymore. He'd spent so long being Van Birch's boyfriend that he wasn't sure he had a life outside that role anymore. Sure, he had his business, but not even the prospect of framing out a new house excited him. And that had always been his favorite part of what he did. Watching plans and drawings and math take physical form. To go from nothing but a pile of wood to a structure in just a few days.

But now, building a house sounded just as tedious as everything else in his life.

He kept remembering what it had been like to come back to Wellville and hear Minnie tell him it was over, to have Rocco bully him off. She had been pregnant then. She could have told him the truth, but because he'd lied to her about Van, she hadn't trusted him enough to even tell him about his child.

Minnie didn't trust Bryant with his own child.

He couldn't get that one thought out of his head. Minnie didn't trust him with his own child.

He scanned his room, looking at the piles of laundry, not sure which ones were clean or dirty, and thinking that he couldn't blame her. He didn't even trust himself to take care of a cat. Bryant fell asleep as he decided that Malcolm was better off with Minnie and Rocco.

He woke to Van bouncing on his bed next to him singing, "Wake up sleepy head, wake up," over and over with no real tune. Bryant felt his stomach lurch and was out of bed and across the hall before he consciously thought about his need to vomit.

All that came back up was whiskey. Bryant couldn't remember the last time he'd eaten. He'd definitely had three glasses of water that morning. Or was that yesterday? He couldn't remember; he couldn't think by the time he stumbled from the bathroom and back into his bedroom, his head pounded so hard.

He collapsed onto his bed and buried his head under his pillow.

Van was still sitting next to him on the bed, the side that had been hers when they'd had their sleepovers. "How you feeling?" she asked, sounding far too chipper.

"Go away," he said from beneath his pillow.

She giggled and bounced. He heard footsteps on the stairs and knew Clay was there too. The two of them never were far apart these days. He heard the clunk of wood on wood and peeked out from under his pillow to see Clay setting down one of Bryant's dining room chairs. He had a bag slung over his shoulder.

"Did you check in here?" he asked.

A sloshing sound came from Bryant's left and he realized

she held the flask that should have been under his pillow with him. "I'd check his dresser too, and maybe the shelf in his closet."

His ancient dresser drawers squeaked as Clay pulled them open. "It's a miracle you have enough clothes to fill the dresser," Clay said. Bryant sat up to see his best friend pawing through his belongings.

"That's where I keep the L.A. clothes," Bryant said. Lord, his head hurt. He wouldn't be able to see, even if he put his glasses on. The pounding in his temples made him feel as though the world would be permanently blurred.

"Aha!" Clay said, and Bryant heard more sloshing. "Why do you have a whole bottle of booze hidden between sweaters?"

"It's to refill the flask," Bryant said, his head in his hands.

"Which flask?" Clay asked. "The one you keep in your bed, or the one you keep in your sock drawer?"

"I don't have a flask in my sock drawer." Bryant looked up to see Clay scowling at him.

"Good to know." Clay circled around to Van's side of the bed and dumped the canvas bag upside down. All Bryant's stash tumbled onto his bed. "Because the one in the spice cabinet, in the end table in the living room, and in your fucking glove compartment were disturbing enough."

"Don't forget above the washing machine!" Van chimed in, bouncing again on the bed.

The sound and the motion had him wanting to vomit again. "Please stop."

She stopped bouncing, but she leaned close and sniffed. "When was the last time you had a shower?" she asked. "You smell like a distillery opened up in one of Clay's work boots."

Bryant could feel Clay's displeased frown.

"What?" Van asked. "I still love you and your stinky feet."

"What are you two doing here?" Bryant asked, not even trying to keep his annoyance out of his voice. "Shouldn't you be planning your world tour wedding or something?"

Van wrapped her arms around Bryant's hunched shoulders from behind and kissed his cheek. "Because we love you, and you have a really big problem."

Minnie came to Bryant's mind. How long had he gone without thinking about her? Five minutes? Could he count the time he'd been asleep? "I assume you've been talking to Minnie?"

"Some," Van said. "But she's not why we're here."

Bryant quirked his head to the side so he could see Van, but his tired eyes wouldn't focus that close. "Then why?"

Clay pulled the dining room chair up next to the bed and sat down. His posture mirrored Bryant's, bent at the waist with his elbows resting on his knees.

"Because we love you," Clay said. One of his hands came to rest on Bryant's shoulder, and Bryant met his eyes. Clay was not a jokester. He was serious more often than not, but Bryant hadn't seen this look in his friend's eyes before. There was sorrow and pain, but there was also love and sadness and such a deep streak of sincerity, Bryant wanted to look away, but he couldn't.

Van kissed his cheek again, then said, "And we want to have you around for a long time."

"Okay," Bryant said. His head still pounded, and his mind was sluggish. "Thanks. You two are my best friends."

Clay's hand tightened on Bryant's shoulder. "Good," he said, "Then maybe you'll listen to us when we tell you that you need help."

Bryant's head swam at the same time his stomach clenched. "I'm fine," he choked out through the panic.

"No, you're not." Van said, still clinging to his back like a spider monkey.

"I'm dealing with a lot," Bryant said. "With the media and Minnie. And finding out I have a son."

"We know," Clay said. "It's a lot."

"And we think you need professional help," Van said.

Bryant rubbed his eyes. "I'm fine. Or I will be once I get rid of this headache."

Clay's grip on Bryant's shoulder turned painful. "Booze hidden all over your house is not fine, Bryant."

"Do you even know what day it is?" Van asked.

"Saturday," he said.

The two of them went silent, exchanging concerned glances. "It's Tuesday," Clay said.

Bryant shook his head. "It's only been a week," he said.

"It's been ten day since you've left this house," Clay said.

"And the only reason we didn't intervene sooner was because the intake at the very discreet rehab resort we booked for you was closed for the holidays."

Bryant jerked his head up. "Rehab? No."

"Yes," Clay said.

"This is your intervention, babe. We need you. And we need you to get better."

"Robin's downstairs with your mom," Clay said. "Phoenix is picking us all up something to eat, and then we're hopping on a plane to Florida."

Bryant was having too much trouble comprehending what they were saying. "Florida?"

"Yes," Van said, "We're going to Florida. Beaches, warm weather, oranges in season, and you're going to go to rehab while the rest of us enjoy a nice, well-deserved vacation."

"I'd rather take the vacation," Bryant said.

"Don't worry, once you're done, we'll take you Disney World," Van said.

"Hurray."

The back door slammed, and Phoenix hollered from downstairs. "Come get your greasy junk food before I eat it all!"

Which made Bryant snort, because Phoenix didn't eat greasy junk food, ever. She'd probably picked herself up a salad.

"Come on," Clay said, standing and releasing his hold on Bryant's shoulder. "Let's get you showered, and then you can eat. Maybe you'll start to feel better."

Van gave him one last peck on the cheek, then disentangled herself from around his body and started scooping the flasks back into the canvas shopping bag.

As Clay pulled Bryant to his feet and pushed him down the hall toward the bathroom, Bryant could hear Van rifling through his things, looking for more hidden alcohol. He didn't have any, unless they hadn't seen his toolbox yet.

"I don't need rehab," Bryant said to Clay as he stripped his shirt off in the bathroom. The material felt grungy in his hands, and he tried to remember the last time he'd changed his clothes. Yesterday? The day before? The day before that? He shook his head, it didn't matter anymore. "I need to talk to Minnie."

"You do," Clay said. "You and she need to have a long, honest discussion about everything that's happened the last couple of years, but she doesn't want to speak to you right now."

Bryant was frozen with shame. "I wasn't very nice to her the last time she was here."

Clay moved past Bryant and turned on the shower. "No, you weren't. Right now, she doesn't think you're very good for her, and she doesn't think you'd be a good father to Malcolm either. And frankly, I agree with her."

"Great," Bryant said, his voice cracking. It was like Clay was trying to break him even more that he already was.

"Hey." Clay's hand clasped Bryant's bicep, hard, and Bryant met his friend's eyes. "That doesn't mean you couldn't be. Things can change, okay? We can fix this, but you need to start taking care of yourself. Understand?"

Bryant hung his head; he couldn't even look at Clay, because his friend was right. Bryant was no good to anyone. But the small, tiny piece of hope that hadn't died inside him still thought that maybe he could be.

"I'm so lost," Bryant whispered.

"I know," Clay said and pulled Bryant into a hug. Bryant could tell the difference between his stale whiskey and B.O. stench and Clay's woodsy soap scent. "But we're here for you, okay? You're not alone. We're all here for you. We're coming with you. Van was adamant she come along so you can tear her inside out in therapy."

"I wouldn't do that," Bryant said.

"You should. I mean, she feels guilty as hell, but she's also coming to realize how unfair of her it was to ask you to do what you did for her. So just know, it's not all on you."

"I don't blame Van," Bryant said, unable to make himself let go of Clay.

"I know," Clay said. With a squeeze, he clapped Bryant on the back, and pushed him away. "Now please get into the shower. Your stench is going to suffocate me."

Bryant almost smiled, and Clay's expression mirrored his as he backed out of the bathroom.

Everyone was crowded around his rarely used dining room table when Bryant came downstairs twenty minutes later. He'd shaved and put on the clean clothes Van had left out on his bed for him. They were all digging into a combination of Skittle's Pizza and Rusty's Burgers. Count on Phoenix to always choose the ultra-local, if questionable, food. Van tossed him a paper-wrapped burger while his mom pulled him down into the chair beside her. She smiled, kissed his cheek, and went back to her pile of french fries.

Bryant swiped one, then kissed her back.

All of these people were here because they loved him. He could see that. He still wasn't wild about the idea of rehab, but Bryant couldn't keep his eyes off the empty chair at the other end of the table near Phoenix, where Minnie should have been sitting. If rehab was the path to getting her back here, then he'd go.

And maybe, giving up alcohol wouldn't be all that bad.

Perhaps it was time for a change.

CHAPTER 26

*M*innie set the last box on the pile in the living room of her old apartment and sighed. She'd been surprised how much she'd accumulated in the two years since she'd moved into Rocco's house, but there it was, a pile of things she wasn't sure she had room for in this tiny apartment. She'd have to deal with it.

Rocco came in behind her, carrying Malcolm and his diaper bag, and shut the door. The sound of the evening rush hour could be heard below. Minnie had forgotten how much louder the street sounds were downtown than out in the new development Rocco lived in. Out there the neighborhood traffic was sparse, with only occasional dogs barking at passing pedestrians.

"You don't have to do this," Rocco said. It had been his refrain since Christmas, when Minnie had told him she needed to move out.

She answered the same way she had for the past month. "Yes, I do."

It wasn't going to be easy, she knew, but moving back

here, living on her own, it was the right thing to do. Erin and Rocco were getting more serious, and they needed room for their relationship to grow. And Minnie needed space to heal. To move on with her life. To remember who she'd been before she'd met Bryant Wilder and figure out who she wanted to be now that he wasn't in her life anymore. She couldn't do that with Rocco constantly judging Bryant for her.

Minnie knew he meant well. Rocco was only angry for her sake, but he was so protective of her and Malcolm that he could be a little self-righteous at times. He didn't see how his disapproval only made Minnie feel worse.

Rocco set Malcolm down on the floor and dropped the diaper bag on the armchair that had been pushed there to make room for all the boxes. He sighed, looking down at his son. Malcolm had become familiar with the space over the last few days. Minnie had been there cleaning and painting after her last tenants had moved out. She'd set up a bed for Malcolm and moved the rocking chair she'd always nursed him in into the spare bedroom.

"I'll help finish setting up Malcolm's room then," Rocco said.

They'd mostly worked out a schedule for Malcolm between the two of them. Rocco would have him during the day three days a week and overnight on his nights off from the plant. Malcolm would go to daycare two days a week while they were both at work, and Minnie would have him the rest of the time. It was a pretty even split—and it wasn't like they wouldn't spend at least some of that time together. Minnie was thankful that there would be some breathing room.

She'd felt like she'd been suffocating all month. Ever

since Bryant had kicked her out of his house, had rejected her, and had said he didn't want to know Malcolm. Had chosen his pride over his son. Over the both of them.

Minnie hadn't seen that coming. She'd expected him to be angry with her. To some extent, Minnie felt she deserved his anger, even his resentment, but she hadn't expected him to not want to get to know Malcolm.

She'd handled it all wrong, of course.

That hadn't been the time to bring up his alcoholism.

But there hadn't been a good time. She'd been trying to find a time to ask him to stop. To find some help, but there had never been a good time. It would have always spoiled the mood, started a fight, and ended their time together. There hadn't been room for Minnie and sobriety in his life, and now there wasn't any room for either.

And with him, she had lost all of her new friends too.

They'd said they'd keep in touch, but by the time a week had gone by, their texts and phone calls had stopped almost completely. The paparazzi photos showed them all hanging out on the beach in Florida instead of dealing with the ten inches of snow a storm from Denver had dropped on Wellville last week.

Lucky them.

Minnie tried not to be bitter, but she missed them. Especially Phoenix.

Phoenix had been Team Minnie from the start, before anyone had even known about her and Bryant.

Minnie needed someone on her side right now. She just had herself and Malcolm. That was all she could count on.

Even her dad, who'd been hounding her to bring Bryant to meet him since Thanksgiving when those first pictures of them came out had stopped calling. Minnie couldn't tell if he'd given up on her, or if he'd distracted himself with something else for the time being. He didn't even know she was moving back into the apartment. She'd have to remember to leave a voicemail for his assistant. Maybe he'd call after that. She was so lonely, she'd even welcome a phone argument with her father over simply listening to the traffic outside her window.

Minnie had been tempted to stream the latest season of *Pop Star* just so she could see Bryant again, but she wouldn't. Not yet.

Instead, she coaxed Malcolm to his feet and led him to the spare bedroom by his hand. "Come on, let's help Daddy set up your new room."

Rocco stayed most of the evening. They ate macaroni and cheese, which was Malcolm's favorite meal, though Rocco steamed some vegetables to go along with it. Malcolm didn't touch them, and Minnie couldn't blame him. She'd barely forced them down herself. Then they'd put Malcolm down to bed together before Rocco had given Minnie a long hug.

"I'm gonna miss having you around," he said and kissed the top of her head.

"I'm going to miss you making me breakfast in the morning."

"I bet you will," he said. "It'll be back to cereal and yesterday's coffee for you."

She swatted his back, but she knew it was true. She never gave herself enough time in the morning to eat properly before she had to show up at Revival. She had to get up so damn early to get the baking done for open.

"Thank you for everything," she said, strangely unwilling

to let him go now that it was time, even though she'd been yearning to be away from him for weeks.

"I'll be by in the morning to pick Malcolm up, yeah?"

She nodded against his chest, ready to cry, but refusing to do so. "Yes. In the morning."

Rocco kissed her forehead one more time, then left.

Minnie spun in a slow circle, sighed, then fished the box cutter off the top of the refrigerator where Rocco had hidden it from Malcolm and started unpacking.

Rehab had not been what Bryant had expected. He wasn't sure why scenes from *One Flew Over The Cuckoo's Nest* had been playing in his mind on the way down to Florida, but that's where he had been. Instead, he had a decent private room. Structured activities each day kept him busy, as well as private and group therapy sessions. The first week had been hell, the withdrawal, even with the drugs, had made him feel like shit. The second week the physical symptom had withdrawn, but he'd lived in a fog. It had helped when he'd been cleared for light exercise. He'd taken walks on the beach, hit the treadmill in the onsite gym, and taken day passes to go to yoga with Van and Phoenix, which had been humiliating but also, oddly soothing.

Bryant wasn't sure how he felt.

Physically he felt better. He'd realized how skinny he'd become over the last few months. He hadn't been paying much attention. He could still see his muscles below his skin, that had been enough, but he hadn't realized it was because he'd lost all his padding, along with a good bit of his muscle mass. He'd wanted to start gaining weight, start

MARLA HOLT

lifting weights. His doctor wanted to wait another week but had upped Bryant's meal portions.

Bryant went to bed most nights with a headache, not from withdrawal but from spending so much time in his own brain. Something he'd spent most of his adult life trying to avoid. Possibly the headaches were also from so much crying.

His throat had been raw for days. He'd cried in therapy, he'd cried with Van, he'd cried in his room at night looking at pictures of Minnie and Malcolm on his phone.

He wanted to tell her what he was doing. He wanted her to be proud of him. He wanted to call her so badly, but he didn't. He'd told his therapist all about Minnie. He'd mentioned wanting to call her. She'd ask him if he wanted to call her for her sake or for his. Bryant realized he'd wanted her praise, but that there was nothing he could offer her. He wasn't even ready to apologize to her. Not yet.

He missed her, but he was still so angry about her keeping Malcolm from him.

That and his fake relationship with Van had been the main topics of his private therapy. Group therapy had been more about understanding what made him turn to alcohol, and it had been helpful, but Bryant hadn't realized how angry he'd been. Or for how long. And it helped to talk about it.

He'd even asked about going back on his ADHD meds, without prompting. His doctor was reluctant to put him on the same medication he'd been on before, because the drug had been a stimulant, and they didn't want Bryant to tilt toward an addiction in the other direction, but his team was discussing options with him, and he liked that they were open and honest and sharing different directions with him as if the choice was his.

When he'd said as much to his therapist one afternoon, she'd blinked at him. "The choice is yours, Bryant. You have the ultimate say in all of this. Don't let anybody tell you differently."

He'd chewed on that one for days. The choice was ultimately his. Not just on which meds he took or how long he stayed at the resort, but what he did with his life, what decisions he said yes and no to, and whether he forgave Minnie.

All of that was up to him.

Ultimately, he stayed in rehab for six weeks—two weeks after Clay, Van, and Phoenix had had to go back to their lives. It had been Bryant's choice to give it that extra two weeks.

When he went back to Kansas and decided *not* to call Minnie. That had been his choice too.

CHAPTER 27

*A*t the beginning of March, Minnie suddenly became Phoenix's best friend. She wasn't producing Van's newest reality show, so Minnie suspected Phoenix was at odd ends about what to do now that Van was busy filming that. Phoenix did talk a lot about Van and Clay's wedding in May. *That* would be filmed for *Pop Star*, so not only did Phoenix have to fill the role as best friend and show producer, she was also fulfilling the roll as Van's right hand and making all of Van's dreams come true the way she always did, by working herself to the bone.

It sounded like the most involvement Van had in the planning of her own wedding was saying where and when, and Phoenix was taking care of the rest. While it might have annoyed Minnie, as far as she could tell, Phoenix preferred things that way. But by the way Phoenix simply moved her work space from the conference table in Revival during the day to Minnie's kitchen table in her apartment in the evenings, Minnie wasn't sure it was healthy. She wondered if Phoenix was suffering from making the Van Birch machine work for so long, much in the same way Bryant had. Only Minnie couldn't detect the same amount of strain on Phoenix as she had on Bryant.

Sure, on the nights when Malcolm was with Rocco, Phoenix and she drank their fair share of wine together, but on other nights, it didn't seem to be an issue. Minnie had the sneaking suspicion there was more going on with Phoenix than she was letting on. She and Minnie had talked about their insufferable parents a time or two. Phoenix's were part of the well-to-do hippie set. They married to please their parents when Phoenix had been conceived, so they didn't lose their trust funds, and divorced by the time Phoenix was six. Her mother lived in San Jose. Her father lived in a tiny town a couple hours north of her mom, and she barely ever saw him. Her mother had remarried when she was in junior high, and of course, that had been what had introduced Phoenix's infamous stepbrother.

"I was afraid for a long time that Clay would do the same to Van," Phoenix confessed to Minnie late one night. "I saw the desire there, but I think my vision was too clouded by my own experience to also see the love."

Now Phoenix seemed okay with Clay, if only because he'd made Van happy. The man she currently loathed, which Minnie pretended not to know, was Robin. Phoenix only referred to him as "The Ex". To listen to Phoenix talk about him, she painted him as a heartless villain.

Minnie wasn't quite sure she believed Robin was that dastardly. Was he intimidating as hell? Yes. As a tall, well-built man with intense eyes who rocked the silver fox look better than George Clooney, he was not someone Minnie would want to get on the wrong side of. But every time she'd seen him interact with his family, he'd seemed intelligent, understanding. Minnie might even say kind, but she didn't know him that well. At the same time, he'd obviously done something to wound Phoenix so deeply that she couldn't let it go. Minnie just wished she knew what it was, so that she might be able to offer her friend some measure of comfort.

According to Phoenix, "The Ex" was the kind of man who made excuses for bad behavior. He was part of that set that wanted to be in with the good ole boys who drank scotch and talked about women's bodies like they were possessions. Women were prizes to be won rather than people to be respected. He was the enemy, and Minnie respected that whatever had happened between the two of them, Phoenix would not be granting forgiveness anytime soon.

Henry Bishop was awaiting trial for kidnapping Van. Minnie might be called as a witness, though she hadn't seen anything. Van had just been abducted from behind her shop, but Minnie was willing to do whatever she could to see that Van's attackers got what they deserved. Especially Bishop. Minnie had seen the photos, the ones of the bruises from the night of The Incident. It was so much worse than what had happened to Minnie in New York, and still, Minnie would have strung up that lacrosse player the same way Phoenix wanted to string up "The Ex" if she could.

Minnie had asked once, "Did he ever hurt you? The Ex?"

Phoenix had tsk-ed. "Never physically. He was never that kind of man. His game was manipulation. He has a sharper tongue than the devil himself."

Minnie could only imagine the words Robin Birch might whisper into a lover's ear. He was so commanding. Maybe Minnie had read too many romance novels, because when Minnie pictured Robin's tongue, it was saying and doing very naughty things. Minnie had turned bright red and tried to purge the thoughts from her mind, but Phoenix had been so full of wine and righteous indignation, she didn't even notice.

Phoenix had been at Minnie's house so often over the last month that she'd learned Malcolm's schedule and had witnessed many a dinnertime hand-off between Minnie and Rocco. She'd become a friendly distraction during that time. Malcolm didn't always adjust well to transitioning between one parent and the other. He didn't understand why things had changed, and it broke Minnie's heart every time Rocco had to pry a crying Malcolm's arms from around her neck before he left.

Really, it was a relief to have Phoenix there to act as a buffer. She even lived close now. Phoenix had rented one of the apartments in the one building her dad had been able to convince the historical society to allow him to renovate. He'd wanted to demolish, but instead, he'd been wrangled into renovating the old warehouse into lofts and offering them at a discounted rate to displaced families through one of the grants Van and Phoenix had set up after the tornado. Phoenix paid full price for hers, and Minnie liked that her father had done something worthwhile for a change.

Phoenix had just wanted to get away from Robin's house. She'd said she couldn't handle living with the love birds any longer, but Minnie suspected she couldn't handle the daily proximity to Robin even more than that.

Minnie had gathered that Phoenix and Van weren't speaking as much as they used to, and that was probably part of the reason Phoenix was spending most of her evenings at Minnie's apartment. Minnie wasn't offended.

She was just glad to have a friend, though she was sorry if Phoenix was feeling lonely.

"How do you feel about this whole Bryant situation?" Phoenix asked one night as they waited for Rocco to show up for his night with Malcolm.

They hadn't even broken out the wine yet.

"What situation?" Minnie asked.

"We all know he's Malcolm's bio dad," Phoenix said.

Minnie fidgeted, couldn't they keep on pretending nobody knew who Malcolm's biological father was the way Minnie kept pretending she didn't know "The Ex" was Robin?

"I don't see how that matters. He doesn't want anything to do with me or Malcolm. He said so after Christmas."

"Hmmm," Phoenix said. "So he hasn't called you then?"

Minnie raised her eyebrows. "No. He hasn't."

"You know he got sober, right?"

Minnie's heart stopped. "No. I did not. When?"

"What did you think the trip to Florida was about? Fun? We so didn't have time for a month-long trip to the East Coast. It did help with publicity though. Pap shots of Van and Clay with virtually no clothes on is always good for business, but we were there for Bryant."

"Wow," Minnie said, leaning back against her chair. "I had no idea."

Phoenix's mouth formed the most self-satisfied smirk Minnie had ever seen. "Of course you didn't. I am very good at my job."

"How long has he been back?" Minnie asked.

Phoenix tapped her finger to her lips. "About a month, give or take. He's doing good. Staying on track, showing up to work, seeing his therapist. He's even back to treating his

ADHD again. He's doing really, really well." Phoenix paused. "I can't believe he hasn't called you. He hasn't called you?"

"Nope," Minnie said. Her heart, which had originally been buoyed by the news that Bryant had finally sought help for all the troubles he'd borne, now sank. He'd been to rehab and back, and he still didn't want to know Minnie or their son.

Had she hurt him that badly? Or worse, had the time they'd had together meant that little to him in retrospect?

When Rocco knocked on the door and let himself in a moment later, Phoenix barely allowed Malcolm time to raise his arms to his dad for a hug before she asked, "You knew Bryant went to rehab, right?"

Rocco blinked, but shifted Malcolm to his hip, greeting his son before saying, "Yeah, we had coffee last week. He told me all about it."

"The two of you. You and Bryant Wilder met for coffee?" Minnie asked. She couldn't picture it. The only time the two of them had done anything together, it had ended in aggressive comments or fisticuffs.

"Yeah, he called and wanted to apologize for giving me a black eye, so I thought the least I could do was hear the guy out. It takes a lot of guts to admit when you've got a problem and try to make amends, you know."

"Bryant called you," Minnie said again.

"Yeah," Rocco searched for Malcolm's overnight bag, and found it in the kitchen chair next to Minnie. "Is that okay?"

Minnie's eyes went wide as she shook her head. "It's fine. I'm just shocked he called you of all people."

Rocco shrugged. "It was no big deal, Mins."

"Did you guys talk about Malcolm?"

Rocco shook his head. "I sort of got the impression he

was saving that conversation for you. He just said that he shouldn't have hit me and that he'd been working through his own stuff and that he was glad that I'd been there for you when he couldn't be. He never mentioned Malcolm."

Rocco shifted Malcolm to the other hip. Malcolm asked about getting chicken nuggets for dinner, and Minnie reminded him that he'd already had chicken and rice and vegetables for dinner, but Malcolm returned with a specific request for "Donald's" that had Rocco blushing. They'd agreed to steer clear of fast food a long time ago.

"It was no big deal, Minnie," Rocco said. "I'm sure he'll call you soon. If he's making amends, you've got to be on his list. You just might be last, you know, because he hurt you the most."

But even as Van and Clay's wedding approached a month later, Minnie still hadn't heard from him.

CHAPTER 28

"*H*ellooooo," Van voice called from the other side of the fence. Then Bryant heard the creak of the old gate opening. "Your truck is here, but does that mean you are?" Two sets of footsteps echoed through last autumn's leaves as Van, and probably Clay, made their way toward Bryant's garage. "I mean, if you went out for a motorcycle ride without me on a gorgeous day like this, I'll never forgive—"

Van cut herself off a she rounded the corner and stopped inside the open garage door. "Nice, you are here." She strolled on into the garage with not Clay, but Butch, behind her.

"Hey," Bryant said, then nodded toward Butch.

"Nice bike," Butch said. It wasn't really, just an old beater he'd bought and slowly fixed up over the years, but he still didn't ever see himself selling it.

"Thanks. I've kind of been neglecting it lately. Thought it was time to change that." Bryant had barely ridden over the past couple of years. When he'd first bought the motorcycle, it had been a weekend ritual of tuning it up and going for a ride. He had just finished changing the oil in it for the first time in far too long.

Van dusted off the ancient desk chair in the corner with an old towel, and took a seat. "Nice, we can take your bike out to the lake. Butch can follow with the fishing poles."

Bryant studied Van, who was giving him hopeful puppy dog eyes. "What do you mean 'fishing poles?'" he asked.

"I thought we could go fishing this afternoon. You know, head out to the lake, eat a bunch of cookies, and bond over cans of worms and our five-foot marlins."

Bryant laughed. Even Butch tried to hide a chuckle at that. "Have you ever even been fishing?"

"I mean, I read that Ernest Hemmingway book, so I'm basically an expert."

"You do know that there aren't marlins in man-made lakes though?"

Van rolled her eyes. "I'm not an idiot. I figured we'd photo shop in the deep-sea fish as a joke. Nobody gets excited about trout."

"Why fishing?"

"I don't know, because I wanted to spend time with you, and it seemed safe. And my dad had my grandpa's old fishing stuff in the basement."

Bryant sighed and grabbed a rag and wiped the oil off his fingers. "Butch, can we get a minute?"

The big man nodded, and Bryant waited until his footsteps faded to the far side of the yard before pulling up an old, overturned bucket, and taking a seat next to Van. Despite his still slightly grimy fingers, Bryant grasped Van's hands between his, then leaned over and placed a kiss on her forehead.

"Do you really want to go fishing?" he asked.

Van shook her head. "I mean, I'd go with you if you wanted to, but you'd have to do all the work. Worms freak me out." She shuddered at the idea, and Bryant chuckled.

"You are not obligated to think of things for us to do that don't involve alcohol, Van. If you want to hang out, just text me, and we'll figure out what to do together."

"Yes, but I feel like after everything I've put on you, it's the least I can do."

"You don't owe me anything."

"I know I don't. But I am still dealing with my own guilt, and I want to spend time with you. I miss you."

"Fair enough," Bryant squeezed her hands again. "I miss you, too." They hadn't been spending nearly the same amount of time together as they'd used to. But they were both busy with other things. Van was working, planning a wedding, building a relationship with Clay, and Bryant was learning how to be himself again. Rediscovering parts of his life he'd forgotten or finding new things he hadn't realized he would like to do. Like saving his motorcycle from neglect and learning how to cook more than toast and eggs.

"I asked Clay if he minded if you and I still had sleepovers every now and then, and he said something very rude."

That made Bryant laugh. "Yeah, I don't see Clay going for that ever, and that's fine. We can make something else our thing."

Van perked up. "So you *do* want to go fishing."

"Nah, worms freak me out too." They didn't, but it made Van giggle, and Bryant had never had the particular urge to fish. "I have an idea. Do you have a guitar with you?"

Van's expression turned incredulous. "I don't take a guitar with me everywhere I go."

Bryant gave her his most skeptical frown.

"Fine, my guitar is in Butch's truck, but that's only because I figured I'd get bored with traditional fishing and figured I could serenade the fish up into our bucket."

Bryant pulled Van to her feet. "Go get it and meet me upstairs."

Van's face lit up. "Oh my God, you didn't!"

"Only one way to find out," he said with a waggle of his eyebrows.

Van raced off with a squeal. Bryant stopped in the kitchen to wash his hands and had just finished positioning his stool in the spare room when Van came crashing in with her acoustic guitar already slung over her shoulder and a delighted smile so bright, she shone like a star.

Bryant picked up the sticks that were resting on his snare drum and twirled them. "I'm a little rusty."

"Oh shut up. I'd fire Zach in a heartbeat if you decided you wanted to travel with us." Zach was the drummer in her band.

Bryant smiled but shook his head. Joining Van on the road was the exact last thing he needed in his life right now. "I'm happy here," he said. Van grinned as Bryant twirled his sticks into position then started the intro to "Seven Nation Army" and scrambled to position her guitar so she could do her best Jack White impression.

They'd spent hours like this in high school, learning every song they could with their favorite drum and guitar parts. Only this time, Butch showed up in the doorway, nodding his head along to the beat. Then he had a cell phone out, recording them, and Bryant couldn't blame the guy. Seeing Van perform live had always been magical. Even if it was in Bryant's spare bedroom, being backed by him on his dusty drum kit.

It had been a long time since Bryant had seen Van smile so unabashedly for so long. It had been a long time since he'd done the same, but his cheeks ached and sweat was dripping into his eyes from the exertion by the time she set her guitar aside. Bryant wiped his forehead with his already dirty shirt then high-fived Van as she danced in a circle around his drum set to the music that was still going on in her head. "We need to do this more often."

"Agreed," Bryant said. "But can I ask you to do something?"

Van stopped dancing, sobering immediately. "Anything."

"Can we plan ahead in the future, instead of you just dropping by? Having a schedule, knowing what to expect, it really helps me."

Van lit up again and socked him playfully in the bicep. "Look at you, setting boundaries and asking for what you need." Bryant felt himself blush. It was all still new for him. Van threw her arms around his shoulders. "I'm so proud of you." Bryant had been about to squeeze the life out of her, because those were words he still had trouble hearing, though he needed to hear them, but her stomach growled so loud and hard, he could feel the vibration, and they broke apart laughing.

"Maybe we should order a pizza?" she asked.

"Or I could make you dinner," Bryant said. "I've had some pork chops marinating in the refrigerator most of the day; it's way more than I could eat myself."

Butch, who was still leaning against the doorjamb,

perked up at the mention of pork chops, and Van said, "Since when do you know how to marinate things?"

Van pushed his glasses up his nose, then ruffled his hair. Bryant wished he wasn't still hesitant to share all the new parts of his life, but he needed to reintegrate with his friends and family, and Van was here. She was trying, so he would too. "I watched a lot of cooking shows in Florida, and I've been trying to eat healthier, gain back some muscles mass, so I've been making all my own meals lately." The pork chops had been supposed to last him the rest of the week, but he didn't mind sharing. He had about three dozen other recipes he'd been dying to try.

Van's phone pinged as they descended the stairs, which meant it was Clay. Van had kept everybody else, even Phoenix, on mute until she and Clay got together. Like clockwork, she asked, "Do you mind if I invite Clay?"

"Of course not," Bryant said as he started gather ingredients from around the kitchen. "Invite Phoenix too if you want. We can make a night of it."

"Phoenix is having dinner with Minnie tonight," Van said as she opened his refrigerator door, then flinched like she'd been tripped up and tried to recover by saying, "Holy hell, there's *food* in your refrigerator. And like, a whole army of sparkling water."

Bryant shrugged, grabbed a bottle of the sparkling water and held it out to Butch, then grabbed one for himself before sliding out the tray of pork chops. "I told you, I've been cooking."

"Your entire adult life, all that's been in that refrigerator have been two bottles of ancient mustard, a mostly empty jar of pickles, and a carton of expired milk—probably the same carton of expired milk."

"Yeah, well. Things change."

"I guess they do. I never thought I'd see arugula in Bryant Wilder's refrigerator," Van said in wonder, then grabbed her own bottle of water before taking a seat next to Butch at the breakfast table.

She messed with her phone for a few minutes while Bryant heated up the oven and prepped the rest of his dishes. He planned to roast apples with the pork and serve it all with a wilted salad made with the arugula Van was so impressed by.

Then, Van broke the silence. "She's invited to the wedding, you know." When Bryant didn't say anything, she said. "Minnie, I mean."

"I knew who you meant."

"Are you okay with that? I know you haven't talked to her since, well, you know."

"Since my breakdown," he said.

"Yeah."

"It's your wedding, Van. And she's a friend of yours; she should be invited."

"I don't want to unwittingly do something that's going to hurt you." Van spun her still-sweating water bottle.

"Minnie coming to your wedding is not going to hurt my feelings," Bryant said. "And I'm not going to fall off the wagon just from seeing her." Would he *want* to drink? Probably. But he wouldn't. He'd made the choice not to drink every day since January, and he wasn't going to start just because Minnie showed up somewhere.

He found himself missing her more and more lately. The way she always fell asleep with her chin on his chest and the blankets pulled up past her nose. The way she'd knock her hip against his whenever they stood next to one another, the way her fingers had absently tickled his scalp whenever they sat next to one another. The way she almost always knew what book he was talking about, even if she hadn't read it. Bryant found himself just wanting to talk to her. Not to impress her with his recovery or to show off his new culinary skills but just because he'd always enjoyed being in her presence.

"I actually think it would be a good thing for me," he said.

Van gave him a soft, encouraging grin, and Bryant tried not to let himself think about the possibilities.

CHAPTER 29

*B*ryant hadn't been this nervous possibly ever. He'd been sweating from anxiety most of the day, and the stupid tux was too hot. He'd shed his jacket and rolled up his sleeves by the time they'd gotten to the toast and dancing portion of the evening. But he'd stuck to his sparkling water.

Had he been tempted by the table full of champagne flutes? Yes. But he'd promised Van that she didn't need to make her wedding dry just because of him. He'd appreciated that she'd offered though. That sort of thoughtfulness was why she would always be his best friend.

But he'd been able to identify why it was he'd wanted a drink. It wasn't for the alcohol, and it wasn't for his nerves. It had been because he wanted to feel included. But as he raised his glass of Perrier during his toast, he had been included. He wasn't missing out on anything by not drinking, and Van's wedding, instead of turning into a major temptation, had given him one more reason to stay sober.

The biggest reason, though, was because he couldn't

mess this night up. For Van and Clay? Of course. For Minnie? Absolutely. But more than anything, Bryant needed to do this for himself.

He'd held himself back too long. It was possible he'd waited too long. Phoenix said Minnie hadn't moved on, that she'd moved out of Rocco's house and was living on her own with Malcolm. She'd said that Minnie wanted to hear from him. That at the very least she'd be happy to hear from his own lips that he was sober, that he was taking care of himself again.

Bryant wasn't so sure. He'd been awful to her at Christmas. He'd been so wrapped up in his own downward spiral that he hadn't been able to focus on the ways Minnie had moved to protect herself and her child.

Just her child.

That had been one of the biggest mental hurdles Bryant had to overcome since Clay and Van had dragged him to rehab. That Malcolm wasn't his son. True, Minnie had taken that choice away from him, but the reality was that Malcolm *was* Minnie and Rocco's son. But that didn't mean that Bryant couldn't have a relationship with him.

"You're procrastinating." A hand came to rest on Bryant's shoulder. Only two people ever touched Bryant that way. It was funny, they weren't related by blood, but Robin and Clay were truly father and son. Another example that blood didn't necessarily have anything to do with it.

Bryant offered a weak smile over his shoulder to Robin. Robin squeezed his shoulder, and the two of them looked back out over the dance floor to where Minnie and Phoenix danced together. Bryant had promised himself he would talk to Minnie by this day. He'd been out of rehab for ninety days, sober for 120. It was time. But he couldn't bring himself to leave the stage, cut through the crowd, and break up the fun Minnie was having with Phoenix. She looked like she was having a genuinely good time, and Bryant liked that.

His gut told him that his attention would make her smile fade.

"I don't want to ruin her good time," he forced himself to say aloud.

"I would really like to dance with Phoenix," Robin said.

Bryant raised an eyebrow. "Yeah?"

Robin nodded. "Pathetic, isn't it. She's barely spoken to me in ten months, and I still love her." They'd talked about this at dinner. Robin had even proposed the plan he was now giving Bryant a hard time for procrastinating on, but he hadn't confessed to being in love with Phoenix.

"You should tell her," Bryant said. "She might not know."

"I think she knows. She just doesn't want to hear it." Robin clapped Bryant on the shoulder again. "What do you say we stop stalling, son and go put our hearts on the line?

"Yeah." It was the only word Bryant could manage. Partially because his entire body sang with nervous energy and partially because he would probably do anything Robin asked him to do when he called Bryant "son."

Robin offered him an encouraging grin before cutting through the crowd and sidling up to Phoenix and Minnie just as the music changed. Bryant could see Phoenix's demeanor shift from across the room, then he watched Robin turn to Minnie and take her in his arms, leading her in an actual waltz across the dance floor. He traced them until Robin had danced them close to the exit, and Bryant guessed that was his clue. He cut along the edge of the dance floor until he stood behind Minnie, tapped on her shoulder, and in his most gentlemanly voice, asked, "May I cut in?"

Minnie's bottom lip was caught between her teeth when she faced him, her eyes large yet guarded. She held out her hand and instead of pulling her into his arms so they could sway on the dance floor, Bryant wrapped his fingers between hers and pulled her out the door into the flowering garden.

The courtyard had always been a feature of the old downtown building, but before the tornado, it had just been a stone path with a couple of mossy benches and an archway where you could choose to have your wedding ceremony. After the tornado, it had been transformed by so many shrubs and so many other manicured flowers that Bryant almost felt he was walking onto the grounds at Pemberley rather than an empty lot in downtown Wellville.

"I haven't been out here since everything bloomed," Minnie said, pulling on his arm as she tried to turn in a circle to take in all the flowers. "It's lovely."

Bryant caught the sparkle of her dress in the fading sunlight, and said, "It is."

As if she knew he'd been talking about her, she faced him with a curious expression. "What are we doing out here?"

Bryant had to clear his throat. Then he adjusted his glasses and realized he was still procrastinating, so instead he pulled her down onto the nearest bench, now sealed wood instead of mossy stone, and just launched into it. "I wanted to apologize to you for all the bullshit I've put you through these last couple of years," he said.

Minnie opened her mouth, but Bryant shushed her with a finger to her lips. They were still full and pillowy soft, just the way he remembered, and Bryant wanted permission to devour them—but not yet. "Just, please, I need to say this."

Minnie nodded and pulled the hand at her lips into her lap, gripping it between both of hers. The gesture tugged at the corners of Bryant's mouth. Maybe not all was lost.

Bryant apologized for lying to Minnie about making her think he was only a small-town contractor, about his relationship with Van, about not fighting for her when she'd believed the role he'd played in the media, about not fighting for her and for Malcolm when he'd found out the truth.

"I wasn't in a good place last winter. It's not an excuse. Just the truth. If Van and Clay hadn't called everyone together and hauled me off to rehab, I think—" he stopped and sniffed back the tears stinging at his eyes. "I didn't have a plan or anything, but if they hadn't intervened, I think I might have drunk myself to death."

Minnie choked on her own sob, and Bryant wiped a tear from her cheek. "I'm really glad you didn't," she said in a whisper.

"Me too." Bryant kept his hand on Minnie's jaw, running his thumb over her cheekbone, as he geared up for the truly difficult part. "I know my sobriety is new, and I know I don't have any right to ask, but I'd really like the opportunity to be a part of Malcolm's life, and maybe, if you can forgive me, a part of yours too."

Minnie gripped his hand at her cheek and pressed her nose into his palm. "I'm sorry I didn't tell you about Malcolm sooner. I was afraid. From the moment I found out I was pregnant, I have been so afraid."

Another tear escaped down her cheek, and Bryant brushed that away. He wanted to crush her into his arms and pepper kisses over her tear tracks and tell her that she never needed to be afraid again. That she could trust him now. That he would be there in every way he could for her and Malcolm forever. But Bryant knew that would be premature. He barely trusted himself again yet.

That Bryant's daily routine remained consistent was part of his treatment plan. He woke, exercised, ate breakfast, went to work. After work he either had a counseling session or a meeting, and on the days he didn't have those, he journaled and read and ate a quiet dinner he'd made himself. He had sparkling water delivered by the pallet and though he was starting to feel guilty about the amount of glass and aluminum cans he was recycling, he told himself he could only tackle one problem at a time. Every night, he was always in bed by ten o'clock.

One of Bryant's favorite things about his new life was sleep. He'd never realized how much better he slept when he hadn't been drinking. He had more energy for lifting weights, more energy for his workday. He drank less coffee and ate as much as he wanted.

But even though he was in bed at ten every night, ready to sleep and recover, he always fell asleep wishing Minnie was next to him.

When he'd spoken to his therapist about wanting to see Minnie again, about wanting to be a part of her and Malcolm's life, she had advised him to take it slow. To not place too much of his happiness on the choices of others, while at the same time acknowledging that speaking to Minnie was something Bryant probably needed to do.

"I have missed you so much," Minnie said.

"So…?" Bryant asked.

"Of course we want you in our lives," Minnie said. "To stay."

Bryant lost the battle with his own tears and rested his forehead against Minnie's as relief and gratitude washed over him.

EPILOGUE

Two Years Later

*R*evival was quiet when Bryant arrived. Only the lights in the front window displays were on and the front doors were locked. He shifted Malcolm to his other hip and fished his keys out of his pocket to unlock the door. Malcolm had spent the day with Rocco and Erin. They'd taken him to the zoo and the park and worn him out. He was awake, but his cheek rested on Bryant's shoulder as he eased them in the front door of the bookshop.

The only light inside came from the kitchen, where Minnie was packing up the pieces of the cake they'd be bringing with them to California. She had done nothing but fret about this cake for weeks. No matter how many times Bryant had reminded her that it was for a one-year-old's birthday party, Minnie had insisted that a baby's birthday wasn't for the baby, it was for the parents.

She stopped fussing with the million pounds of plastic wrap around each layer and tucked it away in her cake carrier when Bryant appeared in the door. The same words they'd said about this trip over and over again to one another passing between their eyes.

Bryant still sighed as she washed her hands. She opened the drawer next to the sink and replaced the wedding band on her finger. He liked that she was worried about their niece's birthday cake, but he hated it when she worked herself into a state of worry over anything. Especially lately.

"Are you coming up to bed?" he asked as Minnie tossed her used apron into the dirty bin in the corner. "Because this guy is beat." He bounced Malcolm in his arms, as he said it, and Malcolm whined, "No, Papa B," and pressed on Bryant's shoulder until he was still again.

Papa B.

That was what Malcolm had decided to call him all on his own. He and Minnie hadn't even been engaged yet. Bryant had only spent a few hours a week with Malcolm when the little boy had used it the first time, but Bryant had cherished the name.

Minnie stretched, and her shirt rode up over her navel. Bryant's fingers itched to spread over the soft skin and pull her into his embrace. "I'm pretty exhausted myself," she said on the tail end of a yawn.

"Come on. Upstairs."

They'd been living in Minnie's apartment since they'd gotten married last year, a quick ceremony under the rose arbor at the courthouse only a few short hours before their niece, Paloma, had been born.

Bryant loved his extended family, but he was feeling a fair bit grumpy about dragging his immediate family halfway across the country for three days for a birthday party when all he wanted to do was lock them in the apartment and spend three uninterrupted days enjoying their company.

Minnie preceded Bryant up the stairs and unlocked the door. They went through the motions of putting Malcolm to bed together. Then Bryant collapsed onto the sofa, his arms and abs pleasantly sore from that morning's workout.

Minnie handed him a cold bottle of Perrier, and with a quick kiss to his forehead, she disappeared into the bathroom to wash the day's flour and sugar off her body. Bryant picked the novel he'd been reading off the side table, an advance copy of Robin's latest thriller.

He wasn't sure when he'd drifted off, but he felt the book being lifted from his hand and the empty water bottle clinked against the side table as Minnie cleared it away. Then a warm, well-lotioned body straddled his lap. Lips tickled at his neck. Bryant's half-asleep hands found their way to Minnie's middle. You couldn't tell when she was dressed, but Bryant could feel the curve of her new baby bump beneath his hands.

Pride and excitement roused him into opening his eyes. He loved noting the changes in Minnie's body as their baby grew inside her. Her breasts were heavier, more rounded, which was basically a miracle. She joked that she had porn boobs, but Bryant told her she had the breasts of a goddess. And her stomach poked out just the slightest bit. Bryant had missed her pregnancy the last time. He wasn't going to miss the tiniest detail this time around.

"You're naked," he said.

"I don't usually bathe with clothes on. Do you?" She didn't seem all that interested in an answer as she began to tug on Bryant's belt. Taking the hint, he pulled his shirt over his head so he'd be able to feel her skin on his.

"I vote you should go around without clothes on all the time," Bryant said. His fingers closed gently over her sensitive breasts. Minnie sucked in a breath, then relaxed into his touch as she rolled her hips over his thighs. She hadn't been feeling particularly amorous since she'd become pregnant, and Bryant had been missing the intimacy.

He didn't blame her. She spent half her mornings throwing up. Bryant wouldn't want someone trying to come on to him when he felt like shit either. But he couldn't help himself now that she wanted him. He sucked one of her darkened nipples between his lips, setting his teeth ever so gently against the bud as his hand sneaked between his wife's legs. She was still warm and wet from her shower, and his fingers parted her folds with ease to slip inside her. Minnie groaned and arched her back, pressing both her mound and her breast further into the places where Bryant held her.

One of her hands still rested on his erection, though she'd only managed to open his belt. Two of her fingers dipped behind his fly, caressing his tip, and his hips surged toward her. Minnie found enough motivation to finish freeing him from his jeans. He released her long enough to help her push them to the floor before she was straddling him again and sinking down onto his cock.

Minnie hissed while Bryant cursed. She was his heaven, his new addiction. He'd never been able to get enough of her. It was how she'd gotten pregnant again only a month after her birth control had run out. Not that it hadn't been a conscious decision on their part, but just like with Malcolm, they hadn't expected her to conceive so quickly. Perhaps they should have known better.

Bryant didn't care. He loved his wife. He wanted to have as many children with her as she would let him create. He wanted to be the father he'd never had, the partner he'd always longed to be during the years he'd only been play acting. He loved this woman, this strange family they had made together, the child they were growing now, the ones that would come after.

"You feel so good," Minnie moaned as she rode him. Bryant could only grunt in response. Speaking would distract him from his goal of giving her as much pleasure as possible before the orgasm he could already feel building inside him.

His thumb found the nub between her legs and his other hand caressed the small of her back, coaxing her into the rhythm he'd come to recognize as her favorite. He caught the nipple of the breast he'd neglected before between his teeth, and with a gentle bite, had her fucking him hard enough to lose himself in the frenzy of sensation.

Minnie was repeating, "Bry, Bry, Bry," over and over again, which was something she only ever called him mid-coitus. She'd confessed one time that it was only because she was usually too excited to pronounce the second half of his name. Bryant was only more enthralled by her abbreviation. His goal was to pleasure her to the point where she couldn't speak anymore at all.

Bryant pressed harder against her clit and flexed his cock inside her. Minnie smashed her tits into his face and Bryant feasted as her words turned unintelligible and her cries grew loud enough to wake the neighbors. He felt her pussy start to clamp around him, and Bryant lost all his restraint as her heat swallowed him whole.

Minnie lay draped over him a few minutes later, limp and exhausted. She was delicious and warm, but he could hear her breathing slowing to an even a pace. He squeezed her hip. "Come on," he said. "Let's get you to bed. It's going to be a long weekend."

"I am so excited about it though." Minnie's words came slow and almost slurred.

Bryant ran his fingers through her damp hair. "I miss Van and Clay too," he said.

"And Fe."

"Of course Fe," Bryant said. Even though he missed Clay the most, he knew Phoenix was Minnie's best friend.

Bryant and Minnie were the only ones of the whole family who still lived in Kansas full-time. Even Robin split his time between Kansas and California these days. Bryant had been happy to leave his paparazzi days behind him for the quiet life with Minnie, but he did miss his friends.

"We'll see them all tomorrow."

"I hope Paloma likes her cake."

"I'm sure she'll have a magnificent time smashing it," Bryant said.

When Minnie showed no sign of rising on her own, he shifted her in his arms so he could cradle carry her to their bed where he could sleep beside her until morning.

THANK YOU FOR READING!

I hope you enjoyed reading *The Deception Incident*. When I started developing *The Van Birch Incident*, I knew Bryant and Phoenix would have their own love stories, but I had no idea what Bryant's looked liked until a cute bookstore owner turned up with a baby on her hip, and then I got excited. I knew I could do so many twisty turny things when I took a secret baby storyline and mashed it up against the absolute turmoil Bryant was already going through. I hope the experience of reading was as cathartic and cleansing for you as it was for me. Missed Van and Clay's story? It's not too late to pick up a copy of *The Van Birch Incident*. Look for Robin and Phoenix's story in *The Betrayal Incident*, coming out in September 2020. Or learn how Van got to be where she is in the prequel novella, *Love, Van B*.

Want to Connect with Me?
I am @marlaholtauthor on Instagram. I'd love to see your bookstagram posts or just chat about the book. I can't wait to meet you!
Finally, leaving reviews is one of the best ways you can support the Indie Authors you love. I'd be forever in your debt if you took the time to review *The Deception Incident*

Neither Bryant nor Minnie have a sign off, their noses are stuck in a book (or between each other's legs. You are welcome to use your imagination.)

ACKNOWLEDGMENTS

ALSO BY MARLA HOLT

When Abe Met Lane: The Prequel Novella to The
Other Lane
The Other Lane: A Modern Fairy Tale

ACKNOWLEDGEMENTS

Thank you to everyone who has been asking for this book. Your love and support for *The Van Birch Incident* and general rally cry that you couldn't wait for Bryant's book kept me going when I didn't think I'd ever be able to write a second book that would live up to the first. You are what kept me breathing through my panic attacks.

Thank you to my sister, Audrey, for reading two books back to back and providing last minute feedback to allay my fears that this book was not going to be a total disaster.

Thank you to my husband for listening to Walk the Moon on repeat for weeks on end while these two characters worked out their issues in my head

Thank you to my Instagram fam for being such wonderfully badass author babes and supporting each other every single day. Thank you to Suite Six Studios for finding *the perfect* cover model for Bryant. I don't know how you pulled him directly out of my head, but you did. Thank you to Jackie Hritz for her fantastic and thorough editing skills. It truly makes all the difference.